WILLIAM MORRIS was a staggeringly talented man. He was architect, sculptor, author, musician, artist and translator extraordinary; he designed fabrics, glass, furniture, musical instruments, and undoubtedly, many a labor-saving device around the house. For he believed in the wholeness of life, he admired the simplicity of an earlier day and deplored the industrial revolution— of which he saw only the beginning. In his writing he attempted to hark back to a simpler, wiser time, to values that seemed to be disappearing from his own world.

With THE SUNDERING FLOOD, Ballantine Books brings you the last of the great prose romances William Morris lived to complete. This superbly crafted adult fantasy enhances and embellishes the medieval enchantments it was his joy to re-create.

THE SUNDERING FLOOD is a charming coda to the rich magnificence of his masterwork, THE WELL AT THE WORLD'S END.

Adult Fantasy

Also by William Morris

THE WELL AT THE WORLD'S END
Volumes I and II

THE WOOD BEYOND THE WORLD

THE WATER OF THE WONDROUS ISLES

Published by Ballantine Books

THE
SUNDERING
FLOOD

William Morris

Introduction by
Lin Carter

BALLANTINE BOOKS • NEW YORK

Introduction copyright © 1973 by Lin Carter

All rights reserved.

SBN 345-03261-6-125

First Printing: May, 1973

Printed in the United States of America

Cover art by Gervasio Gallardo

BALLANTINE BOOKS, INC.
101 Fifth Avenue, New York, N. Y. 10003

Contents

*About The Sundering Flood
and William Morris:*

Osberne Dwarf-friend

WILLIAM MORRIS was a man of prodigious energy and the record of his achievements is not only prodigious, it is astonishing. His career encompassed many very different fields of endeavor, and in each of these fields his accomplishments were important, successful and numerous. Take the field of poetry, for example. In "The Defense of Guinevere" he created what has been hailed as "one of the pearls of Victorian verse"; in *The Earthly Paradise* he wrote one of the most successful and lastingly popular single books of verse in the language; his book-length poem *Sigurd the Volsung* was acclaimed by no less important a literary figure than George Bernard Shaw as the greatest epic written since Homer. So important a figure was Morris among the poets of his time that, the Poet Laureateship having fallen vacant, the government passed over Swinburne himself to privately sound out Morris as to whether or not he would accept the post. He politely but firmly declined the honor, and to his family he remarked wryly that he could not quite see himself "sitting down in crimson plush breeches and white silk stockings to write birthday odes in honour of all the blooming little Guelfings and Battenbergs that happen to come along."

But verse is only one of the fields into which he charged lustily. His accomplishments in pictorial art and design and decoration, in the art of printing and publishing beautiful books, in the rigorous art of translation and its attendant scholarship, in political reform and politics itself, and even in such recondite fields as architecture and the restoration of ancient buildings—in all of these, and even other fields,

William Morris left his mark. In some of them it was a high-water mark; in none of them is his name ever likely to be forgotten.

In the last few years of his life he turned to the writing of novels. In his hands they became amazingly beautiful reincarnations of the great prose romances of the Middle Ages, a period he loved and whose artistic achievements he admired and emulated. I have elsewhere* gone rather deeply into the thesis that, in the crafting of these remarkable romances, he invented, almost by accident, and certainly in an offhand manner, the modern fantasy novel as we know it today—the tale of quest or war or adventure in imaginary worlds or kingdoms where magic works and dwarves and dragons are reality, not legend.

Some critics find fault with his prose. They complain that Morris wrote affectedly, that he concocted a deliberately archaic and artificial style, and that this style is not only difficult to read but bad writing as well, since, in their opinion, the style of a book or story ought not to get in the way of the plot but, rather, should efface itself. The style, they believe, should not attract attention to itself, thus detracting from the story. James Blish has a neat phrase which characterizes this sort of stylistic eccentricity; he calls it the sort of prose that is to be "intoned through the nose" rather than read.

I certainly agree with those who argue that plot is the important thing, or ought to be. If you don't have a strong and interesting story, style alone, however charming, is not going to win you any readers, or hold the ones you have. On the other hand, as a reader and as a fantasy writer I am particularly interested in style, and the unusual style of certain authors, like that of Lord Dunsany and E. R. Eddison, Clark Ashton Smith and Jack Vance, completely intrigues and fascinates me. In such cases as these, arguments preferring the use of clear, lucid, everyday prose to a prose-style deliberately chosen or created to suit the subject are irrelevant. Moreover, in the case of Morris at least, criticism of his style becomes a somewhat *de facto* argument: it is

*See my Introduction to Morris' *Wood Beyond the World* (Ballantine, 1969).

not Morris' fault that reading tastes have changed in the three-quarters of a century since he died. We cannot blame Morris for the effect of Ernest Hemingway and Raymond Chandler on modern prose; to fault him thus in retrospect is highly unfair—it would be like complaining that Homer's verse is all very well, but that the plot of *The Iliad* would be better told in a novel, a form unknown in Homer's day.

Yet there is something to be said for the position of Morris' critics. His prose is rather difficult—though far less difficult than that of Eddison, say, or Charles Williams, or William Hope Hodgson at his most eccentric and self-indulgent. However, the thing that saves Morris' fantasies from being nothing more than quaint but unreadable antiques is the simple fact that he told a good story, even while decking it out with obsolete verbal ornaments. To fully appreciate Morris you have to understand what he was really doing, or trying to do: he was not *trying* to write modern novels; he was deliberately trying to breathe some life into English prose by salvaging from the reefs of time the good things in the old prose romances. He was trying to prove that the spirit of Sir Thomas Malory was not dead in England.

And Morris does indeed tell a whacking good story. The book to hand is one of the best (perhaps the very best) examples of superbly-crafted storytelling in his *oeuvre*. The plot and sub-plots are complexly interwoven: there is the subsidiary theme of the growing love between the youth Osberne and the maiden Elfhild, woven like a thread of warm scarlet through the larger tapestry of wars and battles, treasons and alliances, quests and adventures; there is the bright gold thread of the coming-of-age of the boy Osberne, as the pure metal of manhood enters his soul through hard times and harsh adversity; and there is the shadowy and mysterious, subtle but ever-present influence of unseen or scarcely-glimpsed supernatural forces as they shape and mold the flow of the grand adventure, from Osberne's childhood friendship with the dwarves to the appearance, at intervals throughout the story, of the mysterious traveler who gives Osberne two gifts—the enchanted sword Boardcleaver, and the might of manhood, passed to him, in the manner of the heroes of olden time, by the laying-on of hands.

It's a good story, a strong story, a gripping and entertaining story, to which the old-fashioned style is wholly appropriate—a style which, far from diminishing the power of the book, enhances and embellishes the medieval enchantment Morris sought to re-create.

We began our program of reviving the noble and history-making romances of William Morris in 1969, with the first new edition in far too many years of *The Wood Beyond The World*—the very first major fantasy novel written in modern times. This was followed in 1970 with a two-volume edition of William Morris' acknowledged masterpiece, *The Well at the World's End*, and with *The Water of the Wondrous Isles* a year later.

We turn now to the very last of the great prose romances Morris lived to complete: *The Sundering Flood*. Morris was dying even as he wrote it, and perhaps, looking back at the high deeds and golden times and huge enterprises of his life, he embued his last achievement with something of the glow of the happy comradeship he had once known, the excitement of the battles he had waged—the rich nostalgia we feel toward lost happy days. There is a warm aura that clings about the ringing pages of this superb romance. A tang of adventure breathes through its pages like the bouquet of some rare old wine.

But Morris' strength was failing him towards the end. The strong hand that had wrought great beauty in stone and wood, in glass and woven cloth and written words, could no longer grasp the pen. The very last lines were dictated with laboring breath to his friend Cockerell on the eighth of September in the year 1896.

His strength ebbed from day to day—even that indomitable, robust, iron vigor that had never wearied before. His faculties lapsed; congestion settled in his left lung; he was hardly able to speak.

"It is an astonishing spectacle," a witness to these events recorded in his journal. "He sits speechless waiting for the end to come . . . darkness soon will envelop all the familiar scene, the sweet river, England green and grey, Kelmscott House, the trees . . . the press, the passage, the bindery, the light coming in through the windows, the old books on the shelves. . . ."

The days passed, one by one. Old friends came to visit, lingered to mourn. Arnold Dolmetsch came with antique musical instruments to play old music from the Renaissance for the dying giant; he played a 16th-Century pavane of Byrd's and Morris gave a cry of joy at the sweet, piercing beauty of its opening phrase.

Then, on the 29th, according to Cockerell's diary:

> W. M. said he felt much better. It was a bright morning, and we took him out in the bathchair. We went into Ravenscourt Park and round by the library. . . . W. M. was in good spirits and declared that he was not a bit tired, and that he felt able to do some walking. At 4:45 I went to the post and on returning found W. M. upstairs with blood streaming from his mouth. . . .

Cockerell and F. S. Ellis got Morris downstairs and into bed and fetched the doctor. Four days later, on the third of October, at the age of sixty-two, William Morris was dead. He had finished work on *The Sundering Flood* only twenty-five days before he died.

It remains one of the most astonishing and delightful works of this astonishing and delightful man.

LIN CARTER

Editorial Consultant:

The Ballantine Adult Fantasy Series

Hollis, Long Island, New York

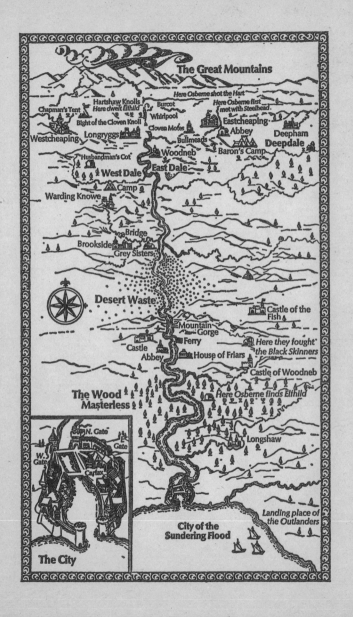

I

Of a River Called the Sundering Flood, and of the Folk that Dwelt Thereby

IT is told that there was once a mighty river which ran south into the sea, and at the mouth thereof was a great and rich city, which had been builded and had waxed and thriven because of the great and most excellent haven which the river aforesaid made where it fell into the sea. And now it was like looking at a huge wood of barked and smoothened fir-trees when one saw the masts of the ships that lay in the said haven.

But up this river ran the flood of tide a long way, so that the biggest of dromonds and round-ships might fare up it, and oft they lay amid pleasant up-country places, with their yards all but touching the windows of the husbandman's stead, and their bowsprits thrusting forth amongst the middens, and the routing swine, and querulous hens. And the uneasy lads and lasses sitting at high-mass of the Sunday in the great village church would see the tall masts dimly amidst the painted saints of the aisle windows, and their minds would wander from the mass-hackled priest and the words and the gestures of him, and see visions of far countries and outlandish folk, and some would be heart-smitten with that desire of wandering and looking on new things which so oft the sea-beat board and the wind-strained pine bear with them to the dwellings of the stay-at-homes: and to some it seemed as if, when they went from out the church, they should fall in with St. Thomas of India stepping over the gangway, and come to visit their uplandish Christmas and the Yule-feast of the field-abiders of midwinter frost. And moreover, when the tide failed, and there was no longer a flood to bear the sea-going keels up-stream (and that was hard on an hundred of miles from the sea), yet was this great river a noble and wide-spreading water, and the down-long stream thereof not so heavy nor so fierce but that the barges and lesser keels might well spread their sails when the south-west blew, and fare on without beating; or if the wind were fouler for them, they that were loth to reach from shore to shore might be tracked up by the draught of horses and bullocks, and bear the wares of the merchants to many a cheaping.

Other rivers moreover not a few fell into this main flood, and of them were some no lesser than the Thames is at Abingdon, where I, who gathered this tale, dwell in the House of the Black Canons; blessed be St. William, and St. Richard, and the Holy Austin our candle in the dark! Yea and some were even bigger, so that the land was well furnished both of fisheries and water-ways.

Now the name of this river was the Sundering Flood, and the city at the mouth thereof was called the City of the Sundering Flood. And it is no wonder, considering all that I have told concerning the wares and chaffer that it bore up-country, though the folk of the City and its lands (and the city-folk in special) knew no cause for this name. Nay, oft they jested and gibed and gabbed, for they loved their river much and were proud of it; wherefore they said it was no sunderer but a uniter; that it joined land to land and shore to shore; that it had peopled the wilderness and made the waste places blossom, and that no highway for wheels and beasts in all the land was so full of blessings and joys as was their own wet Highway of the Flood. Nevertheless, as meseemeth that no name is given to any town or mountain or river causeless, but that men are moved to name all steads for a remembrance of deeds that have been done and tidings that have befallen, or some due cause, even so might it well be with the Sundering Flood, and whereas also I wot something of that cause I shall now presently show you the same.

For ye must know that all this welfare of the said mighty river was during that while that it flowed through the plain country anigh the city, or the fertile pastures and acres of hill and dale and down further to the north. But one who should follow it up further and further would reach at last the place where it came forth from the mountains. There, though it be far smaller than lower down, yet is it still a mighty great water, and it is then well two hundred miles from the main sea. Now from the mountains it cometh in three great forces, and many smaller ones, and perilous and awful is it to behold; for betwixt those forces it filleth all the mountain ghyll, and there is no foothold for man, nay for goat, save at a hundred foot or more above the water, and that evil and perilous; and as is the running of a winter millstream to the beetles and shrew-mice that haunt the greensward beside it, so is the running of that flood to the sons of Adam and the beasts that serve them: and none has been so bold as to strive to cast a bridge across it.

But when ye have journeyed with much toil and no little peril over the mountain-necks (for by the gorge of the river, as aforesaid, no man may go) and have come out of the mountains once more, then again ye have the flood before you, cleaving a great waste of rocks mingled with sand, where groweth neither tree nor bush nor grass; and now the flood floweth wide and shallow but swift, so that no words may tell of its swiftness, and on either side the water are great wastes of tumbled stones that the spates have borne down from the higher ground. And ye shall know that from this place upward to its very wells in the higher mountains, the flood decreaseth not much in body or might, though it be wider or narrower as it is shallower or deeper, for nought but mere trickles of water fall into it in the space of this sandy waste, and what feeding it hath is from the bents and hills on either side as you wend toward the mountains to the north, where, as aforesaid, are its chiefest wells.

Now when ye have journeyed over this waste for some sixty miles, the land begins to better, and there is grass again, yet no trees, and it rises into bents, which go back on each side, east and west, from the Flood, and the said bents are grass also up to the tops, where they are crested with sheer rocks black of colour. As for the Flood itself, it is now gathered into straiter compass, and is deep, and exceeding strong; high banks it hath on either side thereof of twenty foot and upward of black rock going down sheer to the water; and thus it is for a long way, save that the banks be higher and higher as the great valley of the river rises toward the northern mountains.

But as it rises the land betters yet, and is well grassed, and in divers nooks and crannies groweth small wood of birch and whiles of quicken tree; but ever the best of the grass waxeth nigh unto the lips of the Sundering Flood, where it rises a little from the Dale to the water; and what little acre-land there is, and it is but little, is up on knolls that lie nearer to the bent, and be turned somewhat southward; or on the east side of the Flood (which runneth here nigh due north to south), on the bent-side itself, where, as it windeth and turneth, certain slopes lie turned to southwest. And in these places be a few garths, fenced against the deer, wherein grow rye, and some little barley whereof to make malt for beer and ale, whereas the folk of this high-up windy valley may have no comfort of wine. And it is to be said that ever is the land better and the getting more on the east side of the Sundering Flood than on the west.

As to the folk of this land, they are but few even now, and belike were fewer yet in the time of my tale. There was no great man amongst them, neither King, nor Earl, nor Alderman, and it had been hard living for a strong-thief in the Dale. Yet folk there were both on the east side and the west of the Flood. On neither side were they utterly cut off from the world outside the Dale; for though it were toilsome it was not perilous to climb the bents and so wend over the necks east and west, where some forty miles from the west bank and fifty from the east you might come down into a valley fairly well peopled, wherein were two or three cheaping-towns: and to these towns the dalesmen had some resort, that they might sell such of their wool as they needed not to weave for themselves, and other small chaffer, so that they might buy wrought wares such as cutlery and pots, and above all boards and timber, whereof they had nought at home.

But this you must wot and understand, that howsoever the Sundering Flood might be misnamed down below, up in the Dale and down away to the southern mountains it was such that better named it might not be, and that nought might cross its waters undrowned save the fowl flying. Nay, and if one went up-stream to where it welled forth from the great mountains, he were no nearer to passing from one side to the other, for there would be nought before him but a wall of sheer rock, and above that rent and tumbled crags, the safe strong-houses of erne and osprey and gerfalcon. Wherefore all the dealings which the folk on the east Dale and the west might have with each other was but shouting and crying across the swirling and gurgling eddies of the black water, which themselves the while seemed to be talking together in some dread and unknown tongue.

True it is that on certain feast days, and above all on Midsummer night, the folk would pluck up a heart, and gather together as gaily clad as might be where the Flood was the narrowest (save at one place, whereof more hereafter), and there on each side would trundle the fire-wheel, and do other Midsummer games, and make music of string-play and horns, and sing songs of old time and drink to each other, and depart at last to their own homes blessing each other. But never might any man on the east touch the hand of any on the west, save it were that by some strange wandering from the cheaping-towns aforesaid they might meet at last, far and far off from the Dale of the Sundering Flood.

II

Of Wethermel and the Child Osberne

DRAW we nigher now to the heart of our tale, and tell how on the east side of the Sundering Flood was erewhile a stead hight Wethermel; a stead more lonely than most even in that Dale, the last house but one, and that was but a cot, toward the mountains at the head of the Dale. It was not ill set down, for its houses stood beneath a low spreading knoll, the broader side whereof was turned to the south-west, and where by consequence was good increase of corn year by year. The said knoll of Wethermel was amidst of the plain of the Dale a mile from the waterside, and all round about it the pasture was good for kine and horses and sheep all to the water's lip on the west and half way up the bent on the east; while towards the crown of the bent was a wood of bushes good for firewood and charcoal, and even beyond the crown of the bent was good sheep-land a long way.

Nevertheless, though its land was fruitful as for that country, yet had Wethermel no great name for luck, and folk who had the choice would liever dwell otherwhere, so that it was hard for the goodman to get men to work there for hire. Many folk deemed that this ill-luck came because the knoll had been of old time a dwelling of the Dwarfs or the Land-wights, and that they grudged it that the children of Adam had supplanted them, and that corn grew on the very roof of their ancient house. But however that might be, there was little thriving there for the most part: and at least it was noted by some, that if there were any good hap, it ever missed one generation, and went not from father to son, but from grandsire to grandson: and even so it was now at the beginning of this tale.

For he who had been master of Wethermel had died a young man, and his wife followed him in a month or two, and there was left in the house but the father and mother of these twain, hale and stout folk, he of fifty winters, she of forty-five; an old woman of seventy, a kinswoman of the house who had fostered the late goodman; and a little lad who had to name Osberne, now twelve winters old, a child strong and bold, tall, bright and beauteous. These four were all the folk of Wethermel, save now and then a hired man who was hard pressed for livelihood would be got to abide there some six months or so. It must be told further that there was no house within ten miles either up or down the water on that side, save the little cot abovesaid nigher to the mountains, and that was four miles up-stream; it hight Burcot, and was somewhat kenspeckle. Withal as to those Cloven Motes, as they were called, which were between the folk on either side, they were holden at a stead seven miles below Wethermel. So that in all wise was it a lonely and

scantly-manned abode: and because of this every man on the
stead must work somewhat hard and long day by day, and
even Osberne the little lad must do his share; and up to this
time we tell of, his work was chiefly about the houses, or
else it was on the knoll, or round about it, scaring fowl
from the corn; weeding the acre-ground, or tending the old
horses that fed near the garth; or goose-herding at whiles.
Forsooth, the two elders, who loved and treasured the little
carle exceedingly, were loth to trust him far out of sight
because of his bold heart and wilful spirit; and there were
perils in the Dale, and in special at that rough and wild end
thereof, though they came not from weaponed reivers for
the more part, though now and again some desperate out-
cast from the thicker peopled lands had strayed into it; and
there was talk from time to time of outlaws who lay out
over the mountain-necks, and might not always do to lack
a sheep or a neat or a horse. Other perils more of every-day
there were for a young child, as the deep and hurrying
stream of the Sundering Flood, and the wolves which haunted
the bent and the foothills of the mountains; and ever moreover there was the peril from creatures seldom seen, Dwarfs
and Land-wights to wit, who, as all tales told, might be well
pleased to have away into their realm so fair a child of
the sons of Adam as was this Osberne.

Forsooth for the most part the lad kept within bounds, for
love's sake rather than fear, though he wotted well that beating abode bound-breaking; but ye may well wot that this
quietness might not always be. And one while amongst others he was missing for long, and when his grandsire sought
him he found him at last half way between grass and
water above the fierce swirling stream of the river; for he
had clomb down the sheer rock of the bank, which all
along the water is fashioned into staves, as it were organ-
pipes, but here and there broken by I wot not what mighty
power. There then was my lad in an ingle-nook of the
rock, and not able either to go down or come up, till the
goodman let a rope down to him and hauled him on to the
grass.

Belike he was a little cowed by the peril, and the beating
he got for putting his folk in such fear; but though he

was somewhat moved by his grandam's tears and lamentation over him, and no less by the old carline's bewailing
for his days that he would so surely shorten, yet this was
not by a many the last time he strayed from the stead away
into peril. On a time he was missing again nightlong, but in
the morning came into the house blithe and merry, but exceeding hungry, and when the good man asked him where
he had been and bade him whipping-cheer, he said that he
cared little if beaten he were, so merry a time he had had;
for he had gone a long way up the Dale, and about twilight
(this was in mid-May) had fallen in with a merry lad somewhat bigger than himself, who had shown him many merry
plays, and at last had brought him to his house, "which is
not builded of stone and turf, like to ours," saith he, "but
is in a hole in the rock; and there we wore away the night,
and there was no one there but we two, and again he showed
me more strange plays, which were wondrous; but some
did frighten me."

Then his grandsire asked him what like those plays were.
Said Osberne: "He took a stone and stroked it, and mum-
bled, and it turned into a mouse, and played with us nought
afraid a while; but presently it grew much bigger, till it was
bigger than a hare; and great game meseemed that was, till
on a sudden it stood on its hind-legs, and lo it was become
a little child, and O, but so much littler than I; and then it
ran away from us into the dark, squealing the while like a
mouse behind the panel, only louder. Well, thereafter, my
playmate took a big knife, and said: 'Now, drudgling, I shall
show thee a good game indeed.' And so he did, for he set
the edge of the said knife against his neck, and off came
his head; but there came no blood, nor did he tumble
down, but took up his head and stuck it on again, and then
stood crowing like our big red cock. Then he said: 'Poultry,
cockerel, now will I do the like by thee.' And he came to
me with the knife; but I was afraid, and gat hold of his
hand and had the knife from him; and then I wrestled with
him and gave him a fall; but I must needs let him get up
again presently, whereas he grew stronger under my hand;
then he thrust me from him and laughed exceeding much,
and said: 'Here is a champion come into my house forsooth!

Well, I will leave thine head on thy shoulders, for belike I might not be able to stick it on again, which were a pity of thee, for a champion shalt thou verily be in the days to come.' After this all his play with me was to sit down and bid me hearken; and then he took out a little pipe, and put it to his mouth, and made music out of it, which was both sweet and merry. And then he left that, and fell to telling me tales about the woods where big trees grow, and how his kindred had used to dwell therein, and fashioned most fair things in smith's work of gold and silver and iron; and all this liked me well; and he said: 'I tell thee that one day thou shalt have a sword of my father's father's fashioning, and that will be an old one, for they both were long-lived.' And as he spake I deemed that he was not like a child any more, but a little, little old man, white-haired and wrinkle-faced, but without a beard, and his hair shone like glass. And then—then I went to sleep, and when I woke up again it was morning, and I looked around and there was no one with me. So I arose and came home to you, and I am safe and sound if thou beat me not, kinsman."

Now ye may judge if his fore-elders were not scared by the lad's tale, for they knew that he had fallen in with one of the Dwarf-kin, and his grandam caught him up and hugged him and kissed him well favouredly; and the carline, whose name was Bridget, followed on the like road; and then she said: "See you, kinsmen, if it be not my doing that the blessed bairn has come back to us. Tell us, sweetheart, what thou hast round thy neck under thy shirt." Osberne laughed. Said he: "Thou didst hang on me a morsel of parchment with signs drawn thereon, and it is done in a silk bag. Fear not, foster mother, but that I will wear it yet, since thou makest such to-do over it."

"Ah! the kind lad thou art, my dear," said the carline. "I will tell you, kinsmen, that I had that said parchment from our priest, and it is strong neckguard against all evil things, for on it is scored the Holy Rood, and thereon are the names of the three Holy Kings, and other writing withal which I may not read, for it is in clerks' Latin." And again the two women made much of the little lad, while the goodman stood by grumbling and grunting; but this time did

Osberne escape his beating, though he was promised a drubbing which should give him much to think on if he went that way again; and the women prayed and besought him to be obedient to the goodman herein.

But one thing he had not told his kinsfolk, to wit, that the Dwarf had given him for a gift that same knife where-with he had played the game of heads-off, and a fair sheath went with it, and he had done him to wit that most like luck would go with it. Wherefore little Osberne had the said knife hidden under his raiment, along with the parchment whereon was scored the Holy Rood and the good words of wisdom written.

III

Wolves Harry the Flock

Now these matters, and other strayings and misdoings of the youngling, befel before the time whereof I now tell, when he was, as aforesaid, passed of twelve years; and it was in latter autumn, when the nights are lengthening. At this time there was a hired man dwelling with them, whose work it was to drive the sheep afield, either up on to the eastern bents or away off down to the water, so as they might not eat the grass of the kine from them. But Osberne, both of his own will and at the bidding of the goodman, went off afield with this man John and helped him to keep the sheep from straying over-far. Now one day at evening, somewhat later than he was wont, when, as it chanced, Osberne had not fared with him, back comes John from the bents, and he looked scared and pale, and he tells the tale that as the light began to fail up there, three huge wolves fell upon the sheep, and slew sundry of them, and it was easy to be seen of him that he had held no very close battle with the wolves, but had stood aloof till they had done their supper, and then gathered what he could of the sheep without going over-near the field of deed. The goodman berated

him for his cowardice, and seemed to begrudge him his
victuals somewhat that night, whereas, what with them whom
the wolves had slain, and them who had perchance fled
away, the flock was seventeen wethers short. John excused
himself what he might, and said that he had no weapon,
nought save his shepherd's staff, and that the wolves had
slain his dog in the first stour: but while he spake, Osberne,
who sat by, deemed him somewhat stark and tall to be so
little-hearted.

However, the next day the goodman and John must needs
go up to the bent to see if they might find aught alive of
the sheep that were missing, and each of them bore a shield
and short spear, that they might make head against the
wolves if that host should fall on them in the middle of the
[day]. Meantime Osberne, by the goodman's bidding, drives
the flock down toward the water, nothing loth, for ever the
wondrous stream seemed to draw the lad to it. And a fair
day he had of it, wandering amidst the sheep and being
friendly with them, whiles drawing out his knife to look
thereon, as oft he did when he was alone; and forsooth it
was a goodly weapon, carven with quaintnesses about the
heft, the blade inlaid with runes done in gold, and the sheath
of silver. Whiles also he stood on the river's lip and looked
across the water, which was there in most places as big as
the Thames is at Reading, but sometimes narrower. But there
was nought stirring within eyeshot on the further bank that
day, save the fowl, and a bull that came running along and
lowing as he went on some errand, whatever it might be,
for he was not followed of any men. So he came back with
the flock before dark all safe; neither had he gone far from
the stead, for so he was bidden of his grandsire.

A little after comes in the goodman with John, neither
of them in very sweet temper; they had seen nought of the
sheep save the hides and bones of a half score, but the
wolves they had not failed to see; they had come to the
same place as the last night, and seemed by no means afraid
of the man-host with its spears and shields, wherefore these
last had turned their backs and run from them stoutly, and
now sat together glowering on each other, and casting now
and again a gibe each at each. But they were at one in this,

that the wolves were huge and fierce beyond measure, and such as any man might fear. But at last John spake and said: "Well, master, it is as they say down the Dale, that this is no lucky house; meseems ye are beset with no common wolves, but with skin-changers who have taken the shape of wolves, whether they be Land-wights or Dwarfs, or ride-a-nights of the outlaws."

At that word waxed the master wood-wrath, as was his wont if any spake of the luck of Wethermel; and he forgot his fear in his anger, and said: "Hearken the fool-talk of him! Thou hadst not the heart for all thine inches to go forward before thy master, and a man on the downward side of years; and now thou must needs make up fairy tales to cover thy cowardice." Said John, grinning, "Keep thy head, master; for sooth it is that thou wert the first to run, and wert the first through the door."

"Thou liest," said the goodman; "but this I tell thee, that whosoever was afraid then, thou shalt be afraid now." And he rose up and smote his man on the face so that he fell to the ground, and John leapt up and would have smitten his master again; but even therewith comes in the good-wife, and Bridget with her, bearing in the supper smoking hot, and something seemed to hold John back from his blow, and he sat down, surly enough but silent. Then said the goodwife: "What is to do here? Hast thou run against the settle-end, John, that thy cheek is red and blue?"

Laughed the youngling thereat, and a word came into his mouth, and he sang:

> All grey on the bent
> There the sheep-greedy went:
> The big spear and shield
> Met the foes of the field,
> But nought the white teeth
> In the warriors gat sheath,
> For master and man
> Full meetly they ran.
> But now in this hall
> The fear off doth fall
> From one of the twain,
> And his hand getteth gain,

> But the other sits there,
> And new groweth his fear
> Both of man and of grey.
> So the meat on board lay,
> Thou on whom gold doth ride,
> Meat-goddess grey-eyed,
> Let the loaf-warden eat,
> And the man whom he beat,
> And the lad that doth lie
> In wall-nook hereby,
> And thou Gold-tree the fair,
> And the milk-mother dear,
> Lest the meat wax a-cold
> Both for bold and unbold.

Hereat all laughed, but the two men somewhat from one side of their mouths. And the goodman said: "See thou to it, kinsman, lest stripes be thy song-pay." But Osberne laughed from a fair and merry face and sang again:

> O lord of the land,
> To the staff lay no hand
> Till the grey ones thou face
> In the wind-weary place.

And therewith he fell to his meat and ate stoutly, and to the women it seemed that their little kinsman had the makings of a champion in him, and his staves they loved dearly in their hearts, and they smiled upon him kindly; and he looked from one to the other, and quoth he:

> Three mothers had I,
> And one is gone by,
> But two are left here,
> Leal, buxom, and dear.

As for the goodman, now the meat was getting into him the wrath was running off, and he thought within himself that presently he should have great avail of his grandson.

IV

Surly John Falls Out with the Goodman

On the morrow comes John to the goodman, and quoth he: "Master, there is small doubt that I shall one day pay thee for the pudding in the pot which thou gavest me yestreen, and after that I shall have to take my soles out of this straightway; so meseemeth I had best go hence today."

"Well," said the goodman, "if thou must go, go, and the devil go with thee. But as to the knock on thy cheekbone, I will boot thee therefor, if thou wilt take boot and abide, for though thou be no hard worker, nor very deft of thy hands, yet the winter is lonely here, and thou wilt be missed somewhat."

Quoth John: "Yea, goodman, but there is this in it withal, that Wethermel liketh me not, though I say nought against thee for a master. I love not thy were-wolves, that are big and gruesome enough to frighten two stout armed men; and I love not thy Dwarfs, who cut off their own heads and stick them on again, and give guesting to little lads, doing them no hurt; for meseems that means that the said Dwarf will be carving guest-quarters here one day, and who knows how soon; and I care not for such an one as a fellow at board. And then there is thy grandson, and a fair boy he is and a good scald, though that be come upon him somewhat suddenly. But he is over bigwordy for me, and I see clearly that soon there shall be two masters in this house, and one is well enough for me. And lastly as to thy kinswomen; I wot well I shall have no good word from them year in year out. So take this for my last word, that I shall turn my back upon thee so soon as thou hast paid me my hire, and shall go seek quarters down the Dale, at some merrier stead than this."

The goodman looked on him sourly, and then turned about and took a bag from the chest, and drew silver from it, and told over certain pieces and laid them before John (who is henceforth called Surly John) and said: "Here is thine hire in good silver. And now I shall not say one more word to thee for good or bad, save this, that thou hadst best look to it that thy silver melt not before many months are over. Take thy soles out of this straightway." So John took up his silver, and stowed it in his pouch, and then he said: "Well, goodman, now that I am paid I think that I had best pay thee for the cheek-knock of last night."

He was a tall man and strong of thirty winters, and the goodman somewhat on in years and not over strong, wherefore the battle seemed like to go all one way. But lo, as he rushed on the goodman, of a sudden he felt his feet pulled away from under him, and fell noseling to the ground; and when he would rise, lo there was on one side of him the goodman with a cudgel in his hand, and Osberne on the other, with his whittle drawn; and the lad laughed and said: "Thou hast been a long while and used many words about going, so belike thou wert best tarry no longer; or wert thou thinking thou wouldst go to bed? Nay, thou hast talked long, but nought so long that it is night yet."

So therewith Surly John arose and shook the dust of the floor off him, shouldered his bag, which he had ready by, and went out-of-doors and down the Dale afoot, for he was too shamefaced to crave the loan of a horse, to which forsooth the kinsmen would have made him welcome.

So the day wore amidst divers matters, and the sheep pastured anigh to the Mel; but ever the goodman said that wolves or no wolves he must drive them up the bent next day. But he said this so often, that it seemed as if he were not over willing thereto; and in the evening he took forth an old sword which he had, a good one, and sat whetting it with a hone. So they fared to bed.

But in the morning ere it was light the goodman deemed he heard goings-on in the house, and he sat up and hearkened. Next then he heard a hand amongst the three shields which hung on the panel the other side of his shut-bed, and thereafter he heard one going to the door; and he smiled thereat and lay down again, and presently there came the sound of the bleating of many sheep. So the carle stands up therewith, and does on his raiment, and takes his spear and shield, and girds his sword to him, and goeth forth and out of the garth, and turns his face up toward the bent, but goes very slow; and day was now just beginning to dawn though the stars yet shone; clear was the morning. Now in the grey light the carle could just see what he looked to see, to wit, the whole flock going together toward the bent, and a little figure of a son of Adam going after them, on whom a red scarlet hue was even dimly to be seen.

The carle smiled, and said to himself, Forsooth, yonder ruffler must needs clothe him in holiday raiment to do his doughty deed! Now will I not follow him to mar his championship, but will leave him alone to his luck, which I see to be great.

So he abode a little in an ingle of the garth wall, while the sheep lessened but grew clearer before him, and the scarlet raiment of his grandson grew brighter; and then he went swiftly, skirting the knoll till he had it betwixt him and the stead, and thereafter he went more leisurely toward the north. And he said to himself, The lad will do well enough; and as to the women, they will make the less outcry, that when they find me and my weapons gone they will think I have fared with him up the bent. So therewith he betook himself well out of the way, keeping near to the bank of the river.

V

Osberne Slays the Wolves

As to Osberne, I will say nought of him till he comes back in the even, driving all his sheep before him, not one lacking, and two of the lost ones found. He bears with him shield and spear, and has the Dwarf-wrought whittle in his girdle. Over his shoulder to boot he bears a biggish bag, well-nigh big enough for so little a carle; of white linen it is, it hath something heavy in it, and is much stained with blood. So he folds the sheep straightway, and then comes into the hall, he and his bag, and throws the same into the ingle of the hearth fire. Then he casts a sack over his shoulders and sits before the bag, so that it may not be lightly seen. By this time it was dusking outside, and inside the hall it was pretty much dark save for the fire, where little flames leapt up now and again as some piece of the firing tumbled over. In the hall was no one, for the women were bringing in the kine, and the goodman was not yet come in from the field.

There he sits quietly, stirring little. And the next tidings is, the goodman comes home alone; he hears the sheep a-bleating, and goes glad at heart to the fold; and there is his joy eked, for by the light of the moon, which is now rising, he can see well enough to tell over the sheep, and finds two more than there were yesterday. So he goes speedily toward the hall, and the women now come up after him, having gotten the kine into the byre; so they all three go into the hall together.

Then cries out the goodman: "Is there aught in the hall now?" Osberne answers from where he sat: "There is but little, for I am little." Then they turn and see him hugging himself up in the sack, and something at his back, they cannot see what; and the goodman says: "What hast thou been about all day, kinsman? Thou art forever foolhardy and a truant; of right, stripes should pay thee for thy straying." Said Osberne: "I have been shepherding sheep; may it not buy me off the stripes that I have found two of the lost ones, and brought back all safe?" "Maybe," says the master; "but did aught else befal thee?" Says the lad: "Will it not buy me off beating that I have also brought home catch?"

"Yea, if the catch be good," says the goodman. "It is but a leash of snipes, which I got me in a corner of the bog up yonder," says Osberne. "Snipes!" says Bridget; "deft art thou, fosterling, to take them without either springe or stone-bow, and they all flittering like butterflies on a March day."

"Yea, auntie," saith he, "but a stone or two might avail without the bow, were one deft enough. Yet with no such weapons did I slay them; ask me what weapons I bore against them." Therewith he stirs and shakes himself, and off tumbles the sack from his shoulders, and therewith his grandam

lights up the candles, and they all see the scarlet and gold
of his holiday raiment; and Bridget says: "This also will I
ask thee, fosterling: do men go out to take snipes in their
holiday raiment?"

"I will tell thee," says the little lad: "the weapons I bore
against the catch were the shield to ward, and the spear to
thrust, and the knife for the shearing of the heads: and I
tell thee that when men go to battle they use to wend in
their fair-dyed raiment."

Then he stood up in the hall, the little one, but trim and
goodly, with gleaming eyes and bright hair, and a word came
into his mouth:

> On the wind-weary bent
> The grey ones they went,
> Growled the greedy and glared
> On the sheep-kin afeared;
> Low looked the bright sun
> On the battle begun,
> For they saw how the swain
> Stood betwixt them and gain.
> 'Twas the spear in the belly, the spear in the mouth,
> And a warp of the shield from the north to the south,
> The spear in the throat, and the eyes of the sun
> Scarce shut as the last of the battle was done.

"Well sung, kinsman!" said the goodman: "now shalt thou
show us the snipes." But ere the lad might stoop to his
bag the two women were upon him, clipping and kissing him
as if they would never have enough thereof. He made a
shift to thrust them off at last, and stooping to his bag he
drew out something and cast it on the board, and lo the
sheared-off head of a great grey wolf with gaping jaws and
glistening white fangs, and the women shrank before it. But
Osberne said: "Lo the first of the catch, and here is the
second." And again he drew out a head from the bag and
cast it on the board; and so with the third in due course.

"Now," said he, "the bag is empty, and deemest thou,
grandsire, that I have bought me off my beating? And thou,
grandam, I pray thee, give me my meat, for I am an-
hungered." So now they had nought but praises and caresses

for him, and they made as it were a new feast of that
November day, and were as merry as if they were feasting
the best days of Yule.

VI

They Fare to the Cloven Mote

AND now the days wore away to winter, and ever thereafter might Osberne do what he would, and go where he
would, for as little a lad as he was; but he worked with a
good will if he were uncompelled, and if he were suffered
to wander at whiles as his will drave him. Forsooth, since
he had no fellows of a like age to him, it was whiles that
he found the open field or the waste gave him better fellowship than the older folk, yea even than the women.

Winter came, and the snow and the frost, which was not
very hard in that land, as many would have been glad if it
were, for then might the Sundering Flood have been laid
with ice, which never betid. On the morning of Yule day,
Osberne and his grandsire and grandam got under way long
before daylight, that they might go to the Cloven Mote, and
hear the Christmass in the church of Allhallows, which had
been builded on the east side of the water to be the church
of the Mote; but on the other side of the water was another
church like to it in all ways, and under the same invocation,
for the Western folk. This was the first time that Osberne
had been boun to the Mote, and withal both the women
were wont to stay at home: but this time nought would
serve the goodwife but she must wend with her man, that
she might show her darling and her champion to the neighbours. It was a matter of seven miles down the water to
the Mote-stead, and they went aslant over the snow-covered
fields, and hit the riverbank about half way, and went thence
along the very lip of the water. And by then it was pretty
much daylight; and Osberne looked over the water and saw
about a half mile off (for the day was clear) two little knolls

rising from the field, and betwixt them and about them a
shaw of small wood; and he asked his grandsire what that
might be, for hitherto he had never been so far down the
water; whereas before he slew the wolves, down the water
was banned to him, and after that he had been busy about
the houses and folds, or driving the sheep to the bents day
by day.

So his grandsire answered him: "That is hight Hartshaw,
and we are told that on the other side of the shaw and the
knolls looking west is a stead with houses inhabited, and the
whole place is hight Hartshaw Knolls." Said Osberne: "I
would we were there a while, for as I look at the stead it
seemeth friendly to me, and I fare to feel that the folk thereof shall come into my life some day." Answered the goodman: "We hear that little dwelleth there save a widow-
woman and her one child, a little maiden. And as to thy one
day, it shall be a long while coming; for long and long shall
it be for any one to encompass the Sundering Flood, save
the Winter of Fear come upon us, and all the land be over-
laid with ice, and the waters of the Flood be stayed; which
may God and Allhallows forfend."

The lad said nought for a while; and then he said: "Goodman, I would we had gone down to riverbank from out our
own door, and gone all along the Flood-side to the Mote;
for it were pleasant to have looked across the Flood, thinking of all there is on the other side, and wondering if we
shall ever get there. Why did we not this, for on the very
bank the going is better?" Said the carle: "We have come
the shortest way this bitter winter morning; that is all."

Herein he lied; for they had gone that slant way to give
the go-by to a certain place of the Flood-bank which the
Dale-dwellers deemed perilous; but thereof he would not tell
the little carle, now that he was become so masterful, deeming that if he heard of any peril toward he would be all
agog to try the adventure thereof, as forsooth was true. Of
this place, which lay now but just behind them, shall more
be told hereafter.

Now they come to the Mote in good time when the sun
was but just arisen, and there was already a throng; and
at their coming the folk on the western side raised a shout,

as the folk on either side were wont to welcome newcomers;
but the very first man they hit upon was Surly John; and
the goodwife, a soft, kind woman, hailed him friendly, and
was fain to have some one whom she knew unto whom to
tell her tale of the champion and the wolves. For indeed it
needs must out to the very first comer, and out it came now,
many worded, and folk, both men and women, gathered
about the twain to hearken; for the goodwife told it all well
and without hitch.

Surly John must needs abide the telling of it, but when it
was done he said: "Well, dame, so it is that I always deemed
the lad kenspeckle; and it has moreover turned out as I
warned you, that you have got a new master over you."
And therewith he turned away; but of those others who
heard the tale there were more than one or two who praised
it much, and deemed it marvellous as might well be that a
child should have faced and slain those three monsters who
had put two stout men to flight. And one man made up
this stave, which was presently sung all about the Eastern
Mote, and went over the water with the tale to the Western
one:

> To run and to fight
> Are deeds free to the wight,
> And John tried in battle
> Had heard the boards rattle,
> But needed to prove
> The race back to the stove;
> So his wightness he showed
> In way-wearing the road.
> While Osberne, who knew
> How the foot-race to do,
> Must try the new game
> Where the battle-beasts came.
> Bairn for fight, but for running the strong man and tall,
> And all folk for the laughter when both are in hall.

When Surly John heard this stave he cursed between his
teeth, but said nought.

But now on either side the churches fell to ringing to
mass, and all folk fared to service. And Osberne sat in a

good place amongst the carles, and forsooth he had both ears and eyes open, both then and all day. Mass over, the cooking-fires were lighted and tents were pitched on either side the water, and in a while they went to dinner; and thereafter, when they had sung a while, came the time of drinking, and folk were paired, men and women so far as might be, for more men there were than women. But whereas all men save Surly John were well with Osberne, there was gotten for his mate a fair young damsel of but seventeen winters, and Osberne, who had looked hard on all the women who were well-liking (for he had seen but very seldom any women save those two of his kinsfolk), was amazed with joy when the dear maid pulled down her hood and pulled off her gloves. And whereas she was shy of him because of his doughtiness, for all that he was but a child, it was not until they had drunk a cup or two that he took heart to set his hand to her neck and kiss her cheeks and her mouth, whereat she blushed rosy red, and all they that were in the tent laughed and cheered. But thereafter they fell to sweet speech and talked much, and he held her hand when the end of the feast was done; which was after this wise, that folk stood on the very lip of the river in one long row, hand in hand, and the loving-cup went down each row, and they cried healths to each other, and then lifted up their voices and shouted all together, and so undid the Mote and parted. And this time (and it was dark save for the fires flaring behind them) it was the maid that kissed Osberne; neither needed she, a tall damsel though she was, to stoop much thereto, for right big and tall he was of his years.

So then all went back each to his own home. And the winter wore away at Wethermel with nought to tell of.

VII

Of a Newcomer, and His Gift to Osberne

Now when spring came again, needs must Osberne drive the sheep up to the bents, though he had liefer haunted the riverside, for sore he desired to cross the Flood and find out tidings there. And though he were a child, yet he would by his own choice have fared to seek out the pretty maiden whose hand he had held on the edge of the river that even, but livelihood drave him to look to the sheep now that the spring grass was growing.

So on a certain day when March was wearing towards April he drave his sheep up over the crown of the bent; and there he went with them a way where, the land still rising, the ground was hard and rocky but clean, and the grass sweet for as scanty as it was, growing in little hollows and shelters round about the rocks. Wherefore the sheep were nimble in their feeding, and led him on long, till they and he were come into a grassy little dale with a stream running through it. There they were neither to hold nor to bind, but strayed all up and down the dale and over the crest of the bent thereof, and would not come to his call; and his dog was young and not very wise, and could do little to help him. So he began to think he had best gather what of the sheep he could, and drive them home and fold them, and then come back and hunt for the rest, perhaps with the help of his grandsire; but as the ones he could get at were all close anigh, and he was hot and weary with running hither and thither and holloaing to sheep and dog, he would go down to the stream and drink and rest awhile first. And even so he did, and lay down by the water and drank a long draught; but while he was about it he thought he heard footsteps coming down the hill-side over the greensward.

Howsoever, he had his drink out, and then rose to his

knees and looked up, and therewith sprang hastily to his feet, for a tall man was coming on toward him not ten yards from the stream. He was not to say afeard by the sight, yet somewhat startled, for the man was not his grandsire, nor forsooth did he seem to be one of the Dale-dwellers. For he was so clad that he had a grey hawberk on him of fine ringmail, and a scarlet coat thereunder embroidered goodly; a big gold ring was on his left arm, a bright basnet on his head; he was girt with a sword, and bare a bow in his hand, and a quiver hung at his back. He was a goodly man, young by seeming, bright-faced and grey-eyed; his hair was yellow and as fine as silk, and it hung down over his shoulders.

Now Osberne put as good a face on the meeting as he might, and gave the newcomer the sele of the day, and he hailed him again in a clear loud voice, and they stood looking on each other across the stream a while. Then the newcomer laughed pleasantly and said: "Hast thou any name that I may call thee by?"

"I am Osberne of Wethermel," said the youngling. "Aha," said the man, "art thou he that slew the leash of great grey wolves last autumn, who had put two armed men to flight the day before?" Said Osberne, reddening: "Well, what was I to do? There fell a leash of hill-dogs on our sheep, and I made them forbear. Was it a scathe to thee, lord?" The newcomer laughed again: "Nay, my lad," said he, "I love them no more than ye do; they were no dogs of mine. But what doest thou here?"

"Thou seest," said the youngling, "that I am shepherding our sheep; and a many have run from me, and I cannot bring them back to me. So I was going home with those that be left."

"Well," says the man," "we can soon mend that. Rest thou here and abide my coming back again, and I will fetch them for thee."

"With a good will," says Osberne, "and I shall can thee many thanks therefor."

So the man strode on and through the stream, and went his ways up the further bent, and Osberne sat down on a stone and abode him in no little wonder. The man was gone somewhat more than an hour, and then Osberne sees the sheep topping the crest of the bent and pouring down into the dale, and the newcomer came next driving them down; and when they came to the stream they stood there and moved no more than if they were penned.

Then the newcomer came through them up to Osberne, and said in a kind voice, though it was loud: "What, art thou here yet? I deemed that thou wouldst have run home."

"Why should I have run?" said the lad. "For fear of me," said the other. Said Osberne: "I was somewhat afeard when I first saw thee, and thou with the grey byrny and the gleaming helm; but then I saw that thou wert no ill man, and I feared thee no longer. Withal I was fain to see thee again; for thou art goodly and fair to behold, and I am fain to remember thee."

Said the man: "Even so have others said ere now." "Were they women?" said Osberne. "Thou art brisk and keen, youngling," said the man. "Yes, they were women: but it was long ago." "Yet thou lookest no old man," said Osberne. "I have seen old men: they be nought like to thee."

"Heed thou not that," said the helmed man; "but tell me, how old a man art thou?" Said Osberne: "When this April is three days old I shall be thirteen years old."

Said the man of the waste: "Well, thou art stalwarth for thy years, and that liketh me well, and meseems that we shall be friends hereafter: and when thou art a grown man I shall seem no older to thee; nay, we shall be as brothers. Belike I shall see thee again before long; meanwhile, I give thee this rede: when thou mayest, seek thou to the side of the Sundering Flood, for meseemeth that there lieth thy weird. Now there is this last word to be said, that I came hither today to see thee, and in token thereof I have brought thee a gift. Canst thou shoot in the bow aught?" Said Osberne: "There is one at home, and my grandsire hath bent it for me at whiles, and taught me how to shoot somewhat; but I am little deft therein."

Then the man betook him the bow which he had in his hand and said: "Here is one that shall make thee deft; for whoso hath this as a gift from me shall hit what he shooteth at if he use my shafts withal, and here be three which I will give thee; and if thou take heed, thou shalt not find them easy to lose, since ever they shall go home. But if ever thou lose two of them, then take the third and go into some waste place where there is neither meadow nor acre, and turn to the north-east and shoot upward toward the heavens, and say this rhyme:

> A shaft to the north,
> Come ye three, come ye forth;
> A shaft to the east,
> Come three at the least;
> A shaft to the sky,
> Come swift, come anigh!
> Come one, one and one,
> And the tale is all done.

And then shalt thou find the arrows lying at thy feet. Now take the bow and arrows, and drive me thy sheep betwixt us to the top of the bent that looks down on Wethermel."

Then Osberne took the bow and shafts, and he all quivering with joy and delight, and then the two of them together went back across the waste with the sheep before them, and as they went side by side the man said many things, and this at last: "Now that I know thy name, it is like that thou wouldst know mine and who I am; but my very name I may not tell thee, for thy tongue has no word for it, but now and when we meet again thou mayst call me Steelhead: and thou shalt know that when next we meet I shall be arrayed all otherwise than now. In that array I deem thou wilt know me, but look to it that thou show no sign thereof before other men; and as to the bow, thou wilt not be eager belike to say of whom thou hadst it. Lo now! we have opened up Wethermel; fare thou well, bold bairn, and forget not my redes."

And therewith he turned about and gat him gone into the waste again, striding hugely; and the lad was sorry to lack him, for he deemed him the goodliest and best man that he had ever met.

VIII

The Goodman Gets a New Hired Man

Now when he came home to Wethermel he found tidings there, for the goodman had gotten a new hired man, and he showed him to Osberne, who greeted him well: he was a tall man, mild of aspect and speech, flaxen-haired and blue-eyed, and seemed a stark carle. He had come to the stead that morning while the goodman was away, and had craved guesting of the women, who made him welcome and set him down to meat. He told them that his name was Stephen, that he had been born in the country-side, but had gone thence in his early youth to Eastcheaping, which was the market town whither that folk had resort; and that he had grown up there and there wedded a wife; but that when she died in childing with her first bairn, and the bairn had not lived, he loathed the place, and came back again into the Dale.

So when the goodman came home this Stephen offered himself to him, and said that he deemed he could do as good a stroke of work as another, and that he was not for any great wage, but he must not be stinted of his meat, whereas he was a heavy feeder. The goodman liked the looks of him, and they struck the bargain betwixt them straightway, and Stephen had hansel of a second dinner, and ate well thereat; and henceforth is he called Stephen the Eater.

Now when the goodman saw Osberne bring in his new weapon, he asked him whence he had it, and the lad told him that he had been far in the waste, and had found it there. The goodman eyed him, but said nought. Forsooth he misdoubted him that the bow was somewhat unked, and that the lad had had some new dealings with the Dwarf-kin or other strange wights. But then he bethought him of Osberne's luck, and withal it came into his mind that now he had gotten this victual-waster it would not be ill if his lad should shoot them some venison or fowl now and again; and by the look of the bow he deemed it like to be a lucky one. But Stephen reached out for the bow, and handled it and turned it about, and spake: "This is a handy weapon, and they who made it were not without craft, and it pleases me to see it; for now when it brings home prey in the evening, the goodman will deem my maw the less burdensome to him. By my rede, goodman, ye will do well to make thy youngling the hunter to us all, for such bows as this may be shot in only by them that be fated thereto." And he nodded and smiled on Osberne, and the lad deemed that the new man would be friendly to him.

So then was supper brought in, and Stephen the Eater played as good a part as if he had eaten nought since sunrise.

But the next day, when Stephen was boun for driving the sheep to the bent, he said to Osberne: "Come thou with me, young master, to show me the way; and bring the bow and arrows withal, and see if thou canst shoot us something toothsome, for both of feathers and fur there is foison on the hill-side." So they went together, and betwixt whiles of the shepherding Osberne shot a whole string of heathfowl and whimbrel; and ever he hit that which he shot at, so that the arrows were easy indeed to find, since they never failed to be in the quarry.

The goodman was well pleased with his catch, and Stephen licked his lips over the look of the larder. And the next day the lad let Stephen go alone to the hill, and he himself took a horse and went up the water a ten miles toward the mountain, and there he slew a hart of ten tines with one arrow, and brought the quarry home across the horse, to the joy of all the household, and the goodman was not rueing his bargain with Stephen the Eater. So it went on that every two or three days Osberne fared afield after catch, and but seldom came home empty-handed, and the other days he did as he would and went where he listed. And now he began to follow the rede of Steelhead, and went oftenest by the side of the Sundering Flood, but as yet he had gone up the water and not down.

IX

The Bight of the Cloven Knoll

AND now it was mid-April, and the goodman dight him to ride to a mote of the neighbours at a stead hight Bullmeads, where the Dalesmen were wont to gather in the spring, that they might ride thence all together to the town of Eastcheaping and sell the autumn clip of wool and do other chaffer. So the carle goes his ways alone, and will be one night at Bullmeads and two at Eastcheaping, and then another at Bullmeads, and be back on the fifth day. And when he was gone comes Stephen to Osberne, and says: "Young master, I am going presently to the hill with the sheep, and thou needest neither to go with me nor fare a-hunting today, since the house is full of meat; so thou art free, and were I in thy shoes I would go straight from this door down to the water-side, and see if thou mayst not happen on something fair or seldom seen. But hearken to my rede, if thou comest on aught such, thou hast no need to tell of it to any one, not even to me. [And it were not amiss to do on thy coat of scarlet.]"

Osberne thanks him, and takes his bow and arrows and goes his way and comes to the riverside and turns his face south, and goes slowly along the very edge of the water; and the water itself drew his eyes down to gaze on the dark green deeps and fierce downlong swirl of the stream, with its sharp clean lines as if they were carven in steel, and the curling and upheaval and sudden changing of the talking eddies: so that he scarce might see the familiar greensward of the further shore.

At last, when he had gone thus more than two miles from where he first hit the water, a long straight reach lay before him, and as he looked down it; it seemed as if the river came presently to an end; but in sooth there was a sharp turn to the east by which the water ran, but narrowing much; and this narrowing was made by the thrusting forth of the western bank into a sharp ness, which, from where Osberne now stood, showed a wide flank facing, as it seemed, the whole hurrying stream of the Flood. But the stream turned ere it smote the cliff, and striving for the narrow outgate made a prodigious eddy or whirlpool ere it might clear itself of the under-water foot of the ness and make eastward so as to rush on toward the sea. But in the face of the wall, in the bight where the whirlpool turned from it, was a cave the height of a tall man, and some four feet athwart, and below it a ledge thrust out from the sheer rock and hanging over the terrible water, and it was but a yard wide or so. It was but ten feet above the water, and from it to the grass above must have been a matter of forty foot. But the ness as it thrust forth into the river rose also, so that its crest was a score of feet higher where it went down into the water than its base amidst the green grass. Then came the strait passage of the water, some thirty feet across, and then the bank of the eastern side, which, though it thrust not out, but rather was as it were driven back by the stream, yet it rose toward the water, though not so much as the ness over against it. It was as if some one had cast down a knoll across the Sundering Flood, and the stream had washed away the sloped side thereof, and then had sheared its way through by the east side where the ground was the softest. Forsooth so it seemed to the Dalesmen, for on either side they called it the Bight of the Cloven Knoll.

Osberne stood amazed right over against the cave in the cliff-side, and stared at the boiling waters beneath him, that seemed mighty enough to have made a hole in the ship of the world and sunk it in the deep. And he wondered at the cave, whether it were there by chance hap, or that some hands had wrought it for an habitation.

And as he stood gazing there, on a sudden there came out of the cave a shape as of man, and stood upon the ledge above the water, and the lad saw at once that it was a little maiden of about his own age, with ruddy golden hair streaming down from her head, and she was clad in a short coat of dark blue stuff and no more raiment, as far as he could see. Now as aforesaid Osberne was in his holiday raiment of red-scarlet by the bidding of Stephen. Now the maiden looks up and sees the lad standing on the eastern shore, and starts back astonished. Then she came forward again and looked under the sharp of her hand, for the sun shone from the south and was cast back dazzling from the water. There was but some thirty feet of water between them, but all gurgling and rushing and talking, so the child raised a shrill and clear voice as she clapped her hands together and cried: "O thou beauteous creature, what art thou?" Osberne laughed, and said in a loud voice: "I am a man, but young of years, so that they call me a boy, and a bairn, and a lad. But what art thou?"

"Nay, nay," she said, "I must be nigher to thee; it is over-wide here amidst the waters' speech. Fare up to the top on thy side, and so will I." And therewith she turned about and fell to climbing up the side of the cliff by the broken black staves and the shaly slips. And though Osberne were a boy, yea and a tough one in some ways, he trembled and his heart beat quick to see the little creature wending that perilous upright road, and he might not take his eyes off her till she had landed safely on the greensward; then he turned and went swiftly up the eastern knoll, and reached the edge of the sheer rock just as the maiden came running up the ness on her side.

He spake not, for he was eyeing her closely, and she might not speak a while for lack of breath. At last she said: "Now are we as near to each other as we may be today; yea for many days, or it may be for all our lives long: so now let us talk." She set her two feet together and held her hands in front of her, and so stood as if she looked for him to begin. But the words came not speedily to his mouth, and at last she said: "I wonder why thou wilt not speak again; for thy laugh was as the voice of a dear bird; and thy voice is beauteous, so loud and clear."

He laughed, and said: "Well then, I will speak. Tell me what thou art. Art thou of the Faery? for thou art too well shapen to be of the Dwarfkin." She clapped her hands together and laughed; then she said: "I laughed not as mocking thy question, but for joy to hear thy voice again. Nay,

nay, I am no faery, but of the children of men. But thou, art thou not of the sons of the Land-wights?"

"No more than thou art," said he. "I am a goodman's son, but my father is dead, and my mother also, and I live at home at Wethermel up the water, with my grandsire and grandam."

Said she: "Are they kind to thee?" The lad drew himself up: "I am kind to them," said he. "How goodly thou art!" she said; "that was why I dreamed thou must be of the Land-wights, because I have seen divers men, some old, some young like to thee, but none half so goodly." He smiled, and said: "Well, I thought thou wert of the Faery because thou art goodly and little. I have seen a pretty maid not long since, but she was older than thou, I deem, and far taller. But tell me, how old art thcu?" She said: "When May is half worn I shall be of thirteen winters."

"Lo now," said he, "we be nigh of an age; I was thirteen in early April. But thou hast not told me where thou dwellest, and how." She said: "I dwell at Hartshaw Knolls hard by. I am the daughter of a goodman, as thou art, and my father and mother are dead, so that my father I never saw, and now I dwell with my two aunts, and they be both older than was my mother."

"Are they kind to thee?" said the lad, laughing that he must cast back her question. "Whiles," said she, laughing also, "and whiles not: maybe that is because I am not always kind to them, as thou art to thy folk." He answered nought, and she was silent a while; then he said: "What is in thy mind, maiden?" "This," she said, "that I am thinking how fair a chance it was that I should have seen thee, for thou hast made me so glad." Said he: "We can see each other again belike and make it less of a chance." "O yea," she said, and was silent a while. Said he: I wot not why it was that thou wert in the cave: and tell me, is it not exceeding perilous, the climbing up and down? Why wilt thou do that? Also I must tell thee, that this was another cause why I thought thou wert of the Faery, that thou camest out of the cave."

Said she: "I will tell thee all about the cave; but first as to the peril of going thither and coming thence: wouldst thou be very sorry if I were lost on the way?" "Yea," said he, "exceeding sorry." "Well," said she, "then fear it not, for it is so much a wont of mine that to me there is no peril therein: yet am I glad that thou wert afraid for me." "I was sore afraid," said Osberne.

"Now as to the cave," said the maiden. "I found it out two years ago, when I was very little, and the women had been less than kind to me. And thither may I go whenas I would that they should seek me not; because folk say that it is a dwelling of the Dwarfs, and they fear to enter it. Besides, when I think of my kinswomen coming down the rock to find me therein, and they be tall, and one stiff, as if she were cut out of timber, and the other exceeding fat, that makes me merry!"

And therewith she sat down on the very edge of the cliff with her little legs hanging over the water, and laughed, rocking to and fro in her laughter, and Osberne laughed also. But he said: "But art thou not afraid of the Dwarfs?" She said: "Dear bairn or boy, I had been there many times before I heard tell of the Dwarfs, and I gat no harm, and after I had heard the tale I went still, and still gat no harm; nay I will tell thee somewhat: I gat gifts, or such they seemed unto me. First I had to herd the sheep and take them to the best grass, and whiles they strayed and were wearisome to me, and I came home with divers missing, and then would I be wyted or even whipped for what was no fault of mine. And one such time I betook me to the cave and sat therein and wept, and complained to myself of my harm, and when I went out of the cave I saw on the ledge close to my foot a thing lying, and I took it up, and saw that it was a pipe with seven holes therein, and when I blew into it, it made sweet and merry little music. So I thought it great prize, and went away home with it, with all my sorrows well healed. But the next day I drave my sheep to grass, as my business was, and as oft happened, they strayed, and I followed them and gat nothing done; so I was weary, and afraid of what would betide at home in the stead. So I sat down on a stone, and when I had wept a little I thought I would comfort myself with the music of the pipe. But lo a wonder, for no sooner had a note or two sounded than all the sheep came running up to me, bleating, and mowing, and would rub against my sides as I sat piping, and home I brought every head in all glee. And even so has it befallen ever since; and that was hard on a year agone. Fair boy, what dost thou think I am doing now?" Osberne laughed. "Disporting thee in speech with a friend," said he. "Nay," said she, "but I am shepherding sheep."

And she drew forth the pipe from her bosom and fell to playing it, and a ravishing sweet melody came thence, and so merry that the lad himself began to shift his feet as one moving to measure, and straightway he heard a sound of bleating, and sheep came running toward the maiden from all about. Then she arose and ran to them, lest they should shove each other into the water; and she danced before them, lifting up her scanty blue skirts and twinkling her bare feet and legs, while her hair danced about her, and the sheep, they too capered and danced about as if she had bidden them. And the boy looked on and laughed without stint, and he deemed it the best of games to behold. But when she was weary she came back to the head of the ness and sat down again as before, and let the sheep go where they would.

X

Osberne and Elfhild Hold Converse Together

So when she was rested she fell to speech again: "Dear lad, this was the first gift, and I could not but deem that some one had heard me make my moan unseen and had given me that good gift. So what must I do but try it again, and one day I went down into the cave and fell to bewailing me that I had nought to deck me with, neither of gold nor silver, as other maidens had, for in sooth I had seen them with such things. And when I had done, I went forth on to the ledge, and this time I trod cautiously lest I should

kick the dainty thing into the water, and lo, there lay this
pretty thing." And she drew forth from her bosom a necklace
of gold and gems; gold and emerald, gold and sapphire,
gold and ruby; and it flashed in the sun, and Osberne thought
it a fair toy indeed, but knew not that scarce a queen had
got aught so fair in her treasure. "Ye may wot well that I
dare not show either this or the pipe to my aunts, who
would have taken them away from me and cried horror at
them; for oft would they cry out at the evil things that dwelt
in the ness and all the ills they brought on the children of
men. So I play on the pipe when none are by, and I deck
myself sitting in the sun with this fair necklace. Look thou,
lad, for it is a joy to show me unto thee so decked." And she
did back her raiment from her thin neck, and it was white
as snow under the woollen, and she did on the necklace,
and Osberne thought indeed that it sat well there, and that
her head and neck looked grand and graithly.

Then she said: "One other gift I gat from these cave-folk,
if there be such in the cave. On a day I was ailing, and could
scarce hold up my head for weariness and sickness; so I
stole down hither and clomb with all trouble and peril down
to the cave, and fell to bewailing my sickness, and scarce
had I done ere I felt exceeding drowsy, and so laid me
down on the floor of the cave and fell asleep there, feeling
sick no longer even then. And when I awoke, after some
three hours as I deemed, there was nought amiss with me,
and I climbed up to grass again strong and merry, and making nought of the climb. And even so have I done once
and again, and never have the good folk failed me herein.
Hast thou ever had dealings with such-like creatures?"

Osberne answered, and told her of his meeting with the
Dwarf that time, and held up to her the whittle he had
gat, and flashed it in the sun; and then he was about to tell
her of Steelhead. But he remembered that he was scarce
free to tell any one of him, so he held his peace thereof;
but he said: "Meseemeth, maiden, that thou art not without
might, such friends as thou hast. But tell me, what canst
thou do beside the shepherding?" She said: "I can spin and
weave, and bake the bread and make the butter, and grind
meal at the quern; but the last is hard work, and I would

not do it uncompelled, nor forsooth the indoor work either, for nought but the shepherding is to my mind. But now tell me, what canst thou do?" He said: "Meseems I cannot keep my sheep together so well as thou; but last autumn I learned how to slay wolves that would tear the sheep."

She rose up as if to look at him the better, and strained her hands together hard, and gazed eagerly at him. He saw that she was wondering at him and praising him, so he said lightly: "It is no so great a matter as some think; what is most needed is a good heart and a quick eye. Thus I slew the three of them."

"O," she said, "now I know that thou art that fair child and champion of whom I have heard tell, that thy deed was a wonder; and now thou art so kind that thou wilt wear the day talking to a poor and feeble maiden."

Said he: "I do that because it is my will and it pleases me to see thee and talk to thee, for thou art good to look at and dear."

Then she said: "But what else canst thou do, Champion?" Said he: "Of late I am thought to be somewhat deft at shooting in the bow, so that whatso I aim at, that I hit. Thus I am not like to lack for meat." "Yea," she said, "but that is wonderful; and besides, now canst thou shoot at the wolves from afar without their being able to come at thee to bite thee. But now it is hard to get thee to tell of thy prowess, and I must ask after every deal. Tell me of something else." Quoth he: "At home they deem me somewhat of a scald, so that I can smithy out staves." She clapped her hands together and cried: "Now that is good indeed, since thou canst also slay wolves. But how sweet it would be for me to have thee making a stave before me now. Wouldst thou?"

"I wot not," he said, laughing; "but let me try." So he sat down and fell to conning his rhymes, while she stood looking on from across the water. At last he stood up and sang:

> Now the grass groweth free
> And the lily's on lea,
> And the April-tide green
> Is full goodly beseen,

And far behind
Lies the winter blind,
And the lord of the Gale
Is shadowy pale;
And thou, linden be-blossomed, with bed of the worm
Camest forth from the dark house as spring from the storm.

O barm-cloth tree,
The light is in thee,
And as spring-tide shines
Through the lily lines,
So forth from thine heart
Through thy red lips apart
Came words and love
To wolf-bane's grove,
And the shaker of battle-board blesseth the Earth
For the love and the longing, kind craving and mirth.

May I forget
The grass spring-wet
And the quivering stem
On the brooklet's hem,
And the brake thrust up
And the saffron's cup,
Each fashioned thing
From the heart of Spring,
Long ere I forget it, the house of thy word
And the doors of thy learning, the roof of speech-hoard.

When thou art away
In the winter grey,
Through the hall-reek then
And the din of men
Shall I yet behold
Sif's hair of gold
And Hild's bright feet,
The battle-fleet,
And from threshold to hearthstone, like as songs of the South,
To and fro shall be fleeting the words of thy mouth.

Then his song dropped down, and they stood looking silently at each other, and tears ran over the little maiden's cheeks. But she spake first and said: "Most lovely is thy lay, and there is this in it, that I see thou hast made it while thou wert sitting there, for it is all about thee and me, and how thou lovest me and I thee. And full surely I know that thou wilt one day be a great and mighty man. Yet this I find strange in thy song almost to foolishness, that thou speakest in it as I were a woman grown, and thou a grown man, whereas we be both children. And look, heed it, what sunders us, this mighty Flood, which hath been from the beginning and shall be to the end."

He answered not a while, and then he said: "I might not help it; the words came into my mouth, and meseems they be better said than unsaid. Look to it if I do not soon some deed such as bairns be not used to doing." "That I deem is like to be," she said, "yet it shall be a long time ere folk shall call us man and woman. But now, fair child, I must needs go homeward, and thou must let me go or I shall be called in question." "Yea," said Osberne, "yet I would give thee a gift if I might, but I know not what to give thee save it were my Dwarf-wrought whittle." She laughed and said: "That were a gift for a man but not for me; keep it, dear and kind lad. I for my part were fain of giving thee somewhat: but as for my pipe, I fear me that I could never throw it across the water. I would I might reach thee with my gold and gem necklace, but I fear for it lest the Sundering Flood devour it. What shall I do then?"

"Nought at all, dear maiden," said the lad, "I would no wise take thy pipe from thee, which saveth thee from blame and beating; and as to the necklace, that is woman's gear even as the whittle is man's. Keep it safe till thou art become a great lady."

"Well," she said, "now let me go; it almost seems to me as I might not till thou hast given me leave."

"Yea," said he; "but first, when shall I come to see thee again, and thou me? Shall it be tomorrow?" "O nay," she said, "it may not be, lest they take note of me if I come down here over often. Let it be after three days first: and then the next time it must be longer." Quoth Osberne: "Let the next time take care of itself; but I will come in three days. Now I bid thee depart, and I will go home; but I would kiss thee were it not for the Sundering Flood." "That is kind and dear of thee," said the maiden. "Farewell, and forget me not in three days, since thou hast sung that song to me." "I shall not forget so soon," said he. "Farewell!"

She turned about and ran down the ness with the pipe in her hand, and Osberne heard the sweet voice of the pipe thereafter, and the bleating of the sheep and the paddling of their hoofs as they all ran toward her, and he went his ways home with all that in his ears, and was well content with his day's work; and he deemed that he understood the rede which Steelhead had given him. Withal he had an inkling that Stephen the Eater was somehow his friend in more special way than he was to the rest of the household; so he came home to Wethermel in good case.

XI

Osberne Shoots a Gift Across the Flood

Now when the three days were over he went his ways to the Bight of the Cloven Knoll, and Stephen smiled and nodded to him friendly as he went out of the door, and once more he was clad in his red-scarlet raiment. He had his bow in his hand, and besides the three arrows which the hillman had given, he had two others out of the goodman's quiver. Moreover he had thought over from time to time what he might give to the maiden, and now he had in his pouch a fair gold piece which his mother had given him when he was yet very young, and he thought that this were a fair gift might he but get it over to the other side of the Sundering Flood.

Now when he was within eyeshot of the ness, he looked thither, and saw a little figure on the crest thereof, and knew that the maiden had prevented him and was there already, so he hastened all he might to his own vantage ground, and straightway he gave her the sele of the day, and she greeted him kindly. Then he looks and sees that she is somewhat decked out for this meeting, for not only did the Dwarfs' gift, the necklace, gleam and glitter on her little flat child's bosom, but also she had made her a wreath for her head of the spring flowers, and another had she done about her loins. She stood there saying nothing a while, and it seemed to him that she was waiting for him to praise this new-wrought adornment. So he said: "Thou art in fairer guise than when first I saw thee; is there any high-tide toward at thy stead?"

"Nay," she said; "I did this because I looked to see thee today, whereas the other time we happed on each other unawares. But hast thou done any more great deeds?"

He laughed and said: "Nay, nay, let me grow a few days older yet. Nevertheless there is this new thing, that this morning I have brought thee a gift which I deem I may flit to thee, and I shall give it to thee with a good will if thou wilt promise that thou wilt not part with it ever."

"With all my heart will I promise that," she said; "but tell me what it is; show it to me."

He drew it forth and held it up between his finger and thumb, and said: "It is a golden penny, very fair, and I deem it comes from some far country. My mother gave it to me when I was very young; yet I remember that she bade me part not with it, save I should give it to one unto whom I wished all luck, for that she deemed that luck went with it. Now thou art so fair and so dear, and my only fellow of a like age, that I wish luck to thee as much as luck can be found: so I will flit it to thee this wise, that I will do it up in a piece of cloth and tie it to the head of this arrow (which is of no account), and shoot it over to thee." And therewith he knelt down and fell to wrapping it up in the rag.

As for the maiden, she was all eager, and quivering with joy at the getting of such a gift; yet she spake and said: "O how good thou art to me: yet I deem not that thou shouldst give me thy mother's gift. And moreover why shouldst thou shoot away thy luck? It may be that I am not doomed to be lucky, as surely thou art; and it may well be that thou mayst give me thy luck and make thee less lucky, without eking mine, if unluck be my weird."

Now though he had set his heart on giving the gold to the

fair child, yet her words seemed wise to him, and he said: "What then shall we do?" She said: "Abide a while till I think of it."

So they were silent a while, both of them, till the little maid looked up and said: "Is it a round thing?" "Yea," said he. "What is there upon it?" she said. Quoth Osberne: "On one side be two warriors, and on the other the Rood and certain letters."

She thought again and said: "How much were it marred if it were halved, one warrior and half a cross?" He said: "That hangs upon this, who has one half and who the other." She said: "How would it be, since I can see that thou wishest that I should share thy gift, and belike thy luck also, if thou wert to do it into two halves, and keep one thyself and shoot me the other over the Flood?" He leapt up and fell a-dancing for joy as she spake, and cried out: "O, but thou art wise! Now I can see that this is what my mother meant me to do, to share the gold and the luck."

Therewith he took the penny out of its wrapping and drew forth his whittle, and gat a big stone and set the gold on the steel and smote it, deftly enough; for he was no ill smith for his years. Then he stood up and cried out: "There, it is done, and neither of the warriors is scathed, for there was a waste place betwixt them. Now then for the shaft and the bow!" The maiden looked eagerly with knitted brows, and soon saw Osberne take up the shaft and nock it on the bowstring.

Then he said: "Take heed and stand still and the halfling shall be thine. Look now, I will send the shaft so that it shall go in the grass-grown cleft betwixt the two big stones behind thee to thy right hand." He raised his bow therewith, and saw how she gathered her skirts about her, as if she would not have them hinder the shaft. Then he loosed, and the shaft flew, but she abode still a little; and he laughed and said: "Go, maiden, and find the shaft and the gold." Then she turned and ran to the cleft, and took out the arrow, and did off the wrapping with trembling fingers and gat the gold and looked on it, and cried out: "O the fair warrior! such like shalt thou be one day upon a penny, dear child."

Then she came forward again and said: "Now this is

strange, that neither last time nor now have we told each other our names: now I will tell thee that my name is Elfhild, of Hartshaw Knolls. What is thine?"

"Elfhild my child," said he, "my name is Osberne Wulf-grim's son, and I am of Wethermel, as I told thee. Yet belike it is not so strange that we have not told our names hitherto, and I hope no ill-luck will go with our telling them, for I suppose that people give each other names when there are many of them, and they would know one from another. But as to us, there be only two of us, so that if I call thee Maiden, and thou call me Swain, it had been enough. Nevertheless I am fain of calling thee Elfhild."

"And I am full fain of calling thee Osberne," she said. "Besides, if at any time both thou and I were to depart from this country-side we might chance to meet amongst folk of many names, and thus we might the better know each other —But O!" she said, growing exceeding eager, "dost thou know how good a gift thou hast given me? For the halves of the penny, we shall both keep them for ever, as thou knowest, and by our having them we shall know each other if we meet in the world without and our faces have become changed."

Said Osberne: "I deem not that my face will change very much, at least not till I grow old—nor do I think that thine will either." She laughed merrily: "O bairn Osberne, when thou art become a man and a great man, and art called maybe Earl Osberne Wulfgrimsson, will not thy face have changed, and thou with the beard and the fierce eyes, and the mouth that hath shouted in the battle? As for me, Allhallows grant it that my face may change: look at me, a kind of red crow now, all skinny and spindle-legged, and yet I may grow to be a fair woman; and then indeed I should be fain for thee to see me. For somehow it seems to be shown to me that thou wilt be loved of women & love them somewhat over-much."

"For my part," said Osberne, "I seem to see of myself that I shall have much to do slaying wolves and evil things, and standing before kings and getting gifts of them, so that there will be little time for me to go about loving women— yet thee I shall ever love, Elfhild." And he reddened as he spake this, as though he were a youth before his time. But Elfhild said: "In all ways thou art kind to me, and thee shall I ever love. But now tell me, Osberne, what wouldst thou have me do today to make game and play for thee?" Said he: "Call up the sheep again to thee with the sweet little pipe, for therein is much game." She nodded her head merrily, and drew forth her pipe and played, and the sheep came bundling up as the day before; and she danced and played a long while, and Osberne clapped his hands and laughed and egged her on, and was full fain of her dancing, and forsooth it was a wonder and delight to see her.

At last she was wearied out, and cast herself on the grass at the very edge of the cliff, and said that she could no more. And Osberne thanked her kindly.

So when she had gotten her breath again, she asked him what next she should do for his disport. And he bade tell him of how she lived with those two women, her aunts, and what she did from day to day. So she sat down as on the other day, with her legs hanging down over the grisly flood, and told him full sweetly of her joys and her work and her troubles. And some of the tale was piteous enough, for the two kinswomen, who were by no means old, for the eldest was only of thirty summers, were somewhat hard with the child and right careless of her, as shall be shown afterwards.

But after a little she broke off and said: "But Osberne, dear, these be no fair tales for thee, though thou art kind to hearken to them. I have better tales than that, of champions to wit, and ladies and castles and dragons and the like, that I have heard; some of my kinswomen, some of folk that come to our house at a pinch, for it is a poor house; and some, yea and most and the best, from an old woman who dwelleth in a cot not far from us. And she loveth me and hath learned me much lore; and I will tell thee thereof if thou wilt hearken."

"I will well," said he, "and thanks thou shalt have of me; I would I might give thee some other gift." She said: "My tale reward will be that thou shalt tell me over and over the staves thou madest last time we met, till I have them by heart. And other staves shalt thou make for me if thou wilt."

"Thus is the bargain struck," said the lad, "now get thee to the work."

So the little maiden fell to telling him a tale of the Faery, and when it was done he asked for another; but this was a long one, and wore the day down, so that Elfhild must needs depart ere it was done. Then was a talk of when the next meeting should be, and to Osberne nought was near enough save tomorrow. But Elfhild said that it was nought safe, lest aught should wake up her kinswomen to asking of her whereabouts, and again the meeting was appointed for three days hence; but had it not been for the tale, for which something must be risked, Elfhild said that the time between must be a week. So each of the children departed to their houses well pleased.

XII

Of a Guest Called Waywearer

Now hereafter all went the same way, that from time to time they met on either side the Sundering Flood, save that Osberne came not ever in his fair-dyed raiment, but was mostly clad in russet; but on Elfhild's birthday he was clad in his best. Otherwise nought befel to tell of. Whiles either of the children were ailing, whiles Elfhild was kept at home by her kinswomen, and so they failed each other, but never by their own will. The one who came to the trysting-place and missed the other was sore grieved, and in special Osberne, whose child's heart swelled nigh to bursting with sorrow mingled with wrath, and at such times the Sundering Flood seemed to him like the coils of a deadly serpent which was strangling the life out of him, and he would wend home in all despair.

So wore the days through spring and summer and early autumn, and at Wethermel all went smoothly, and the goodman there was better pleased than ever with his new man, who, if he ate two men's victuals, did three men's work; as for Osberne, he loved Stephen dearly, and Stephen for his part was for ever doing something for his disport, and in two ways in special. For first he was, like Elfhild, stuffed with all kinds of tales and histories, and oft when they were out a-shepherding he would tell these to Osberne day-long; and not unseldom when the tale was under way the lad would cry out: "Fair is thy tale, but I have heard it before, only it is different thus and thus." And in sooth he had heard it from Elfhild. The other matter was that Stephen was a smith exceeding deft, and learned the craft to Osberne, so that by the end of the year he bade fair to be a good smith himself. Moreover, whiles would Stephen take a scrap of iron and a little deal of silver, as a silver penny or a florin, from out of his hoard, and would fashion it into an ouch or chain or arm-ring, so quaintly and finely that it was a joy to look on. And every one of these good things would Stephen give to Osberne with a friendly grin, and Osberne took them with a joyful heart because now he had a new thing to give to Elfhild, and each one he shot across the river unto her the soonest that he might. But whiles, when his heart was full, Osberne would say to the smith: "Thou givest me so much, and doest so well by me, that I know not how ever I am to make it good to thee." And Stephen would say: "Fear not, master, the time will come when thou mayst do such good to me as shall pay for all at once."

Now befel tidings on a day of the beginning of October; for the wind, which had been high and blustering all day, grew greater and greater by then candles were lighted in the hall, till it was blowing a great gale from the south-west, which seemed like to lift the house-roof. Then befel a knocking on the house-door, and Stephen went thereto and opened it, & came back with a man all dripping & towzelled with the storm. He was a tall man, yellow-haired, and goodly both of face and body, but his face much hidden with a beard untrimmed, and he was clad in rags which scarce held together, and never a shoe had he to his foot: yet was he bold and free of mien despite his poor attire. He carried some long thing under his arm wrapped up in cloth which was bound about with twine and sealed every here and there with yellow wax.

The goodman started up when he came in, and made as if he would have the newcomer put out, and he muttered: "We keep no house for the harbouring of runagates." Yet he looked at Osberne withal, for he was now grown so masterful that nought was done in the house without him; and the lad stood up straightway and came to the newcomer and bade him welcome from out the storm. Then he took him by the hand and led him up to the hearth, and spake to his grandam: "Goodwife, this our guest has been in rough weather without, and ere he sits down to meat with us, it were well to take him into the inner chamber and wash his feet, and find him dry raiment." The goodwife looked kindly on the guest and bade him come with her, and he went; but ere his back was turned Osberne looked on him and caught a glance of his eye, and therewith he was sure that despite his rags and wretchedness this was his friend Steelhead. In a while he came back into the hall, clad and shod as well as might be done in a hurry, and Osberne led him into his own seat at the board, and gave him to drink; and Stephen withal served him with all care, so that he was in an hospitable house, save that the goodman cast somewhat grudging glances on him, but whereas he might not gainsay all the rest of his household, there was little scathe therein.

But when the guest sat down, he took that long bundle and gave it into Osberne's hands, and said: "Thou art so friendly to a gangrel man, that I make bold to ask this grace of thee also, to wit that thou wilt heed this bundle, and let none other touch it, and give it back to me tomorrow morning ere I depart." Osberne yeasaid to that and took the bundle and laid it at his bed-head. And therewith the meat was brought in, and the meal was merry; for now the guest seemed so noble-looking a man and so cheerful of countenance and so debonair, that none save the goodman thought any longer of his rags wherewith he had come into the hall out of the storm. But even the goodman was better with him presently, when he saw that though he ate and drank like a tall man, he needed no such abundance for the filling of his maw as did Stephen.

Ere they began drinking the guest said: "I may as well tell you folks my name, since ye are so good to me, and have not asked for it, and ye must know that I am called Way-wearer, and that I wish increase of good unto this house."

Then the cup went round and they drank late into the night, and when they had drunk the voidee cup, Osberne led the newcomer to the guest-chamber, and kissed him with good-night, but made no show of knowing who he was.

XIII

Steelhead Gives Osberne the Sword Boardcleaver

WHEN morning was, the guest came into the hall and found the household there, and he spake to the goodwife and said: "Dame, I would have done off this raiment which ye lent me last night and done on mine and left thine lying there, but mine I might not find."

"Nor thou nor anyone else," she said, "shall find thy rags any more, good guest, unless they come to life when thou risest from the dead on the day of doom; for I have peaceably burned them in the garth this hour ago. God help us if the stead of Wethermel cannot spare a yard or two of home-spun to a guest who cometh in stripped by the storm." The guest nodded kindly to her; but Osberne said: "Which way ridest thou this morning, guest, for I would fain lead thee a little way?" "I wend south from thy door, fair master," said the newcomer; "but as to riding, 't is Shanks' mare must be my way-beast, unless I go stealing a horse."

"There is no need for that," said Osberne, "we can find thee a good horse, and if thou bringest him not back it will be no loss to us, as the less hay-need we shall have through winter. Stephen, go thou and see to it that the horses be ready saddled and bridled when we have eaten a morsel." The guest laughed and looked to the carle-master, and said: "How sayest thou, goodman, is the gift given?" The carle smiled somewhat ruefully, and said: "The gift is given; and soothly it is for the youngling to give since all will come to him, be it more or less." "I will take it then," said the guest, "since good will goeth with it; but look to it, goodman, if I reward thee not therefor, for as ragged as I came into thine house."

Now therewith they break their fast; and the last night's wind has fallen utterly, and the sky is blue and the sun bright, and it is warm for that season. Then Osberne gives the sealed bundle to Waywearer, and he took it and did it on to his saddle-bow, and he mounts, and Osberne also, who is dight in his fair-hued raiment; and they set out up the Dale, and ride swiftly, and are few-spoken together.

So they rode till they were past the last house, the cot to wit above told of, and then they came into a fair little clough with a bright stream running through it toward the Sundering Flood; and there were bushes and small wood up and down the clough, and there Waywearer, that is to say, Steelhead, drew rein, and said to Osberne: "Meseems this is as far as thou needest lead me out, lad, so let us off horse and go down and sit by the brook."

So they did, and tied their horses to a thorn-bush growing thereby; and Waywearer took the bundle off his horse and said to Osberne: "Hast thou any guess at what this good thing is?" Osberne reddened and said: "That is the sword which thou didst promise me last spring." Waywearer laughed and said: "Sharp are thine eyes to see a sword through all this wrappage of cerecloth; surely they be of the warrior kin. But sooth hast thou said; this is thy sword." And therewith he fell to undoing the cloth, while the boy looked on eagerly.

At last the hilts and the sheath showed naked: the pommel and cross were of gold of beauteous and wonderful fashion, such as no smith may work now, and the grip was wrapped about with golden wire. And the sheath wherein lay the deadly white edges was of brown leather of oxhide, studded about with knops of gold and silver, and the peace-strings were of scarlet silk with golden acorns at the ends.

Said Osberne: "O thou art kind to have brought this for me: and may I handle it now and at once?"

"Yea," said Steelhead smiling; "but beware, beware!" for he saw the lad lay his hand to the peace-strings; "do not away the peace-strings, lest thou be tempted to draw forth the blade. For this sword is hight Boardcleaver, and was fashioned by the fathers of long ago; and so wise is he and so eager, that whensoever he cometh forth from the sheath he will not go back again till he hath had a life. So beware ever, for mickle scathe shall come of it if he see the heavens and the earth for light cause."

Somewhat daunted was the bold lad; but he said: "Tell me, thou bright lord, at what times I shall draw forth Board-cleaver?"

Said Steelhead: "Only then when thou hast the foe before thee: then draw and be of good courage, for never shall point and edge be dulled by the eye-shot of the wicked and wizards, as whiles it befals the common blades of today. For a man of might hath breathed on the edges amidst much craft of spells, so that nought may master that blade, save one of its brethren fashioned by the same hands, if such there be yet upon the earth, whereof I misdoubt me. Now then thou hast the sword; but I lay this upon thee therewith, that thou be no brawler nor make-bate, and that thou draw not Boardcleaver in any false quarrel, or in behalf of any tyrant or evil-doer, or else shall thy luck fail thee despite the blade that lieth hidden there. But meseemeth nought shalt thou be of the kind of these wrong-doers. And I say of thee that thou didst well with me last night. For though thou knewest me presently, and that I was not without might, yet at first, when thou tookest me by the hand and leddest me to the fire before all the house, thou knewest me not, and I was to thee but the ragged gangrel body whom thy grandsire would have thrust forth into the storm again; but thou didst to me no worse than if I had been lord and earl."

Now it is to be told, that when Osberne heard these words then first he knew what praise was, and the heart glowed within him, and valiancy grew up therein, and his face was bright and his eyes glistened with tears; and he spake no word aloud, but he swore to himself that he would be no worse than his friend Steelhead would have him to be.

Then he took the sword and girt it to him; and he said: "Master, this is no long sword, but it is great and heavy, and meseemeth my bairn's might may never wield it. Shall I not lay it by till I become a man?"

"That shall be seen to, fair youngling," said Steelhead.

"In an hour thou shalt have might enough to wield Board-cleaver, though doubtless thy might shall be eked year by year and month by month thereafter."

XIV

The Gifts of Steelhead

Now by then it was high noon, and the sun very hot, and as they lay on the grass after this converse the lad looked on the water, and he was besweated, and longed for the bright pools of the stream after the manner of boys; and he said at last: "I were fain to take to the water this hot noon, if it please thee."

"It is well thought of, lad," said Steelhead, "and that the more, as I must needs see thee naked if I am to strengthen thee as I am minded to do." So they did off their raiment, both of them, and went into the biggest of the pools hard by; and if Steelhead were a noble-looking man clad, far nobler was he to look on naked, for he was both big and well shapen, so that better might not be. As for Osberne, there looked but little of him when he was unclad, as is the fashion of lads to be lank, yet for his age he was full well shapen. So Steelhead came out of the water presently, and clad himself, while Osberne yet played a while. Then Steelhead called the lad to him all naked as he was, and said: "Stand thou before me, youngling, and I will give thee a gift which shall go well with Boardcleaver." And the lad stood still before him, and Steelhead laid his hands on the head of him first, and let them abide there a while; then he passed his hands over the shoulders and arms of the boy, and his legs and thighs and breast, and all over his body; and therewith he said: "In our days and the olden time it was the wont of fathers to bless their children in this wise; but for thee, thy father is dead, and thy nighest kinsman is little-hearted and somewhat of a churl. Thus then have I done to thee to take the place of a father to thee, I who am of the

warriors of while agone. And I think it will avail thee; and
it is borne in upon me that before very long thou wilt need
this avail, if thou art to live and do the deeds I would have
thee. Now it is done, so cover thee in thy raiment and rest a
while; and then I will depart and leave thee to the might
which I have given thee, and the valiance which hath grown
up in thine heart."

So they lay down on the greensward and rested; and Osberne had fetched along with him cakes and cheese and a keg
of good drink, and they took their bever there in all content.
But for that time Steelhead spake no more of his folk and the
old days, but about the fowl and fish and other wild things
that haunted that clough, and of shooting in the bow and so
forth. Then they arose and went to their horses, and Steelhead said to Osberne: "How is it with the might of thy
body, lad? Canst thou do better in wielding of Boardcleaver?"
So the youngling stretched himself and took the sword by the
hilts and shook it and waved it about, and tossed it in the
air and caught it again, and said: "Seest thou, master?
Meseems my might is so much eked, that I deem I could
swim the stream of the Sundering Flood and overcome it."
Quoth the hillman, laughing: "Yea, and we know that that
would please thee well; but let it be, my son, I bid thee;
for no race of folk who have dwelt in the Dale from the beginning of the world have ever won across the Sundering
Flood. So now we depart for this present; but as for this
way-beast I ride, thy grandsire shall lose nothing and gain
much by him; for I took him but to pleasure thee, and I
shall send him back to Wethermel ere many days are past.
Farewell, my son!"

So he kissed the youngling, and rode away south across the
stream and over the other side of the clough. Osberne stood
beside his horse, looking after him and the way he had taken,
and then mounted and rode his way homeward, somewhat
downcast at first for the missing of this new father. But
after a while, what for his new gift and his freshly-gained
might, and the pride and pleasure of life, he became all joyous again, as though the earth were new made for him.

Ye may well think that the very next time (which indeed
was on the morrow) that Osberne went to the Bight of the

Cloven Knoll, he went girt with Boardcleaver, and showed it to his friend; and she looked somewhat sober at the sight of it, and said: "I pray thee, Osberne, draw it not forth from the sheath." "In nowise may I draw it," said he, "for I am told never to draw it till I have my foe before me; for ever it will have a life betwixt the coming forth from the sheath and its going back again." "I fear me," she said, "that thou wilt have to draw it often, so that many a tale will be told of it, and perhaps at last the death of thee." And therewith she put her hands up to her face and wept. But he comforted her with kind words, till the tears were gone.

Then she looked at him long and lovingly, and said at last: "I know not how it is, but thou seemest to me changed and grown less like a child, as though some new might had come to thee. Now I may not ask thee who has done this to thee, and given thee the sword, for if thou mightest thou wouldst have told me. But tell me this, hast thou all this from a friend or a foe?" He said: "Dost thou indeed see that I am grown mightier? Well, it is so; and true it is that I may not tell thee who is the giver; but I may tell thee that it is a friend. But art thou not glad of my gain?" She smiled and said: "I should be glad, and would be if I might; but somehow meseemeth that thou growest older quicker than I do, and that it is ill for me, for it will sunder us more than even now we be sundered."

And again he had to comfort her with sweet words; and he shot across to her an ouch which Stephen had given him that morning, so soon she was herself again, and sat and told him a tale of old times; and they parted happily, and Osberne gat him home to Wethermel. But he had scarce been at home a minute or two when there came one riding to the door, a young man scarlet-clad and gay, and his horse was dight with the goodliest of saddles and bridles, and the bit of silver; but for all that, both Osberne and Stephen, who was standing in the door, knew the horse for their own nag, on whom Waywearer had ridden off the yestermorn.

Now the lad cries out: "Is this the stead of Wethermel?" "Yea," said Osberne; "what wouldst thou?" "I would see the goodman," says the swain. "He is yet afield," said Osberne, "but if thou wilt come in and have the bite and the sup thou mayst abide him, for he will not be long."

"I may not," said the swain, "for time fails me; so I will say to thee what I was to say to him, which is no long spell, to wit that Waywearer sendeth home the horse the goodman lent him, and bids him keep the gear on him in his memory." Therewith is he off the horse in a twinkling and out through the garth gate, and away so swiftly that they lost sight of him in a moment. Stephen laughed and said to Osberne: "Waywearer is nowise debt-tough; now will our goodman be glad tonight. But see thou! Look to the nag's shoes! If ever I saw silver to know it, they be shod therewith." And so it was as he said, and the silver nigh an inch thick.

Soon cometh home the goodman, and they tell him the tidings, and he grows wondrous glad, and says that luck has come to Wethermel at last. But thereafter they found that horse much bettered, so that he was the best nag in all the Wethermel pastures.

XV

Surly John Brings a Guest to Wethermel

WEAR the days now till it is the beginning of winter, and there is nought new to tell of, till on a day when it began to dusk, and all the household were gathered in the hall, one knocked at the door, and when Stephen went thereto, who should follow him in save Surly John, and with him a stranger, a big tall man, dark-haired and red-bearded, wide-visaged, brown-eyed and red-cheeked, blotch-faced and insolent of bearing. He was girt with a sword, had a shield at his back and bore a spear in his hand, and was clad in a long byrny down to his knees. He spake at once in a loud voice, ere Surly John got out the word: "May Hardcastle be here tonight, ye folk?" The goodman quaked at the look and the voice of him, and said: "Yea, surely, lord, if thou wilt have it so."

But Osberne turned his head over his shoulder, for his back was toward the door, and said: "Meat and drink and an ingle in the hall are free to every comer to this house, whether he be earl or churl." Hardcastle scowled on the lad, and said: "I am neither earl nor churl, but a man of mine own hand, and I take thy bidding, goodman, for this night, but as to thereafter we will look to it; but as to thy youngling, I will look to him at once and teach him a little manners." And therewith he went up to Osberne and smote him a cheek-slap from behind. Surly John laughed, and made a mow at him, and said: "Ho! young wolf-slayer, feelest thou that? Now is come the end of thy mastery!" But neither for slap nor for gibe did Osberne flinch one whit, or change countenance.

Then Hardcastle said: "Hah! Is that the lad who slew the wolves ye ran from, John? He will be a useful lad about the house." John held his peace and reddened somewhat, and Hardcastle said: "Now show me where to bestow this fighting-gear of mine; for meseems I shall not want it yet awhile in this meek and friendly house." Quoth Osberne over his shoulder: "Things boded will happen, and also things unboded." Hardcastle scowled again, but this time smote him not, for hē was busy doing off his hawberk, which Stephen took from him presently, along with his other armour and weapons, and hung them upon the pins at the other end of the hall. Then he came back and stood before Hardcastle as if waiting some commandment, but the warrior said: "Who is this big lubber here, and what is his name? What does the fool want?" Said Stephen: "I want to serve thee, noble sir, and my name is Stephen the Eater; but I can swallow most things better than hard words." Hardcastle lifted up his right foot to kick his backside, but Stephen deftly thrust out his right foot and gave the man a shove on his breast, so that he tripped him and down went Hardcastle bundling. He picked himself up in a mighty rage, and would have fallen on Stephen; but he saw that the Eater had a broad and big knife in his girdle, so he forbore, being now all unarmed; and Stephen said: "Our floor is somewhat slippery for dancing, fair sir."

But therewith arose Osberne, and came before the guest, and louted to him and said: "Noble sir, I pray thee pardon our man Stephen, for thou seest how clumsy a man he is, and he knoweth not where to bestow his long legs; he is ever in everyone's way." And as he spake the smiles were all over his face, and he louted low again. Stephen stared astonished at him and drew back, and as for Hardcastle, the wrath ran off him, and he looked on Osberne and said: "Nay, thou art not so unmannerly a lad as I deemed; belike I shall yet make something out of thee."

Therewith the meat was borne in and they all sat to table, and Hardcastle was well at ease; and the goodman, if he were not quite happy, yet made a shift to seem as if he were. The guest sat at the right hand of the goodman, and after he had eaten a while he said: "Goodman, thy women here have doubtless once been fair, but now they are somewhat stricken in years. Hast thou in hiding somewhere, or belike lying out in the field or at some cot, anything prettier? something with sleek sides and round arms and dainty legs and feet? It would make us merrier, and belike kinder, if such there were."

The goodman turned pale, and stammered out that these were all the women at Wethermel; and John cried out: "It is even as I told thee, warrior. Heed it not; there be fair women up and down the Dale, and thou shalt have one or two of these with little pains, either for love or for fear." Hardcastle laughed and said: "Thou shalt go and fetch them for me, Surly John, and see which shall serve thee best, love or fear." All laughed thereat, for they well knew his ill temper and his cowardice, and he turned red and blue for rage. But as for Osberne, he could not help thinking of the pretty maid whose hand he had held at the Cloven Mote last winter; and he thought that if Hardcastle did her any wrong, Boardcleaver might well look on the sun in her behalf.

A little after Osberne turns to John and sees his knife lying on the board, a goodly one, well carven on the heft. So he says: "Thy whittle seems to me both good and strange, John, reach it into my hand." John did so, and the youngling takes hold of it by the back near the point with his thumb and finger, and twists it till it is like a ram's horn. Then he gives it back to John and says: "Thy knife is now stranger than it was, John, but 'tis not of so much use as erst." All marvelled at this feat, all save the fool Surly John, who raises a great outcry that his knife is marred. But Hardcastle, whose head was now pretty much filled with drink, cried out: "Hold thy peace, John; doubtless this youngling here hath craft enough to straighten thy whittle even as he has crooked and winded it. By the mass he is a handy smith, and will be of much avail to me." Osberne reached out his hand for the knife, and John gave it to him, and he took it by the point as aforetime, and lo, in a moment it was once more straight again, so to say. Then he hands it back to John, and says: "Let our man Stephen lay his hammer on the blade tomorrow once or twice, and thy knife shall be as good as ever it was." All wondered, but Hardcastle not much, whereas by this time he could not see very straight out of his eyes. So he bids lead him to bed, and the goodman took him by the hand and brought him to the guest-chamber, and himself lies down in an ingle of the hall. So all lay down, and there was rest in the house the night long; save for the goodman, who slept but little, and that with dreams of the cutting of throats and firing of roofs.

XVI

Hardcastle Would Seize Wethermel

WHEN it was morning, and folk were afoot in the house, Hardcastle lay long abed; but when the first meal was on the board, and they were gathered in hall, he came thereto, and sat down and ate without a word and was by seeming as surly as John. But when the boards were taken up, and the women at least, though not the others, I deem, were looking that he should call for his horses and depart, he leaned back in his high-seat and spake slowly and lazily: "This stead of Wethermel is much to my mind; it is a plenteous house and good land, and more plenteous it might be made were I to cast a dyke and a wall round about, and have in here a sort of good fellows who should do my bidding, so that we might help ourselves to what we lacked where plenty was to be had. I will think of this hereafter, but at this present, and till winter is done and spring is come, I will say no more of that. And to you folk, even to the big lubber yonder, I will say this, that ye, women and all, shall be free of meat and drink and bed if ye will but be brisk about doing my will, and will serve me featly; but if not, then shall ye pack and be off, and have no worse harm of me. Have ye heard, and will ye obey?"

The women were pale and trembled, and the goodman quaked exceedingly, while Surly John stood by grinning. Osberne smiled pleasantly but spake not. He was girt with the sword Boardcleaver and clad in scarlet. As for Stephen, he stood before Hardcastle with a face seeming solemn, save that he squinted fearfully, looking all down along his long nose.

Now came forth the goodman and knelt before the ruffler, and said: "Lord, we will even do thy will: but mightest thou tell us where ye got licence and title to take all our wealth from us and make us thy thralls?" The warrior laughed: "It is fairly asked, goodman, and I will not spare to show thee my title." Therewith he drew forth his sword, a great and heavy blade, and cast it rattling on the board before him, and said: "There is my title, goodman; wilt thou ask a better?" The goodman groaned and said: "At least, lord, I pray thee take not all I have, but leave me some little whereby to live, and thereof I will pay somewhat year by year, if the seasons be good."

"My friend," quoth Hardcastle, "by the title that lieth yonder I have gotten thy wealth, and every jot of it might I keep if I would. But see how kind I am to thee and thine. For have I not told you that ye shall live in this house, and eat the sweet and drink the strong and lie warm a-nights, so long as ye do my will."

"Yea," said the goodman, "but we must needs toil as thralls." "Great fool," said Hardcastle, "what matters that to thee? It is like thou shalt work no harder than erst, or no harder than may be enough to keep me as thy guest. Nay, goodman, wilt thou turn me from thy door and deny me guesting? What sayest thou to that, Fiddlebow, my sharp dear?" said he, handling his sword. Now the goodman crept away, and Surly John says that he wept.

But Osberne came forward as smiling and debonaire as erst, and he said: "Fair sir, one thing I crave of thee to tell me, to wit, is there no other way out of this thraldom, for well thou wottest that no man would be a thrall might he help it?" "Well, my lad," quoth the warrior smiling, for now after his talk with the goodman he was in better humour, "when thou growest older thou wilt find that saw of thine belied many wise, and that many there be who are not loth to be thralls. But as to what way there may be out of this thraldom, I will tell thee the way, as I was about to do with the goodman; though whereas he is but little-hearted, and there is none else fight-worthy in the house, save it were this lubber in front—Well thou, why art thou skellying, man, as if thou wouldst cast the eyes out of thine head on either side?" Quoth Stephen: "I was grown so afraid of thee, fair sir, that I wotted not where to look, so I thought my eyes would do me least harm if they looked down along my nose." Quoth Hardcastle: "I begin to see how it will go with thee, great lout, that in the first days of my mastership thine hide shall pay for thy folly." Stephen squinted none the less, but his whittle was yet in his belt.

Now Hardcastle went on speaking to Osberne and said: "Well now, I will tell thee the way out of this thraldom, as thou wilt call it; and the more to thee, bairn, because thou wilt become my man and wilt be bold and deft, I doubt not; therefore thou shouldst learn early the fashions of great and bold men. Hearken! Ever when I offer to some man a lot that seemeth hard unto him, then I bid him, if it likes him not, to pitch me the hazelled field hard by his house, and we to go thereinto and see what point and edge may say to it; and if he slay me or hurt me so much that I must be borne off the field within the four corners, then is he quit, and hath his land again, and hath gained mickle glory of my body. Moreover if he may not fight himself, yet will I meet any champion that he may choose to do battle with me. Now this is a good and noble custom of the bold, and hath been deemed so from time long agone. And indeed I deem pity of it that here today the goodman may not fight nor hath found any champion to fight for him. But three days' frist will I give him to find such a champion—Thou wretch," said he to Stephen, "why wilt thou still skelly at me?"

"Because the champion is found," said Stephen in a snuffling voice.

Hardcastle snorted and his lip-beard bristled, but forth stood Osberne, and he still smiling; and he said: "Thou warrior, three things I offer thee to choose from, and the first is that thou depart hence, thou and thy man; because thou hast not dealt with us as a guest should, but hast smitten me and threatened all of us, and brazened out thy wrong-doing. This is the best way out of thy folly. What sayest thou to it?" But such fury was in the ruffler's heart now, that he had no words for it, but rolled about in the high-seat snorting and blowing. Said Osberne: "I see thou wilt not take this way, and that is the worse for thee. Now the next is that we hazel a field and fight therein. Wilt thou have this?" The champion roared out: "Yea, that will I! But in such wise that thou take sword and shield and I a bunch of birch twigs; and if I catch thee not and unbreech thee and whip thee as a grammar-master his scholar, then will I lay down sword and shield for ever."

Said Osberne coldly: "Thou seest not that I am girt with a sword, and I tell thee it is a good one. Or wilt thou take Surly John's knife this morning and do as I did with it last night? And I did it for a warning to thee, but belike thou wert drunk and noted it not."

Hardcastle's face fell somewhat, for now he did remember the feat of the knife. But Osberne spake again: "I ask thee, warrior, wilt thou enter the field that I shall hazel for thee?" Quoth the ruffler, but in a lower voice: "I cannot fight with a boy; whether I slay him or am slain I am shamed."

Spake Osberne: "Then depart from the house with as little shame as a ruffler and a churl may have. But if thou wilt neither of these things, then will it befal that I shall draw my blade and fall on thee to slay thee, and make the most of it that here stands by me my man Stephen, a true and fearless carle, with his whittle bare in his hand. And this I may well do, whereas, by thine own telling, thou art not in our house but in thine own."

Hardcastle lifted up his head, for he had hung it down a while, and said in a hoarse voice: "Hazel the field for me then, and I will go therein with thee and slay thee." "That may well be," said Osberne, "—yet it may not be." Then he bade Stephen to go hazel the field in the flat meadows toward the river: and therewith he bethought him of his friend on the further side of the water, and how it might well be that he should never see her again, but lie slain on the meadow of Wethermel; and he wondered if tidings of the battle would go across the water and come unto her. But amidst his musings the harsh voice of Hardcastle reached his ears: he turned round with a start and heard how the ruffler said to him: "Let me see the sword, lad, wherewith thou wilt fight me." Osberne took the sheathed blade from his girdle and handed it to Hardcastle without a word, and the warrior fell at once to handling the peace-strings, but Osberne cried out: "Nay, warrior, meddle not with the peace-strings, for who knoweth what scathe may come of the baring of the blade within doors?" "Well, well," said Hardcastle, "but the blade must out presently, and what harm if it be now?" Yet he took his hand from the weapon, and laid it on the board before him.

Osberne looked about him and saw that they two were alone in the hall now, for the others had gone down to look on the hazelling. So he spake quietly and said: "Warrior, is it not so, that thou hast in thine heart some foreboding of what shall befal?" Hardcastle answered nought, and Osberne went on: "I see that so it is, and meseems it were better for thee if this battle were unfought. Lo now, shall we not make peace in such wise that thou abide here this day in all honour holden, and in honour depart tomorrow morn, led out with such good gifts as shall please thee? Thus shalt thou have no shame, and everything untoward betwixt us shall be forgotten." Hardcastle shook his head and said: "Nay, lad, nay, the tale would get about, and shame would presently be on the wing towards me. We must stand within the hazel-garth against each other." Then he spake again, and a somewhat grim smile was on his face: "Awhile agone thou didst threaten to slay me with the help of yonder squinting loon, but now thou standest unarmed before me, and I have thy sword under my hand. Hast thou no fear of what I may do to thee, since so it is that forebodings weigh on mine heart?"

"Nay, I am not afraid," said Osberne; "thou mayst be a bad man, yet not so bad as that."

"Sooth it is," said Hardcastle; "but I say again, thou art a valiant lad. Lo now, take thy sword again; but tell me, what armour of defence hast thou for this battle?"

"Nought save my shield," said Osberne; "there is a rusty steel hood stands yonder on the wall, but no byrny have we in the house."

Said Hardcastle: "Well, I may do so much as this for thee, I will leave all my defences here and go down to the hazels with nought but my sword in my fist, and thou shalt have thy shield; but I warn thee that Fiddlebow is a good blade."

Said Osberne, and smiled: "Well I wot that if thou get in but one downright stroke on me, little shall my shield avail me against Fiddlebow. Yet I take thine offer and thank thee for it. But this forthinketh me, that if thou live out this day thou wilt still betake thee to the same insolency and greediness and wrong-doing as thou hast shown yesterday and this morning."

Hardcastle laughed roughly and said: "Well, lad, I deem thou art right; wherefore slay me hardily if thou mayst, and rid the world of me. Yet hearken, of all my deeds I have no shame at all: though folk say some of them were ugly—let it be."

Therewith came Stephen into the hall, and he did them to wit that the hazels were pitched, and now he squinted no more.

XVII

The Slaying of Hardcastle

So they three went down together into the meadow, and there stood the others by the hazel-garth: the goodman cowering and abject, Surly John pale and anxious, and the two women clinging together in sore sorrow, the grandam weeping sorely. But as they passed close by these last, Stephen touched the grandam and said to her: "Sawest thou ever King David the little?" "Nay," she said sobbing. "Look thou into the hazel-garth presently then," said he, "and thou shalt see him with eye."

So now they two stood in the hazelled field; it was two hours before noon; the sky was overcast with a promise of the first snow of the winter, but as yet none had fallen, and the field was dry and hard. Now Hardcastle has Fiddle-bow bare in his fist, but Osberne takes Boardcleaver from his girdle and unwinds the peace-strings; then he stands still for a moment and looks toward his foeman, who cries out at him: "Haste thee, lad, I were fain done with it." Then Osberne draws forth the blade, and it made a gleam of white in the grey day, and as the folk say who stood thereby, as Boardcleaver came forth bare there came a great humming sound all about. Then Osberne gets his shield on his arm and cries out: "Now thou warrior!" and straightway Hardcastle comes leaping toward him, and Osberne abode him as he came on with uplifted sword, leapt lightly to one side, and thrust forth Boardcleaver and touched his side, so that all could see the blade had drunk a little blood. Fiercely and fast turned Hardcastle about on the lad, but therewith was he within the ruffler's stroke, and Boardcleaver's point was steady before Osberne's breast and met Hardcastle's side and made a great wound with the point, and the warrior staggered back, and his sword-point was lowered. Then cried out Osberne: "What! Thou wouldst unbreech me, wouldst

thou? But now art thou unbreeched." For therewith Boardcleaver swept round backhanded and came back as swift as
lightning, and the edge clave all the right flank and buttock
of him, so that the blood ran freely; and then as Hardcastle,
still staggering, hove up his sword wildly, Osberne put the
slant stroke aside with his shield and thrust forth Boardcleaver right at his breast, and the point went in, and the
whole blade, as there were nought but dough before it, and
Hardcastle, nigh rent in two, fell aback off the sword.

Osberne stood still a while looking on him but Stephen
ran up and knelt beside him, and felt his wrist and laid his
hand on the breast, and then turned and looked up at Osberne, who knelt down beside him also and wiped the blood
off Boardcleaver with a lap of the dead man's coat. Then
he stood up and thrust the blade back into the sheath, and
wound the peace-strings about it all. Then came the word
into his mouth, and he sang:

> Came sword and shield
> To the hazelled field
> Where the fey man fell
> At Wethermel:
> The grey blade grew glad
> In the hands of a lad,
> And the tall man and stark
> Leapt into the dark.
> For the cleaver of war-boards came forth from his door
> And guided the hand of the lacking in lore.
>
> But now is the blade
> In the dark sheath laid,
> His heart o'erfull.
> And the peace-strings lull
> Up dale and down
> The ball-roofs brown
> Hang over the peace
> Of the year's increase.
> No fear rendeth midnight, and dieth the day
> With no foe save the winter that weareth away.

Then he cried out: "Draw nigh, goodman and grandsire,
and take again the house and lands of Wethermel, as ye had

them aforetime before yesterday was a day." So the goodman came to him and kissed him, and thanked him kindly
and humbly, and the women came and embraced him and
hung about him. As for Surly John, he had slunk away so
soon as he saw the fall of his master, and now when they
looked around for him, they saw him but as a fleck going
swiftly down the Dale. Thereat they all laughed together, and
the laughter eased their hearts, so that they felt free and
happy.

"Now," said Stephen, "what shall we do with this carcass,
that was so fierce and fell this morning?" Said Osberne: "We
shall lay him in earth here in his raiment as he fell, since
he died in manly wise, though belike he has lived as a beast.
But his sword I will give to thee in reward for thy trusty
following both now and at other times."

So Stephen fetched mattock and pick, and dug a grave for
that champion amidwards of the hazel-garth, and there they
laid him, and heaped up mould and stones over his grave;
and to this day it is called Hardcastle's Howe there, or for
short, and that the oftenest, Hardcastle.

So they went all of them up to the house, and were merry
and joyful.

XVIII

Elfhild Hears of the Slaying

BUT two days after this was the tryst-day for Osberne to
see his over-water friend, and he went soberly enough, and
came to the water-side and found her over against him; and
she asked him of tidings. "Tidings enough," said he, "for
now have I done a deed beyond my years, a deed unmeet
for a child; to wit, I have slain a man."

"O," she said, "and didst thou sleep after the deed?" Said
Osberne: "Yea, and dreamed never a deal. But I must tell
thee that I was in my right." Said Elfhild: "What did he
to thee that thou must slay him?" Osberne said: "He came

swaggering into our house and would take all to him, and put all of us to the road or hold us in thraldom." She said: "But tell me, how didst thou slay him? Was he drunk or asleep?" "Nay," said he, "I was champion for my grandsire, and the robber had a sword in his fist, and I another, and we fought, and I overcame him." Said the maiden: "But was he mannikin or a dastard, or unskilled in weapons?" Spake Osberne, reddening: "He was a stark carle, a bold man, and was said to be of all prowess."

She said nothing a while, but stood pale and downcast. And he said: "What is this, playmate? I looked to have much praise from thee for my deed. Dost thou know that this man was as the pest to all the country-side, and that I have freed men of peace from a curse?" "Be not wrath with me, Osberne," she said, "indeed I am somewhat downcast; for I see that now thou wilt be no playmate for me, but wilt be a man before thy time, and wilt be looking towards such things as men desire; and that tall maidens come to womanhood will be for thee, not quaint rags of children such as I be."

"Now, Elfhild," said he, "why wilt thou run to meet trouble half way? Am I worser to thee than I was last time?" "Nay," she said, "and indeed I deem thee glorious, and it is kind and kind of thee to come to me ever, and not to miss one of our trysts."

"Now thou art dear," said Osberne; "and wilt thou do something for my disport? Wilt thou pipe thy sheep to thee?"

"Nay," said she, "I will not; I will not skip like an antic, and show thee my poor little spindle legs. If I were a woman grown I should scarce show so much as the ankle of my foot. Besides, thou laughest at my hopping and jumping amongst those foolish woolly beasts, and I would not have thee laugh at me."

"Elfhild my dear," said he, "thou art wrong. When I have laughed it was never in mockery of thee, but for pleasure of thy pretty ways and the daintiness of thy dancing, which is like to the linden leaves on a fresh summer morning."

"But how am I to know that?" she said. "Well, at any rate ask me not to dance today. But I will sit down and tell thee a very sweet tale of old times, which thou hast never erst heard. It is about the sea and ships, and of a sea-wife coming into the dwellings of men." Quoth Osberne, "I were fain to look on the sea and to sail it." "Yea," said Elfhild, "but thou wilt take me with thee, wilt thou not?" "O yea," said Osberne. And they both forgat the Sundering Flood, and how they should never meet, as they sat each side of the fearful water, and the tale and sweet speech sped to and fro betwixt them. So a fair ending had that day of tryst.

XIX

The Winter Passes and Elfhild Tells of the Death of Her Kinswoman

Now Osberne and Stephen both give rede to the goodman, and bid him live somewhat less niggardly, since not only had they good store of victual and clothes and the like, which had been hoarded a long time, but also the gifts of Way-wearer had stood them in good stead, and furthermore, the goodman was much bettered by the spoil of Hardcastle. For he had left much wealth behind him, and chiefly in silver and gold; and all that he had left, save his weapons, had Osberne given to his grandsire. So the goodman heeded their words and let himself be talked over, and while winter was yet young and before there was any snow to hinder, he rode with Osberne down the Dale, and looked into many of the steads, and amongst others, were dwelt the damsel who had been paired with Osberne on the day of the mid-winter Cloven Mote. And he thought her fair and sweet, and she received him joyfully and kissed him; but he was scarce so ready for that as he was aforetime, for he deemed she kissed him as a child and not a man.

So by hook or by crook the goodman got him six hired folk; three men, two of whom were young, and three women, all young and one comely, one ill-favoured, and the other betwixt and between. It must be said by the way, that if he had abided the spring for getting these new folk he would scarce have hired them, for the repute of Wethermel for scant housekeeping had gone wide about; but when folk heard that Master Nicholas was hiring folk from mid-winter on- wards, they were willing enough to go, whereas they deemed he would be changing his mind and becoming open-handed. So Nicholas rides back with his catch (for he had brought nags to horse them), and henceforth is good house kept at Wethermel, as good as anywhere in the Dale.

Again fared Osberne to the mid-winter Cloven Mote, and again was he mated to the above-said damsel, who hight Gertrude; and forsooth this time he deemed that she kissed him and caressed him not so wholly as a mere boy, though of such things ye may well deem he knew little. For she seemed to find it hard when they kissed, as paired folk are bound to do, to let her lips leave his, and when their hands parted at the end of the Mote she gave a great sigh, and put her cheek toward him for a parting kiss, which for- sooth he gave her somewhat unheedfully; for he was look- ing hard toward the other shore to see if he could make out the shape of Elfhild amongst the women there; as he had done whenever he gat a chance of it all day long, but had failed wholly therein.

Three days afterwards he kept tryst with Elfhild, and asked her if she had been at the Mote, and she told him No; that her aunts went every time but always left her be- hind. Then she said smiling: "And this time they have come back full of thy praises, for the tale of thee, and the slay- ing of the robber, has come over to our side; and one of them, the youngest, had thee shown to her by one of the folk, and she saith that thou art the fairest lad that ever was seen: and therein she is not far wrong."

He laughed and reddened, and told for tidings how he had fared at the Mote, and Elfhild belike was not best pleased to hear of the fair damsel who was so fond of kissing; but in all honesty she rejoiced when Osberne told how hard he had looked for her on the other side of the water. So they made the most of their short day, as indeed they had need to do, for through the winter, when the snow was on the earth and the grass grew not, the sheep were all shut up in the folds and the cotes, and there was no shepherding toward; so that Elfhild was hard put to it for some pretence for getting away from the house, and their trysts had to be further between than they had been; and not seldom, moreover, Elfhild failed at the trysting-place, and Osberne had to go sorrowfully away, though well he wotted it was by no fault of his playmate.

So wore the winter tidingless, and spring came again, and again the two met oftener; and great feast they made the first day, when Elfhild came to the ness with her head and her loins wreathed with the winter wolfsbane. It was a warm and very clear day of February, and Elfhild of her own will piped to her sheep and danced amongst them; and Osberne looked on her eagerly, and he deemed that she had grown bigger and sleeker and fairer; and her feet and legs (for still she went barefoot) since they had not the summer tan on them, looked so dainty-white to him that sore he longed to stroke them and kiss them. And this, belike, was the beginning to him of the longing of a young man, which afterwards was so sore on him, to be with his friend and embrace her and caress her.

So they met often that springtide, and oftener as the weather waxed warmer. And nought worth telling befel to Osberne that while save these meetings. But at last, when May was yet young, Osberne kept tryst thrice and Elfhild came not, and the fourth time she came and had tidings, to wit, that one of her kinswomen had died of sickness. Said she: "And it was the one who was least kind to me, and made most occasion for chastising me. Well, she is gone; and often she was kind to me, and before I saw thee I loved her somewhat. But now things will go better, because the other aunt, who was kinder than the dead one, hath taken also into the house that old woman whereof I told thee, who hath taught me lore and many ancient tales; and though she be old and wrinkled, she is kind and loves me: and she is on our side, and I have told her about thee; and she in turn told me strange things and unked, which I will not and dare not tell again to thee. Wherefore now let us be glad together."

Said Osberne: "Yea, we will try to be glad; but see thou, I want more than this now, I want to come across to thee, and tell thee things which I cannot shout across this accursed

Flood; and I want to take thee by the hand and put my arms about thee and kiss thee. Dost thou not wish the like by me?"

"O yea," said the maiden reddening, "most soothly do I. But hearken, Osberne; the carline sayeth that all this thou shalt do to me, and that we shall meet body to body one day. Dost thou trow in this?"

"Nay, how can I tell," said he somewhat surlily, "when thou hast told me so little of the tale?"

"Well," she said, "but I may not tell more; so now, I pray, let us be glad with what we have got of meeting oftener, and a life better and merrier for me. Bethink thee, my dear, that if I live easier and have not to toil so much, and catch fewer stripes, and have better meat and more, I shall grow sleeker and daintier, yea and bigger, so that I shall look older and more womanlike sooner." And she wept a little therewith; so he repented his surliness and set to comfort her, till she laughed and he also, and they were merrier together.

So now time after time was their converse sweet and happy, and true it was that Elfhild grew fairer and sleeker week by week; and she was better clad now, and well shod, and wore her ouches and necklaces openly, though she said she had not shown all to the carline, "not all of thine I mean. But the Dwarf necklace, the glorious one, I have shown her, and she saith that it is such a wonder that it forebodeth my becoming a Queen; and that will be well, as thou shalt be a great man." Thuswise they prattled.

XX

Osberne Fares to Eastcheaping and Brings Gifts for Elfhild

But when June was, Master Nicholas would ride to Eastcheaping, and he took Osberne with him; and a great wonder it was to see so many houses built of stone and lime all standing together, and so fair, as he deemed them, though it was but a little cheaping. Howsoever, without the walls was an abbey of monks, which was both fair and great, and the church thereof as well fashioned as most; and when the lad went thereinto he was all ravished with joy at the great pillars and arches and the vault above, and the pictures on the walls and in the windows, and the hangings and other braveries about the altars. And when he was at high mass, and the monks and the minstrels fell to singing together, he scarce knew whether he were in heaven or on earth. Yet whether in one or the other, he longed to have his friend from over the river with him, that she might see and hear it all, and tell him what she thought of it. Wondrous also was the market wherein they did their chaffer, and the chapmen in their fine coats of strange fashion to him and their outland faces, and the carts and wains of the country folk and their big sleek horses. And when it was all done he found that he had more than a silver penny or two in his pouch; for a deal of the wares sold were his own, to wit the peltries he had gotten by his shooting and his valour. For a great bear had he slain with spear and shield, he by himself, and two more with the help of Stephen the Eater, and wolves and foxes and ermines and beavers a great many. But when he had the money it burnt a hole in his pocket; for he must needs go to the booths and buy for Elfhild, as far as his money went, such things as he deemed he could shoot across the Flood to her, as fair windowed shoon, and broidered hosen and dainty smocks and silken kerchiefs, and a chaplet for her head. And when this was done, he was about with his grandsire in the street, and there came down from the Castle a company of riders, all in jack and sallet and long spears, and two knights in white armour all gleaming in the sun, and the banner of the good town with them. Then his heart rose so high at the sight, and he yearned so for deeds of fame, that he smote his hands together and called good luck on them, and some of them turned about and laughed to each other, and praised the goodly boy, and knew not that he had slain a stouter man then e'er a one of them.

Withal his eyes might be no long while off the gay-clad young women (for it was holy day, and they dressed out in their best), and he stared so downrightly on them that his grandsire rebuked him aloud. And that heard some of the women, and they who were fair amongst them laughed and praised him, for they deemed him right welcome to look on all he might see of them, so fair a boy as he was: and one of them, a goodly woman of some thirty summers, came up to him and bade the old carle hold his peace and not scold at the boy: "For," said she, "the lad is so well-liking that he hath good right already to deal with any woman as he will; and when he groweth older by a half score years, God-a-mercy, which of us shall be able to say him nay! Would I were younger by that tale of years, that I might be able presently to follow him all over the world." And therewith she kissed him betwixt the eyes and went her ways. But as before, he was but half pleased to be so kissed, as a mere child. Shortly to say, there they made great feast for the joy of all these things, and rode back to the Dale in a day or two, and came safe and sound to Wethermel.

Now at the next meeting 'twixt the two children Osberne bore down all those fair things; and he found Elfhild on the ness, and she looking shy and dear, for he had told her that he was going to the cheaping. And now was her hair no longer spread abroad but bound up close to her head, and she was clad in a seemly gown of homespun, with black hosen and skin shoes well laced.

Straightway after the first greetings was great ado about shooting those fair things across the water; and when they were all across, Elfhild undid them, and wept for sheer joy of them and for love of her valiant friend, and at last she sat nigh the edge hugging them all to her bosom, and said: "Now, sweetheart, is the tale on thy side; for thou must tell me all that thou hast seen and done." So he fell to, nought loth, and told everything at large, and the little maiden's eyes sparkled and her face glowed; but when he had told last of all about the women and of her who had kissed him, she said: "Ah, all that is just what my carline saith of thee, that all women shall love thee; and that is most like, and what shall I do then, I who shall be so far away from thee?" Then he swore to her that whatever betid he would always love her, and she made as if she were gladdened again thereby; but in her heart she could not but deem that he made somewhat light of it, and was nought so anxious as she was.

But ere they parted that day, she went aback a little, and did on her all those fair things which he had brought, such as she might get upon her body; and a green gown of fine cloth was one of them, which he had made a shift to cast across bundled up, by dint of his new strength. So dight, she stood for him to look at, and he was well pleased, and praised her in such wise that it was clear he looked at her wisely and closely. So they parted. But when he was gone, she sat down and wept, she knew not why. And in a while she arose and did on her everyday raiment and went home.

XXI

Warriors from Eastcheaping Ride into the Dale

So the summer wears with nought to tell of, and autumn and winter in like manner, and spring was come again, and it was hard on two years since those twain had first met, and Osberne was fifteen years old and Elfhild but a month and a half less, and still they met happily as aforetime. Wethermel throve in all wise this while, and there was deep peace on the Eastern Dale, and never had the edges of Board-cleaver looked on the light of day since the fall of Hard-castle.

But in early May of this year came riders into the Dale, friends, though they rode all-armed, to wit the men-at-arms of Eastcheaping, even such as Osberne had seen riding down from the Castle the last time of his going thither; and the errand they came on was this, that war and strife were at hand for the good town, for the Baron of Deepdale had sent the Porte his challenge for some matter of truage, wherein the town deemed it had a clear right, and seeing that it was nought feeble, it had a settled mind to fight it out. Where-fore it had sent a knight of its service and a company of men-at-arms to see what help its friends of the Dale would give it at the pinch: for it was well known that the dalesmen were stalwarth carles if need were, both a-foot and on horseback, though they were no stirrers up of strife.

With this errand on hand came the men into the Dale, and the very first stead they came to was Wethermel, for it lay first on their road. And now was Wethermel as wellmanned stead, for besides Stephen the Eater, there were twelve carles defensible dwelling there, whereof five were sons of men of estate.

So when the said men-at-arms rode into the garth of a bright May evening, and they all glittering like so many heaps of sunlit ice, all folk came out a-doors, and Osberne stood before them all, clad in scarlet raiment, for Nicholas the goodman hung back somewhat, as was his wont when he deemed he saw peril at hand. Then Osberne hailed the newcomers, and asked no questions of them, and made no words save to welcome them and bid them in; and they got off their horses and entered the house, one score and five all told. And there they unarmed them, and all service was done them, and then meat and drink were set on the board and all folk fared to supper, and it was soon seen that both sides were friendly and sweet together. And Osberne set the Knight who was their captain at his right hand, and they talked merrily together. But when supper was done the Knight spake unto Osberne and Nicholas and said: "Sirs, is it free for me to tell out our errand into the Dale?" Osberne answered: "We should not have asked it, fair sir, if ye had not offered to tell it, but would rather have prayed you to drink a cup or two; but so it is that we be eager to hear your tale, whereas we see that ye are of our friends of Eastcheaping." Then the Knight began, and told them of their quarrel from point to point, and the right they deemed they had therein. And from time to time Osberne put in a question when he would have the matter made clearer to him, and the Knight deemed his questions handy and wise. And at last he said: "Now so it is, neighbours, that we ask help of you; and the help we need is not so much of money or beasts or weapons as of the bodies and souls of stark & stouthearted men. What say ye, who be here, have ye will to ward your cheaping and the place where we have done good to each other, or will ye let all go down the wind as for you?"

"Fair sir," said Osberne, "we will first ask you one question: Ye bid us to ride to battle with you in your quarrel; but do ye bid and command us this service as of right, or do ye crave our help as neighbours, and because there is love and dealings betwixt us? And this I ask because we dalesmen deem that we be free men, owning no service to any lord, or earl, or king."

Said the Knight: "We claim no service of you of right or by custom, but crave your help as bold and free neighbours who for love's sake may be fain of helping friends in need."

Spake Osberne: "Then there is no more to be said but this, that there is one who will ride with you, and that is my own self. And though I be but a lad I have a stroke of work in me, as some hereby can witness; and if thou wilt, I will ride down the Dale with you and give you my furtherance with the goodmen there. But as for these good fellows—which of you will ride with this Knight against the good town's foemen and ours?" They all cried aye to this and rose up and shouted. But Osberne said: "Well, lads, but some one must be left behind to look to the goodman and the women, and husband field and fold. I will take with me but six and Stephen the Eater, my man." And he named them one after the other.

Who were joyous now save the Knight and his men-at-arms, and they all drank a cup to the young master; but sooth to say, some of them wondered how so young a lad would bear him in the fight. But others said, Let-a-be, no man so well beloved as this shall be a dastard.

So merry they were in the hall and drank a bout, but not for long, whereas the captain would not have his men so drunk that they might not ride fast and far on the morrow. So the voidee cup was drunk, and Osberne led the Knight to his bed and gave him good-night. But ere he was asleep came Stephen to his bedside and asked was he fain of a tale; and the Knight yeasaid it; so Stephen told much about the Dale and its folk, and about the Dwarfs and the Land-wights. And at last he fell to talk about his master, the young one, and told much of him and his valiancy and kindness and prowess; and he told at length all the tale how Hardcastle had sped at his hands. And the captain marvelled and said: "I am in luck to see this lad and be his fellow then; for such marvels come not to hand more than once or twice in a ten score years, and this is one of them."

XXII

Osberne Takes Leave of Elfhild

So they rose on the morrow and dight them in their armour; and Osberne did on him Hardcastle's long byrny and gilded basnet, and girded Boardcleaver to him, and took his spear in hand and hung his shield at his back. But his bow and wonder-shafts he gave to Stephen to bear with him; and Stephen and the other men were fairly well bedight; and the captain said that if there was any lack of weapons or armour to any of them it mattered but little, as they had good store of gear at the cheaping.

So they ate a morsel and drank one cup and then rode their ways down the Dale. And the longest tale that need be told of them is that, by the furtherance of Osberne, they sped their errand well at most of the steads of the mid and lower Dales. And they made stay for the night at a stead hight Woodneb, which was some little way up the river from the place where the East and West Dales held the Cloven Mote, and by consequence not over far from the trysting-place of those twain.

At the said house that even they were of one mind to gather a mote there the next morning, and they sent folk that same night to bear the war-arrow to the steads above and below, and all seemed like to go well; and ever Osberne spake his mind without fear or favour to the boldest and wisest that were there. But as he was laying himself down to sleep a pang shot into his heart, for he called to mind that the morrow was the very day of tryst at the Bight of the Cloven Knoll, and longer it was ere he got to sleep that night than was his wont. But when day came he was awake and few were stirring. So he arose and clad him in his war-gear, and went out of the house and out of the garth when it was not yet sunrise, and came down to the river and went up it till he and the sunbeams came together to his place over against the ness, and there he abided. But he had been there a scant half hour ere he saw Elfhild coming up the slope, and she clad in all that fair weed he had given her, wherein this time of spring and early summer she mostly came to the trysting-place, and about her shoulders was a garland of white May blossom. And when she saw him in his shifting grey hawberk and gleaming helm, and Boardcleaver girt to his side and the spear in his hand, she stretched out her hands to him and cried out: "O if thou mightest but be here and thine arms about me! For now I see that some evil hath befallen, and that thou art arrayed to go away from me out of the Dale. And O thy war-coat and thine helm! Thou art going into peril of death, and thou so young! But I had an inkling hereof, for there were two carles in our house last night, and they said that there were weaponed men riding amidst the Eastdalers. Tell me, what is it? Will ye fight in the Dale or go far from it? And then how long dost thou look to be away?"

He spake, and his face was writhen with the coming tears, so sore his heart was stung by her sorrow: "It is indeed true that I am come to bid thee farewell for a while, and this is the manner of it." And therewith he told her all as it was, and said withal: "Now I can do nought save to bid thee gather thy valiance to thee and not to wound my heart with the wildness of thy grief. And look thou, my dear; e'en now thou wert saying thy yearning that mine arms were round about thy body: now are we no longer altogether children, and I will tell thee that it is many a day since I have longed for this; and now I know that thou longest that our bodies might meet. Belike thou wilt deem me hard and self-seeking if I tell thee that there is more joy in me for the gain of that knowledge than there is sorrow in my heart for thy pain."

"Nay, nay," she said, "but for that I deem thee the dearer and the dearer."

"See then, sweetheart," said he, "how might it ever come about that we might meet bodily if I abode ever at Wethermel and the Dale in peace and quietness, while thou dwelt still with thy carlines on the other side of this fierce stream? Must I not take chancehap and war by the hand and follow where they lead, that I may learn the wideness of the world, and compass earth and sea till I have gone about the Sundering Flood and found thy little body somewhere in the said wide world? And maybe this is the beginning thereof."

Now was the maiden a little comforted, and she said, smiling as well as she might: "And belike thou art for the cheaping again? Dost thou remember what a joy it was to thee to bring me those things and shoot and cast them over the water unto me? Now this time when thou comest back to the Dale I will ask thee to bring me one thing more, and then I shall be satisfied."

"Yea, sweetheart, and what shall that be?" And sooth to say it went against the grain with him that at the very moment of their parting she should crave something, like a very child, for a fairing. But she said: "O my dear, and what should it be but thou thyself?" And therewith she could refrain her passion no longer, but brake out a-weeping sorely again, so that her eyes could no longer behold him. But she heard many caressing words come across the water, and many farewells and words of grief, and yet she could not master her tears so that she could see him clearly, neither could she speak one word in answer. But at last she looked up and saw that he was gone from before her, and dimly she saw him yet a little way gone down the water, and he turned toward her and raised his hand and waved it to her. And nought else she saw of him for that time save the gleam of his scarlet surcoat and a flash of his helm in the May sunlight.

But for Osberne, sick at heart at first he was, and he strode hurrying along if that might ease him a little, and after a while he took some deal of courage, but still hastened on leaving the waterside; and then in a while himseemed to hear the voice of a great horn afar off, and he called to mind that the Mote had been summoned; and his mind turned toward what was to do.

XXIII

Osberne Is Chosen Captain of the Dalesmen

So when he was come anigh the stead he saw the gathered folk and the glittering of weapons about a knoll a bowshot without the garth, and made the best of his way toward the Mote. And as he was drawing near, there ran toward him divers men from the skirts of the throng, and cried out to him to hasten, "For now," cried one of them, "the Mote is dealing with thee." So he ran on with them; and when he entered the throng, which for those parts was no small one, there went up a great shout, and they shoved him along up to the foot of the knoll, on the top whereof stood three of the best men of estate, and the Lawman of the Dale, and the captain of the men of Eastcheaping. These called him to come amongst them, and then the Lawman fell to speaking: "Osberne Wulfgrimsson," said he, "thou art late at the Mote, and it is well-nigh done, but this is the heart of the matter, that we have ten score and six of good men pledged them to ride with these friends of Eastcheaping; but they have craved to have a captain to them chosen from us Dalesmen. But whereas there hath been but little war or strife in the Dale since the riding of the White Champion, which is a thirty years ago, we be for the most part little skilled in battle; and we all wot that thou hast a man's heart in thy lad's body, and that thou hast slain a mighty man of war, a man deft in all prowess. Wherefore some of the folk have spoken of thee to be the captain of our company; and I tell thee that I shall presently call for the word of the whole Mote, and if they yeasay it, then must thou needs go as captain of these, will thou nill thou."

Osberne was as red as fire in the face by then the Lawman was done, and he said: "Master, I pray thee consider my youth, and how I have had no schooling herein, and know nought of ordering men or arraying a battle. All this is nought like defending life and livelihood against a robber when there was none to serve at a pinch, and using one's mother-wit in dealing with it." The captain of the East-cheapers smiled upon him kindly and said: "My son, he who can use his mother-wit to any purpose when the edges be aloft hath learned the more part of battle-craft. Withal it is but a few hours agone that I saw thee handling the men of thine household like to a ripe man. Fear not, my son, but that thou shalt do well enough; and moreover I promise that I will learn thee the craft all I may. And know that if thou deny this, then shalt thou take the heart out of these good fellows, who be eager enough to help the good town and be no mannikins, I warrant them. Naysay it not, my lad, naysay it not."

Now was Osberne's heart thumping against his ribs, what for sudden wonder, what for the hope of renown that flashed upon him as a sudden flame of strange light. But withal he thought in himself, and that all suddenly also: If the Sundering Flood is to be encompassed here is indeed the beginning of it, if this good Knight shall be my friend and shall learn me the craft of war, and thereby I become a man of might, to be desired and waged by them who have not either the craft or the courage to fight for themselves face to face with their foemen.

Wherefore now he turned to the Lawman and said: "Master, it is enough; if the Mote of the neighbours will have me captain I may not naysay it: and may my luck be enough to overcome my childish years: and if not, may I lie on the field and not come back again to hear the mothers and maids curse me for having cast away the lives of their sons and their dears."

Then spake the Lawman, after he had smiled on Osberne and laid his hand on the lad's shoulder: "Men of the East Dale, ye be met together to see if ye can in any wise help our friends and neighbours of Eastcheaping, and ye have told off certain men to go in arms for their avail, and will have a captain over them. Now it hath been said to me that he who seems likeliest for the said captain is the young man Osberne Wulfgrimsson of Wethermel, and if this be so, let me hear your voices saying Yea. But even then there will be time for any man of you to name another, if it seem good to him, and that name will be also put to the Mote, and a dozen others if such there be. Now first, what say ye to Osberne Wulfgrimsson?"

Straightway arose a great cheer and the clashing of weapons, and well-nigh every man as it seemed cried out Yea. But when the noise and cry was abated, the Lawman bade any man who would put forth another name. No man spake for a little, till at last Surly John pushes forth to the front and says: "I name Erling Thomasson, a good man and true!" Brake forth then great laughter and whooping, for the said Erling was a manifest niggard, a dastard who sweated in his bed when the mouse squeaked in the wall a nighttime. But one man sang out: "Yea, Lawman, and I name Surly John." Thereat was there fresh laughter, and men shoved John to and fro till they had hustled him out to the skirts of the throng, and there bid him go a-wolf-hunting.

But now the Lawman takes Osberne by the hand and leads him to the edge of the knoll, and stands there and says: "Men of the Dale, ye would go to the war; ye would take a captain to you; ye would have Osberne Wulfgrimsson for your captain. All this ye have done uncompelled, of your own will; therefore take not the rue if it turn not out so well as ye looked for. But now I bid all them that be going this journey to lift up their right hands and swear to be leal and true to your captain, Osberne Wulfgrimsson, in all things, for life or for death."

Even so they did with a hearty good will: thereupon Osberne spake and said, after he had had a word with [the Knight] Sir Medard, apart: "All ye my men, I have but this to say to you: I hold you trusty and valiant, and men unlike to fight soft. But this I know of you, as of all other of us Dalesmen, that ye are most wont to go each after his own will, and it is well-nigh enough to put a man off from doing a thing if another man say to him, Do it. Now this manner ye must change, since ye are become men-at-arms, and if I bid you go to the right or the left, ye need think of nought but which is your right hand and which the left; though forsooth I wot well that some of you be so perverse that even that debate may lead you into trouble and contention. Now look to it that ye may not all be captains, and they that try it, so long as I be over you, are like to wend into wild weather. Now stout-hearts, and my friends, it is now a little past high noon; and we shall abide here no longer than tomorrow morn, and at daybreak we shall be on our way to Eastcheaping, wherefore that time have yet got to see to your weapons and array, and to say farewell, such of you as be not too far off, to your kindred and wives and sweethearts. And now let all we do our best when we come among the edges, so that hereafter one man may say to another: Thou art as valiant as the Dalesmen when they fought in the war of Eastcheaping."

Then all men gave a great shout, and were well-nigh weeping-ripe for high heart and for love of him, though a minute before their faces were all agrin, so wise and valiant and kind they deemed his words and the manner of his speaking.

Therewith the Mote brake up, and the men were busy arraying them for departure: and as for Osberne, he had his hands full of work, in giving and taking commandments, and in learning from Sir Medard the beginnings of the lore of battle; so that what hopes he had of making his way to the trysting-place once more were speedily swept aside. And the next morning betimes they set out together, the Dalesmen and the Eastcheapers, in all good fellowship, and in two days' time came to Eastcheaping; and there were the Dalesmen welcomed dearly, and they were lodged full well by the crafts-masters of the good town. But Sir Medard took Osberne with him up into the Castle and guested him there, that he might the closer teach him his new craft, and an apt scholar he found. Also from the morrow after their coming, the captain, by bidding of the Porte, furnished and arrayed the Dalesmen with weapons, as long spears and good swords and bows and arrows, and jacks and sallets and shields, and they went out into the mead under the Castle to be better assured thereby, and fell to learning how best to handle their weapons. And both their captains and they themselves deemed it best that they should fight a-foot; for though they were good horsemen after their fashion, they would have to learn all in the craft of fighting a-horseback.

XXIV

A Skirmish with the Baron of Deepdale in the Marshes

Now I have nought to do to write a chronicle of the good town of Eastcheaping, or a history of this war of them of the town with the Baron of Deepdale, or else a long tale I might make of it. So here follows all that shall be told of the said war.

In somewhat less than a month from their coming to Eastcheaping they had sure news that the Baron was on the way to the town with a great company of knights and men-at-arms; and thereafter it was known that he was riding with a light heart and little heed. Wherefore Sir Medard turned the matter over in his mind, and, whereas if any one knew well the roads and the fields about Eastcheaping, he, Sir Medard, knew them better, he deemed he might give this great lord a brush by the way. So he rode out a-gates with but a small company of men-at-arms, five score to wit, all in white armour, and rides with them along the causeway. But early in the night, ere he set out, he had bidden a twelve score footmen make their way quietly in knots of five and ten and thereabout to a certain place fifteen miles as the highway led from Eastcheaping, where the said causeway, craftily made, went high raised over a marish place much beset with willow and alder, an evil place for the going of heavily-laded horses. But of these same footmen, some half had bows, and the rest spears and swords; all the Dalesmen went with these, and Osberne was the captain of the whole company, but with him was an old grey-beard, a sergeant tried in many wars, and a guileful man therein, and to him and Osberne Sir Medard showed what should be done.

So now the Baron and his came riding along the causeway, ten hundreds of men in all, lightly and in merry fashion, for they had said that they would go knock at the door of Eastcheaping and see what the carles were about there; and it was hard on noon. And first came riding an hundred or so of tall men well armed in white armour, their basnets new tinned; and they came to a certain place where on either side was abundance of thick alder bush and the ground soft between, and there was the causeway wider by a spear-length than its wont for some two score yards. Well, this hundred passed by on their way, but when they were clean out of sight, and the next company not yet come, up rise a half dozen of men from out the alders on either side, and come on to the causeway: they are clad in homespun coats and hoods, though if any had looked closely he had seen hawberks and steel hoods under the cloth. These men lay some things down on the causeway in the very midst between the narrows, and then get them back into the marsh again.

No sooner are they gone but there comes the sound of weaponed men going, and presently there is the head of a much bigger company coming on to the wide space betwixt the narrows, three hundreds of men at least. They were armed and mounted as well as might be, but kept not very good order. When the first of them came to the place where the marsh-lurkers had been, they found lying athwart the causeway, one on each side, two dead porkers, two dead dogs, two hares, and in the very midst a fox, these also dead. The first men wonder at this, and get off their horses and handle the carcasses; then they call others to look at them; and some deem this the work of dwarfs or fairies or such like; and others say this is a sign or token of the up-country folk to rise upon them, and that they had best send men a-foot to search the marsh; and others that they should send tidings to the rearward folk. And some say one thing, some another, and all the while their fellows are thronging into the wide place till they are all crowded together, and not a third part of them know what has befallen, and deem that something has gone amiss; and the rearward fall to drawing their swords and crying out, To it, to it! Slay, slay! Deepdale,

Deepdale! till scarce a man knew his right hand from his left.

But amidst all this turmoil a great voice (and it was Stephen the Eater) cried out from the marsh at the right hand: "Go back, ye swine, to Deepdale." Then another sang out from the north: "If ye can, ye dead dogs." Then Stephen again: "This time ye must run like hares." "Learn lore of the fox next time, if ye can," cried the northern voice. And even therewith was the twanging of bowstrings from either side, and the whistle of shafts and spears, for the foemen were near enough, and men and horses fell huddling on the causeway, and the shafts rained on without abatement, and the Deepdale riders were in sorry case indeed; and many of them were good knights well tried in the wars.

Then some gat off their horses and entered the marsh, and found no better hap there, for they were speedily slain by axe and sword of the Eastcheapers; or they squattered in the mire and yielded them to whomsoever was before them, of whom Stephen gat a good knight full-armed. But Osberne was otherwhere. For some of the Baron's men spared not to turn their backs and ride all they might rearward; but they went but a little way into the narrows ere they saw steel before them, and there across the causeway stood the company of the Dalesmen, even such as were not with the bowmen. Desperately they drave at them; but it was all for nought, for the first four fell, they and their horses, before the long spears of the Dalesmen, and the others were cumbered with the wounded and the slain, so that they might not come on a-horseback. Howbeit, some dismounted and fell on sword in hand. Then forth from the ranks of the Dalesmen came a slim warrior in a long hawberk and bright basnet and a shield on his arm, and he put his hand to his left side and drew, and it was as if a beam of fell blue flame flashed in the sun; and he cried out: "For the Dale! For the Dale! Hasten, fellows, and follow on, for Boardcleaver crieth for a life." And therewith he entered among the Deepdale folk and smote right and left, and with each stroke hewed a man, and they fell back before him; and then the Dalesmen were by his side instead of the foes, and still he went forward and men fell before him, and still came on

the spears of the Dalesmen; and now all they of Deepdale,
whether a-foot or on horseback, turn and flee away toward
the place of the first slaughter.

Then Osberne cried to his men: "Off the causeway now,
all ye Dalesmen; these ye shall not chase, they shall fall in
with chasing enough anon; and now must the causeway be
clear of all but foemen if I know aught of Sir Medard's mind.
Ye have done well." Therewith he gat him quietly from off
the causeway, and all they followed; they went but a little
way, and then about on the tussocks around the alder bushes,
and turned toward the causeway and awaited new tidings.

Speedily they befel; for anon they heard a confused noise
of crying and shouting and thundering of horse-hoofs, and
clattering of weapons and war-gear, and then burst out from
a corner of the causeway all the throng of fleers, spurring
all they might, weaponless, many of them jostling and shoving each other, so that every now and then man and horse
fell over into the marsh and wallowed there, till the Dalesmen came up and gave them choice of death or rendering.
And came great cries of Eastcheaping! For the Porte! and
A Medard, a Medard! and the riders of Eastcheaping came
thrusting amongst the fleers, and with the first of the chasers
was Medard himself bareheaded, so that all might know him,
and after him his banner of a Tower and an Eagle sitting
therein; and then came the banner of the good town, to wit,
three Wool-packs on a red ground; and then the rest of the
riders. And all that went by in a minute or two, and thereafter came the bowmen, all bemired with the marish waters,
but talking high and singing for joy. Said Osberne: "Come
we now, fellows, and join ourselves to these, for they will
not run away like to the horses. Now belike has Sir Medard
done the business, so we may follow him fair and softly."
"He may yet have somewhat to do," quoth a man who was
of that country; "for in a while this marish ends and the
causeway comes out on to fair and soft meadows, and there
we may look yet again to come on the Baron and his."
"Sooth is that," quoth the sergeant from amongst the bowmen on the causeway; "yet is not the good Knight so hare-
brained as not to abide ere he falls on, save he see no defence in what is left of the Baron's array. Ye shall see; but

come thou up, Master Osberne, with thy Dalesmen, and let us get on to the said sunny meads out of this frog-city."

So Osberne and his Dalesmen scrambled up, and they all went on together at a pretty pace; and Osberne had not yet sheathed Boardcleaver, but bore him on his shoulder all bloody as he was.

So in an half hour they saw the hard meads before them, and then they set up a shout and ran all together, for they heard the noise of battle, and saw some confused running and riding, and knew not what it might mean. So on they ran till they had come up on to the crown of a long but low ridge whence they might see the whole plain, and straightway they set up the whoop of victory. Forsooth what they beheld was the two banners of Sir Medard and the Porte following on the last of the fleers, and beyond them the whole host of the Baron flowing away as men discomfited; so they rested to catch their breath on the top of the ridge, and of all of them that went out from Eastcheaping the night before there was not one man lacking. Then they set off again toward the battle, their weapons on their shoulders and their horns blowing; and they went speedily, and presently they saw that Sir Medard and his had slacked in the chase and were standing together about the banners with their faces to the foe. Wherefore they also went slower, and they met together with many glad cries; and then Osberne came to Sir Medard and hailed him joyfully, and therewith thrust Boardcleaver back into the sheath and said: "Meseemeth, Captain, that the battle is done. But [how] came their whole host to flee away?" Said Sir Medard: "We drave the rout along the causeway, and they, when they came on to the hard meadow, might not stay them; and the rest, who saw them coming on the spur and our banners in the chase, knew not how many or how few were following on them, and they turned also, deeming they were safest at home. And so now we will gather the spoil together and wend fair and softly back to Eastcheaping."

Even so they did, and great spoil they gathered, and all the footmen gat them horses and rode with the others; so that they all came back safe to the good town before sunset. Thus ended the first riding of the Baron of Deepdale.

XXV

Stephen Tells of an Adventure in the Camp of the Foemen

THEREAFTER the Baron gathered his men again, and rode abroad divers times in the summer and autumn, and was now gotten warier, so that he gat no great overthrow. Yet was he often met by them of Eastcheaping, and not seldom had the worse. Osberne and his were in the field as oft as any, and gave and took, but ever showed them valiant. Osberne was hurt twice, but not sorely, and ever he waxed in manhood, and was well accounted of by all men; and the Dalesmen began to be well known to them of Deepdale and were a terror to them.

Thus wore summer and autumn, and Osberne saw no face of the hope of getting home to the Dale before spring. The winter came early, and was with much frost and snow, and they of Eastcheaping kept them within their walls perforce, but they held the Yule-feast merrily and with good heart.

When winter was gone and the snow and the floods, and spring was come again, there began again skirmishing and riding; and now one, now the other prevailed; and Osberne fell to learning all the feats of chivalry under Sir Medard. And in one fray he paid his master back for the learning, and somewhat more; for the Knight thrust too far forth amongst the foemen, and was unhorsed and set on by many; and had not Osberne been [nigh], who bestrode him with Boardcleaver in his fist, and thrust and hewed all around till some of theirs came up to help, the good town had lost its captain. So he rehorsed Sir Medard, and somewhat hardly they came forth of the throng, and were not ill beaten that day.

But when May was, the Baron of Deepdale had waxed so mighty that he gathered a great host together, and came therewith against Eastcheaping, so that they had nought to do save draw within their walls: and the Baron sent a herald, and bade thereby yield them, on such terms, over and above paying their truage according to his will, that they should batter down their walls, and take his men into their castle and have his burgreve over them, and moreover that they give over ten of their best to his mercy. This challenge they naysaid in few words, for the town was well victualled and manned. Wherefore on the morrow early the Baron assailed the walls with many men, but gat nothing thereby save loss of good men; and the assault over, Medard and his opened the gates and went forth on the foemen while they were yet in disarray, and won much and lost little.

Thereafter the Baron assailed the walls no more, but cast a dyke about the town and sat down before it; and he had abundance of victual coming in to him from his country-side, so that his men lacked nothing. But whereas his dyke and the towers of earth and timber which he let build there-on were scarce manned so well as they should have been, because there was so much of them, the Eastcheapers did not leave them wholly in quiet, but fell on oft and hard, and slew the Baron many men and did him much scathe. And men in the town were in good heart, and said one to the other, that if things went no worse than this they might hold out merrily till winter should break up the leaguer. But in the last of these skirmishes Osberne was hurt sorely, and though he was brought off by his fellows, and lost not Boardcleaver, as well-nigh betid, he must needs keep his bed somewhat more than a month ere he was well healed.

But on a day in September, when he was much amended and was growing strong again, came to him Stephen, whom he had not seen for some days, and seeing that there was no man in the chamber save they two, spake to him and said: "Captain, I would have a word with thee if I might."

Said Osberne: "Speech is free to thee, Stephen." And the Eater said: "I have been out a-gates of late, for I deemed that if I might find adventures it would be for thy health." Said Osberne, laughing: "Yet maybe not for thine, Stephen. I were loth to come to Wethermel without thee." Said Stephen: "At this rate it may be long ere we come to Wethermel." "I would we might hasten the homecoming," said Osberne, knitting his brows, "but I wot not how that may be since the Baron is yet so strong." "Ah, but I have a deeming how it may be done," said Stephen: "but there is peril in it." Osberne stood up and said: "What hast thou been about, runagate?"

"Master," said he, "I will tell thee. Five nights ago I did on raiment of the fashion of them beyond Deepdale, and I had with me a fiddle, and was in a manner of a minstrel; and thou wottest that I am not so evil a gut-scraper, and that I have many tales and old rhymes to hand, though I am no scald as thou art. Well, I got out a-gates a night-tide by the postern on the nook of the south-east tower, the warden whereof is a friend of mine own, and bade him expect me by midnight of the third day; and then by night and cloud I contrived it to skirt the dyke and get me about till I came north-west of our north gate, and then somehow I got up over the dyke, which is low there and was not guarded as then, and in a nook I lay still till morning came. And there I let myself be found by one of the warders, and when he kicked me and challenged me, I told him what I would as to myself, and he trowed it, and he brought me to his fellows, who, a five of them, were cooking their break-fast, and they gave me victual and bade me play and sing for their disport, and I did so, and pleased them. Thereafter one of them took me along with him toward the west side of the dyke, and I played and sang; and so, to make a long story short, I worked round the dyke that day till I was come to the south side of the leaguer, and there I lay that night in good entertainment; but on the morrow I went on my way, and before evening I had come back again to the north-west, just where I had started from. There I fell in with the man-at-arms who had kicked me up the morning before, and he fell to speech with me, and showed me many things, and amongst others the great bastide wherein, said he, the Baron of Deepdale was lodged, and that it was little guarded, which mattered nothing by day, but by night he deemed it something rash of the Baron to suffer so few men of his anigh him.

"Now while we spake together thus there was a stir about us, and we and others rose up from the grass where we were lying, and lo it was the Baron who was come amongst us, so we all did him reverence. He was a dark man, rather little than big, but wiry and hard-bitten; keen and eager of face, yet was there something lordly about his bearing. As luck would have it he came straight to where we stood together, and stayed to look upon me as something unwonted to him, for I was wholly unarmed, save for a little knife in my girdle; and I was clad in a black gown and a cotehardy of green sprigged with tinsel, and had my fiddle and bow at my back. We louted low before him, and he spake to my friend: 'Is this big fellow a minstrel?' 'Yea, lord,' said the other. Said the Baron: 'Looking at his inches, 't is a pity of him that he hath not jack and sallet and a spear over his shoulder. How sayest thou, carle; what if I were to set thee in the forefront of the press amongst the very knighthood?' 'Noble lord,' quoth I, 'I fear me if I came within push of spear thou wouldst presently see me running, so long are my legs. I am a big man, so please you, great lord, but I have the heart of a hare in me.' He looked upon me somewhat grimly, then he said: 'Meseems thou hast a fox's tongue in thee, carle, and I promise thee I have half a mind to it to hand thee over to the provost-marshal's folk, to see what they could make of whipping thee. Thou man-at-arms, hast thou heard him lay his bow over the strings?' 'Yea, lord,' said the man; 'he playeth not ill for an uplander.' 'Let him try it now before us, and do it well withal if he would save the skin of his back.' Speedily I had my fiddle in my hand, and fell to, and if I played not my best, I played at least something better than my worst. And when I had done, the Baron said: 'Friend, how many such tunes canst thou play? And canst thou sing aught?' 'It would not be so easy to tell up the tunes I can play, lord,' said I; 'and sing I can withal, after a fashion.' Said the Baron to the man-at-arms: 'Bring thou this man to my lodging tonight some two hours before midnight, and he shall play and sing to us, and if we be not sleep-eager he shall tell us some old tale also; and I will reward him. And thou, I shall not make thee a man-at-arms this time, though trust me, I misdoubt thy hare-heart. There is no such look in thine eyes.' And he turned away and left us. So we wore the night merrily enough till the time appointed, what with minstrelsy and some deal of good wine.

"To the Baron's lodging I went, which was not right great, but hung goodly with arras of Troy. And I had the luck to please the lord; for I both played and sang somewhat near my best. And he bade give me a handful of silver pennies, though I must needs share them with my soldier friend, unto whom the lord forgat to give aught, and bade me come the next night at the same time; which I did, after I had spent the day in looking into everything about that side of the leaguer. But when I came forth with my friend from the lord's lodging that second night (and I the richer therefor), I did him to wit that the next morning early I should take my soles out of the leaguer and make for my own country, whatever might happen, so that no so many questions might be asked if I were missed on the morrow, as belike I was. Well, the end of this long story is, that a little before midnight I crept away and over the dyke and came to the postern and my friend, who let me into the town, and here I am safe and sound. Now, Captain, canst thou tell me why I took so much trouble in my disport, with no little peril withal?"

Now for some time Osberne had been walking to and fro as he hearkened to the tale, and now he turned about sharply to Stephen and said: "Yea, I know; thou wilt mean it in a day or two that we should go, we two, by night and cloud to the Great Bastide and carry off the Baron of Deepdale, that we may give him guesting in the good town."

Stephen smote his palms together and said: "Wise art thou, child of Wethermel; but not so wise as I be. We shall go, we two, but not alone, but have with us four stout fellows, and of wisdom enough, not Dalesmen, for too simple are they and lack guile. To say sooth I have chosen them already, and told them how we shall fare, and they are all agog for it."

"Well," said Osberne, "and when shall it be? Of a sooth thou lettest no grass grow under thy feet. But hast thou told any one else?" Said Stephen: "Tomorrow night is the time appointed, and I have bidden my friend the warder of the postern to hold ready a score of men well-armed against the hour we are to be looked for to knock at the door with our guest, if so be that we should need them, but I have not told him what we are about. Well now, what sayest thou? Have I done anything to amend thine health?" "Thou hast made me whole and well, friend," said Osberne; "and now I think we shall soon look upon Wethermel, and I shall never be sick or sorry again."

The Eater smiled, and they fell to talking of other matters as folk came into the chamber to them; and all that came in wondered to see the captain looking so much mended in health.

XXVI

They Bring the Baron into Eastcheaping

So on the morrow just before midnight came Osberne and Stephen and the four others to the postern above-said. Osberne and the four were clad, over their armour, in frocks and hoods of up-country fashion; but Stephen was in his minstrel's raiment, save that he bore no fiddle, and had a heavy short-sword girt to him under his cotehardy. The night was moonless, but there was little cloud, so that there was a glimmer of starlight. As they opened the door, came forth from the ingle a tall man, unarmed as it seemed, and clad as a gangrel carle, and Stephen without more ado stretched out his long arm and caught him by the breast of his coat. The man stirred not nor strove, but said softly: "Dost thou not know me, Stephen the Eater? I come to see the child of Wethermel; he shall know me by the token of the Imposition of Hands. And I am come to help him and all you." That heard Osberne and spake softly to the others: "This is a friend and a stout-heart; he shall be of all avail to us."

"Speak not," said Stephen, "but hold we on, and go crouching till we be under the lee of the dyke." Even so did

they, and Stephen led the way, but Osberne came next and
Steelhead with him; they spake not together, but Osberne
felt the stronger for having him beside him, and his heart
was full of joy.

So they clomb the dyke, and as they topped it they saw a
weaponed man on his feet betwixt them and the sky. Stephen
stood up straightway and fell a-whistling a merry tune, but
softly enough, while he made a sign to the others to fetch a
compass and go creeping past this man. So did they, while
Stephen and the warder walked toward one another; but so
soon as they met, the warder knew his friend, and hailed him
and said: "Well, minstrel, thou art back again pretty soon;
what is toward, man?" Said Stephen: "Sooth to say, I went
not all the way home; for it came into my mind that maybe
the Baron might call for me again; and when it rains florins
I am fain to have my hat under the spout." Said the warder:
"Thou art come in time, for the Baron is somewhat ailing,
and whiles he sleeps not well a-nights; it was but last night
when it was so, and he sends for me and asks me of thee, and
biddeth me fetch thee; and St Peter! the uproar when I told
him that thou wert gone; and it was hardly that I escaped a
whipcord supper. Howsoever, his wrath ran off him in a little, and then he bade me look out for thee, and if I find thee
I am to bring thee to him at any hour of day or night wherein the armour is off him: wherefore, see thou, in happy hour
art thou come. So abide me till I go and fetch a fellow to
keep my watch, and then will I go on with thee to my
lord."

"Wait a while," said Stephen; "to say sooth I have hereby an old carle, my uncle, and his son, a young swain, and
both they are good at song, and the older man a very poke
stuffed full of old tales: how were it if I brought them along?"

"It were good," said the warder, "for it shall, see thou,
make a change of disport for our lord, and that will please
him the more. So go now, bring up hither thy kinsmen, and
I will see to my watch and we will meet here straightway."

So then Stephen went to his folk, who were creeping
nigher and nigher to the Great Bastide, and were as now
in broken ground somewhat bushed, a good lurking-place to
wit. There he finds them, and bids the four abide their com-

ing back with their prey, which now he nowise doubted of, and takes Steelhead and Osberne along with him, and brings them to the warder; who laughed when he saw Steelhead, for he went for that time all bent and bowed, and, as he deemed by what he could see under the dim sky, ragged and wretched. Said he: "Minstrel, thou wert scarce in luck to happen on this rag of a kinsman of thine. Hast thou no better, man?" Said Stephen, grinning in the dark: "Abide till ye have proved him. Trust me, he hath something better than sour curds in his belly." "Well," said the warder, "let-a-be! As for the young man, he seems like enough. Now then, fellow, for a pull at the florin-tree."

So they went, the four of them, toward the Great Bastide, and none hindered them, deeming that they were of the service of the Baron. Even at the door of the Baron's lodging the warder (there was but one and a chamberlain) nodded friendly to the soldier and let them pass unquestioned. They entered the chamber, wherein now was no man, as the Baron would have it whenas he listed to sleep. The soldier went forward on tip-toe, but Stephen trod heavily, and Steelhead laughed aloud, and went straight up to the great man's bed-head, and fared to pass his hand over his face from his forehead to his chin, just touching him, but the sleeping man waked not. As for Osberne, he stood betwixt the door and the soldier, and drew his sword forth from under his carter's frock, but it was not Boardcleaver, for he had left him at home. The soldier looked from one to another, and stared astonished at their demeanour. Straightway then he had both Stephen and Osberne on him at once: nor had he any senses nor might to strive with them, who stripped his coat off over his head, gagged him, and tied him hand and foot. By then they had done this, Steelhead had taken up the naked Baron and set some of the warder's raiment on him, and done on him the said warder's coat and sallet over all; and there stood the man of worship, waked up now, as it seemed, but looked before him as if he saw naught, even as a man who walks in sleep. Stephen the meantime unstrung his fiddle and began to play a slow sweet tune thereon, and let his big but melodious voice go with it, and thus they brought the lordship of Deepdale to the door, and still he seemed of no avail, save to walk on as Steelhead would have him.

So out they fared, and none hindered them any more than when they went in; and they came to the bushed ground where lay the four townsmen and stirred them, and so went on all seven with their new fellow the Baron, who still walked on like a man in his sleep.

They made a compass about the warder who had taken the place of Stephen's friend, so that he might not challenge them, and came fair and softly to the dyke, and thereafter to the postern. There Stephen knocked after the manner appointed, and the door opened and showed the passage all full of armed men. But Stephen cried out: "All's well, friend Dickon, and there shall be no sally out tonight, only take us in, and bring me and Captain Osberne to Sir Medard, for we have somewhat to show him."

So they gat them into the town, they and their new guest; but ere the door was shut, Steelhead took Osberne by the skirt and drew him a little aside and said: "Lad of Wethermel, in all ways hast thou shown thy valiancy, and I am glad of thee. Now I have come from the hill-sides and the crannies of the rocks to look upon thee, and I must get me back at once; for within a builded town I may not be. But I can see that it will not be long till we meet in the mountains. So I tell thee, when thou deemest thy need and thy grief to be as great as it may be, hie thou to the little dale where first we met, and call on me by the token of the bow I gave thee then, and presently thou shalt have tidings: now farewell."

"Yea, but hold," said Osberne, "wilt thou not enter, even if it be to go forth at once by another gate with much company? Else wilt thou be tangled amongst all these foemen."

"Trouble not thyself about me," said Steelhead; "it shall not be hard for me to go where I will in despite of any foeman."

XXVII

They Parley from the Walls

THEREWITH he was gone and Osberne entered the town after his fellows, and the Baron of Deepdale was brought to Sir Medard in the great tower. There they would have served him with all honour, but he was not yet come out of that trance; so they laid him to rest in Sir Medard's own bed, and had warders both within the chamber and without; and Osberne sat talking with Sir Medard in the said chamber till dawn was, when the Baron awoke really and fairly, and called for drink. And Sir Medard brought it unto him with his own hand, and the Baron stared at him and said: "Art thou of the service tonight? I know thee not." Quoth Sir Medard: "And yet we have been near enough together ere this, Lord Baron; thou shouldst know me, meseems." The Baron looked hard on him and then round about the chamber, and cried out: "Holy Mary! 't is Medard the carle-leader. Where am I, and where is the evil beast of a minstrel? Hath he beguiled me?" Said Medard: "Lord, at this present thou art in a chamber of my poor house in Eastcheaping. Doubtless tomorrow, after we have had some talk together, thou and I and the Porte, thou mayst go back home to Deepdale, or abide here a while to see how we can feast, we carle-warriors, and to be holden in all honour."

Now came forth Stephen the Eater and said: "Lord, lo here the evil beast of a minstrel who hath verily beguiled thee; but, Baron, it is to thy gain and not thy loss. For to-morrow shall the war be ended, and thou shalt be free to go back again to the fair women of Deepdale whom thou lovest so much, and shalt save thy men-at-arms, and thy weapons and tents and timber, and victuals and drink a great heap; and all this I deem, and more maybe, wouldst thou have lost hadst thou gone on sitting perversely before Eastcheaping all for nought. So I will not say pardon me, but make friends with me rather for being good to thee." And therewith he reached out his great hand to the Baron; but Osberne drew him back by the girdle, and chid him for mocking a captive, while the Baron turned his face to the wall and covered up his head with the bed-clothes.

But ye may judge if there were riding and running in the leaguer next morning when they could find the Baron nowhere; and one said this and the other that; and he cried Kill and slay, and he cried Flee ere we all come to like end; and great was the doubt and the turmoil. Amidst of which comes Sir Medard on to the battlement of the northwest tower, and beside him a squire bearing a white banner, and a herald with a trumpet, which herald presently blew a loud blast, but such an one as sounded not of war but of parley. So when the captains and leaders heard the said blast and saw the white banner of peace, they deemed that new tidings were toward, and a half score of them crossed over their dyke bearing a white banner with them, and came close under the tower whereon stood Sir Medard; and the chiefest of them, an old hoar man and very wise, hight Sir Degore, stood before the others all unhelmed and said: "Is it Sir Medard that standeth up there?"

"Yea verily," said the Knight; "and what art thou? Art thou a leader of the host that sitteth about us?" Said the other: "I am Sir Degore, of whom thou wilt have heard; under my lord the Baron of Deepdale I am the leader of this host, and I have come to ask what thou wouldst of us." Said Sir Medard: "I would see the Baron of Deepdale."

"He is sick this morning," said Sir Degore, "and may not rise; but if thou wouldst render the town and the castle unto him, it is all one, thou mayst make me serve thy turn; I know his mind full well."

Sir Medard laughed: "Nay," said he, "we will wait for that till we may see the Baron himself. But tell me, Sir Knight, what is all this stir and hubbub in thine host this morning?"

Said Sir Degore, without tarrying the word one moment: "There is a great aid and refreshment come to us out of the East country, both of victual and men, and our folk be welcoming the men and sharing the victual."

"There is nothing in this, then, that we have heard, that

ye cannot find your Duke, and are seeking him up and down?"

"Nay, nothing," said the greybeard, wagging his head. But the folk that were with him look on each other and thought within themselves how wise the old man was. And Sir Medard spake when he might for his laughter: "Sir, thy lord did well to make thee captain under him, for thou art a wise and ready liar. But so it is that thou speakest with one who knoweth the tale better than thou. Ho ye, bring forward my lord."

Straightway came two squires, who led a lean dark man between them, unarmed and clad in a long furred black gown. He took off his hat, and thereupon Sir Degore and all they below knew him for their lord. He spake at once and said: "Sir Degore and ye others, my lords and captains, can ye hear me?"

"Yea, lord," said Sir Degore.

Then said the Baron: "This then is my word and commandment, that ye give leave to all our folk-in-arms to depart each one to his own house, and to bear away with him his weapons and armour and three horses if he be of the knighthood, and one if he be of the sergeantry; but the others, archers and villeins, may take one horse between three to bear their baggage and ease them on the journey. But the flour and wheat and wine, and all the neat and sheep, ye shall leave behind; for the folk of this country-side and the good town have occasion for them. But as to mine own matters which are of mine own person, as arms and raiment and jewels and the like, ye shall bring them unto me here in the good town, where I am minded to abide two or three days that I may hold counsel about weighty matters with the Porte and the Burgreve. Moreover, I would have thee, Sir Degore, and a five of my counsellors and a half score of my servants, come hither to me to aide with me for my aid and service while I tarry in Eastcheaping. Now this is my will and pleasure, and I shall be no wiser later on; wherefore do thou, Sir Degore, go straightway and tell my will to the captains and sergeants and the knights, so that the hosts may presently break up."

Ye may deem how Sir Degore and the other Deepdalers

were abashed when they knew that their lord was a captive
in the hands of the foemen; yet they seemed to think that
the terms of the good town were not so hard as might have
been looked for, since they had gotten this so great advan-
tage.

Now Sir Degore spake and said: "Sir Medard, wilt thou
suffer me to come up to thee, so that I may speak with my
lord privily?" "To what end," said Sir Medard, "since thou
hast heard thy lord's commandment? Wilt thou not obey
him?" "Yea," said Degore, "if I have heard his last word;
nevertheless I were fain to come and speak with him."
"Come up then," said Sir Medard; "yet I must warn thee
that it may be easier for thee to come in to Eastcheaping today than to go out therefrom. Moreover, bethink ye if ye
dally how it would be were we to open our gates and fall upon you with all ours, and ye disarrayed and leaderless."

Therewith he gave word to open the postern to Sir Degore, who entered and was brought to the top of the tower,
and there he went up to the Baron and bent the knee to him
and might not refrain his tears; but the Baron laughed,
yet somewhat hardly. So they two went aside into an ingle of
the tower toward the town, while Sir Medard and his stood
aloof a while. Then turned back Sir Degore to them of
Eastcheaping, and said: "Sir Medard, I pray thee leave to
depart to my host, that I may do after the bidding of my
lord."

"Yea, go," said Sir Medard; "yet I would have thee remember that I pray for a long life for the Baron of Deepdale,
since he hath become so good a friend to our town, and that
thou wilt be in the wrong if thou do aught to shorten it."

So Degore went his ways, and he and those counsellors
and leaders went back sadly to the leaguer, and fell to work
to undo all they had done the six months past. And it was no
long time ere the stout men-at-arms of Deepdale began to
flow away from before Eastcheaping, and the men of the
town held good watch all the while; and ere it was evening
divers bands of them went out-of-gates in good order to see
that none of the Deepdalers abode in array in the leaguer,
and found nothing there which they had cause to dread. And
they took much spoil of that which the Baron's host must

needs leave behind. Meanwhile Sir Medard and his made what cheer they might to the Baron; and Sir Medard showed Osberne unto him, and told him all the tale of the wolves and the slaying of Hardcastle, and did him to wit that much of the valiancy which they of Eastcheaping had shown in the war came of this lad of Wethermel. And the Baron marvelled, and looked upon Osberne and said: "Well, lad, if ever thou art hard bestead, come thou to Deepdale, and we shall find somewhat for thee to do; and I bid thee thrive hale and well!"

Howbeit Sir Medard told not to the Baron that Osberne had been one of them that bore him off the last night. Yet somehow he came to know it in time to come; I wot not through whom or how.

XXVIII

The Baron of Deepdale Makes Peace

So now the war was over, for the next day the Baron of Deepdale signed the deed of peace which gave up to the Porte of Eastcheaping all that for which they had withstood him; and withal some deal of ransom he had to pay for his own body, how much my tale-teller knoweth not, but deemeth that they would scarce put the snepe upon him as to bid but a squire's or knight-bachelor's ransom for a free baron, a lord of wide lands, who had under him towns, tolls, and markets.

So the ransom being paid, or some deal of it, and pledges left for the remnant, the Baron went his ways in no very evil mood, and it was soon seen that they of Eastcheaping would no longer need the men they had waged over and above those who were due to them for service, wherefore leave was given to such waged men to depart, and the Dalesmen amongst others. But gifts were given them largely, over and above their war-pay, and to Osberne and Stephen the Eater in especial. Unto whom, amongst other things, the Butchers' gild of the good town did on the eve of his departure bring a great and fair ox, white of colour; and they had gilded the horns of the beast, and done him about with garlands: but on a scroll between the horns was fairly writ the words, The Eater's Ox. Which gift Stephen received as it was given, very lovingly, and many a cup they drank together over him; but Stephen said ere his friends departed: "Yet look ye, lads of Eastcheaping, though this ox be mine, yet shall he not be the ox of the Eater; for slay him will I never, but let live on and on for love of our friends of Eastcheaping so long as I may buy, beg, or steal a cow's grass for him."

As for Osberne, though he bought in the booths a pretty many of such things as were goodly and little, of goldsmiths' work and the like, to flit to his friend across the Sundering Flood, yet no gift would he take, save a very fair armour of the spoils of Deepdale: and this was no gift, said Sir Medard, but what he had earned himself by hard toil enough.

All loved him, but Sir Medard in especial, who had fain dubbed him knight; but Osberne would not, and said that such had been no wont of his fathers before him; and he looked never to go very far from the Dale and for no long while. "And even if I may not live there," quoth he, "I look to die there;" and he reddened therewith till the eyes looked light in the face of him. But Medard said: "Wheresoever thou livest or diest thou wilt live and die a great-heart. But this I bid thee, whenso thou hast need of a friend who may show thee the road into the world of deeds, when thou hast aught to hide or aught to seek, come thou unto me, and be sure that I shall not fail thee."

Osberne thanked him from his whole heart, and they kissed and departed with all love; and as the Dalesmen rode down the street toward the western gate, it was full of folk shouting out praises and blessings; and the windows were full of women who cast down flowers on them as they went along, saying that but for these stout-hearts they might have had neither town nor honour nor children, and that nought was good enough for such friends as these. Thus rode the Dalesmen out of Eastcheaping.

But of the ten score and six that had ridden out of the

Dale, two score and two were lacking, who had either been slain in battle or so sorely hurt that they were no longer fightworthy; but sixteen had dropped in by ones and twos and threes to fill the places of these, so that they rode back but little fewer than they came.

XXIX

Osberne and His Men Return to Wethermel

Now on a fair evening a little ere sunset of the beginning of October, came those Dalesmen amongst the black rocks and rough places that crowned the bent which looked down west over the Dale. And now, though they had been talking merrily and loud for the last three hours, their hearts were so full within them that scarce a word might they say one to another. And when at last they had won through that rocky tangle and had opened Wethermel, and nought lay before them but the grassy slopes and the wide-spread valley cleft by the line of the Sundering Flood; now, when they saw in the clear air the grey houses of Wethermel lying together, and the smoke of the evening cooking-fires going up to the heavens, and the sheep wending on, thick and huddling before the driving of three tall men, and the kine moving towards the byre and the women amongst them, then this befel: that whereas they had been all of one mind that when they came to the crown of the bent, they would spur on and race merrily toward Wethermel, yet now when it lay before them, and there was so little a way betwixt them and its hearth, they all of them with one consent drew rein and sat still on their horses, as if they had suddenly come face to face with the host of the foemen. Yea, some there were, and they rather of the oldest than the youngest, who might not refrain them, but fell a-weeping and sobbing, whether it were for joy or sorrow, or a blending of both, may scarce be said.

Osberne wept not: sooth to say, the turmoil of hope and

fear within his heart ate up somewhat the softness that might else have mastered him at this new sight of his fathers' house. He rode forth before the others, and lifted up his voice and loudly and clearly cried a blessing on the Dale and the dwellers therein, and then rode on soberly down the bent, and the others followed him still silently. But when they were drawn anigh, and every soul, man, woman and child, ran forth from the garth to meet and welcome them, then at last their joy brake forth, and they gat off their horses and gave themselves up to the caresses of the women and the embracing of the carles, and loud was the speech and the laughter amongst them.

Osberne was met first by Nicholas his grandsire, who kissed and embraced him, and then gave him up to his grandam and the fostermother, and one or other of these twain would scarce let go of him a long while.

But now was riding and running after victual for so big a company of men; for nought would serve the folk of Wethermel but that the whole fellowship must abide there that night. But all was got ready in a while, and meanwhile the stay-at-homes might not have enough of praising and caressing the folk returned, and everything they said or did was a wonder.

At last the feast was arrayed, and the hall was thronged as much as might be, and folk fell to meat, and now they were all exceeding merry; and when they had done eating, the boards were drawn to make more room, and they fell to the drink, and after the first cup to Christ, and the second to Allhallows, the third was drunk to the home-comers from the war. Yet were not the stay-at-homes to be put off with so little, and they called a cup for Osberne the Captain of the warriors; and when it had been drunk, then all folk looked toward the captain to see what he would do; but he rose up and stood in his place, his cheek flushed and his eyes sparkling: and the word came into his mouth, and he sang:

> The War-god's gale
> Drave down the Dale
> And thrust us out
> To the battle-shout;
> We wended far

To the wall of war
And trod the way
Where the edges lay,
The rain of the string rattled rough on the field
Where the haysel was hoarded with sword-edge & shield.

Long lived the sun
When the play was begun,
And little but white
Was the moon all night;
But the days drew in
And work was to win,
And on the snow
Lay men alow,
And at Yule fared we feasting in war-warded wall
And the helm and the byrny were bright in the hall.

Then changed the year
And spring was dear,
But no maid went
On mead or bent,
For there grew on ground
New battle-round,
New war-wall ran
Round houses of man,
There tower to tower oft dark and dim grew
At noontide of summer with rain of the yew.

Neath point and edge
In the battle hedge
We dwelt till wore
Late summer o'er;
In the autumn night
We steered aright
The wisdom-bark
Through the steel-thronged dark,
The warrior we wafted from out of the fray,
And he woke midst the worthy and hearkened their say.

Now peace is won
And all strife done,
And in our hands
The fame of lands
Aback we bear

> To the dale the dear,
> And the Fathers lie
> Made glad thereby.
> Now blossometh bliss in the howes of the old
> At our tale growing green from their tale that is told.

Loud was the glee and the shouting at his song, and all men said that every whit thereof was sooth, and that this was the best day that had ever dawned on Wethermel; and great joy and bliss was on the hall till they must needs go to their rest. So changed was Wethermel, the niggard once, and that, it might be deemed, was but one youngling's doing.

XXX

Osberne Goes to the Trysting-Place

BUT on the morrow ere the day was old, the guests departed in all contentment each to his own folk, and Osberne and the Wethermel men led them out with blessings.

When they were all gone and the unwonted stir was over, it seemed to Osberne as if he were awaking from a dream, and his heart was in a turmoil of hope and fear, so that he knew not what to do till he was once more at the Bight of the Cloven Knoll. He tarried for nought save to take up the gifts of Eastcheaping, and he had no weapon with him save his bow and arrows wherewith to flit the said gifts across the water, but he was gaily clad in a coat of green, flowered with gold, which he had bought him at Eastcheaping; and a fair and lovely youth he looked, as he strode along at his swiftest toward the trysting-place, his face flushed, his brows a little knit with mingled trouble and joy, his lips parted with his eager breathing. Whiles as he went he said to himself, How many chances and changes there were, and how might he expect to find Elfhild there again? And next, when he had enough afflicted himself with thinking of her sick, or dead, or wedded, his strong heart of a youth threw it off again, and he thought, How could evil such as that befal him, the stalwarth and joyous?

So he fared till he came within sight of the ness, and saw no figure there on the top of it: yet he straightway fell to running, as though he knew she had been waiting for him a long while; but as he ran he kept his eyes down on the ground, so that he might not see her place empty of her. But when he came to his place he lifted up his eyes, and there to his great joy saw her coming up the slope of the ness; and when she saw him she uttered a great cry and spread out her arms and reached out to him. But as for him, he might make neither word nor sound a great while, but stood looking on her. Then he said: "Is it well with thee?"

"O yea, yea," she said, "and over-well as now."

"Art thou wedded?" said he.

"Yea," she said, "unto thee."

"O would that we were, would that we were!" said Osberne.

"O!" she said, "be not sad this morning, or wish for aught so that it grieve thee. Bethink thee how dear this moment is, now at last when our eyes behold each other."

"Hast thou come here often to look for me?" said he. She said: "It was the fourteenth of May was a year that we parted; now is this the eighth day of October. That makes five hundred and eleven days: not oftener than that have I come here to look for thee."

So piteous-kind she looked as she spake, that his bosom heaved and his face changed, and he wept. She said: "I wish I had not said that to make thee weep for me, my dear." He spake as his face cleared: "Nay, my dear, it was not all for thee, but for me also; and it was not all for grief, but for love." She said: "With this word thou givest me leave to weep;" and she wept in good sooth.

Then in a while she said: "And now thou wilt sit down, wilt thou not? And tell me all thy tale, and of thy great deeds, some wind whereof hath been blown to us across the Sundering Flood. And sweet it will be to hear thy voice going on and on, and telling me dear things of thyself."

"Even so will I do," said Osberne, "if thou wilt; yet I were fain to hear of thee and how thou hast fared this while; and thy words would I hear above all things." The voice of him quavered as he spake, and he seemed to find it hard to bring any words out: but his eyes were devouring her as if he could never have enough of looking on her. Forsooth there was cause, so fair she was, and he now come far into his eighteenth year. She was that day clad all in black, without any adornment, and her hair was knit up as a crown about her beauteous head, which sat upon her shoulders as the swan upon the billow: her hair had darkened since the days of her childhood, and was now brown mingled with gold, as though the sun were within it; somewhat low it came down upon her forehead, which was broad and white; her eyes were blue-grey and lustrous, her cheeks a little hollow, but the jaw was truly wrought, and fine and clear, and her chin firm and lovely carven; her lips not very full, but red and lovely, her nose straight and fine. The colour of her clear and sweet, but not blent with much red: rather it was as if the gold of her hair had passed over her face and left some little deal behind there. In all her face was a look half piteous, as though she craved the love of folk; but yet both mirth and swift thought brake through it at whiles, and sober wisdom shaded it into something like sternness. Low-bosomed she was yet, and thin-flanked, and had learned no tricks and graces of movement such as women of towns and great houses use for the beguiling of men. But the dear simpleness of her body in these days when the joy of childhood had left her, and a high heart of good longing was ever before her, was an allurement of love and far beyond any fooling such as that.

Now she said: "How thou lookest on me, dear Osberne, and thy face is somewhat sober; is there aught that thou likest not in me? I will do as thou biddest, and tell all the little there is to tell about me, ere thou tellest me all the mickle thou hast to tell about thee."

He said, and still spake as if the words were somewhat hard to find: "I look upon thee, Elfhild, because I love thee, lovely, that I fear for thee and me, that I desire more than is half agone and become a woman, and I see thee so fair and lovely, that I fear for thee and me, that I desire more than is my due, and that never shall we mend our sundering; and that even what I have may be taken from me." She smiled, yet somewhat faintly, and spake: "I call that ill said; yet shalt thou not make me weep thereby, such joy as I have of the love in thy words. But come, sit thou down, and I shall tell thee my tidings."

So they sat down each as nigh unto the edge as they might; and Osberne spake no more for that while, but looked and listened, and Elfhild said: "Day by day I have come hither, sometimes sadder and sorrier than at others, whiles with more hope, and whiles with less, whiles also with none at all. Of that thou wottest already or mayst bethink thee. Of tidings to call tidings the first is that my kinswoman, my mother's sister, has changed her life: she died six months ago, and we brought her to earth by the church of Allhallows the West, hard by the place of the Cloven Mote. Needs must I say that, though she was the last one of my kindred, the loss of her was no very grievous sorrow to me, for ever she had heeded me little and loved me less, though she used me not cruelly when I was little; and her burial was a stately one as for a poor house in the West Dale. Now furthermore, as for the carline who is the only one left to look after me, by my deeming she doth love me, and moreover she hath belike more of might than were to be looked for of so old and frail-seeming a woman, and that besides her mickle wisdom. Whereof hearken this, which is the second tidings of note I have to tell thee. It is now some two months ago, when summer was waning into autumn, that on an evening just after sunset we were sitting after our wont in our house, which, though it be neither grand nor great, is bigger than we need for us twain. Comes a knock on the door, and the carline goes thereto, and is followed back into the chamber by a tall man, clad neither as one of our country-side nor as a warrior, but in a long black gown with furred edges. He had no weapons save a short sword and a whittle in his girdle; he was not ill-looked, black-bearded and ruddy-faced, and seemed strong-built, a man of about five and forty winters. He hailed us courteously, and asked if he might abide with us till morning, and we naysaid him not, if he might do with such cheer as we might make him. He smiled, and said any cheer was better worth to him than the desert as at that time:

and he said withal that he had a way-beast without who was
as weary as was he; and says he, there is a pair of saddle-
bags on him, which many would not deem overmuch of a
burden, if they had not very far to carry it.

"So I went out a-doors with him to see after his nag and
saddle-bags; and I led the horse into the same stall where
was winter quarters for our two horses; but this was a very
big stark beast, grey of colour, such as we have not in this
land; and I gave him hay and barley, but the saddle-bags he
brought back with him into the chamber. And he kept ever
by my side on the way there and back, and looked at me oft
in the failing light, though I was but in my sorry old raiment with bare feet, in such guise as thou hast not seen me
for years, my dear. Howsoever, I heeded it not at the time,
and we both came back into the chamber, where Dame Anna
had now lighted the candles. Shortly to say, we put what
meat and drink we might before our guest, and he seemed
well content therewith; and he was merry with us, and
showed himself a man of many words deftly strung together,
and spared not to tell us many things about tidings of far and
noble countries, and the ways of men both great and small
therein. And he said that he was a chapman journeying after
gain, and looked to buy wares in the Dale, and therewith he
asked us if we had aught to sell him, but Anna laughed and
said: 'Fair sir, were ye to buy all this and all that is in it,
from groundsell to roofridge, and all our kine and sheep and
horses to boot, little would the tide of gold ebb in thy bags
yonder.' 'I wot not,' he said; 'who may say what treasure ye
have been hoarding here this long while?' He looked on me
as he spake, and I reddened and looked down, for in my
heart I was thinking of the pipe and the gemmed necklace
which the Dwarfs had given me. And yet more than all, of
thy gifts, Osberne, which have been so dear to me: for
soothly to say, of these matters I had never told Dame Anna,
though she knoweth that I go oft to look upon thee here
and that I love thee. However, that talk ran off, and presently the chapman got to asking Anna about the matters of
the Dale, and the ways of its folk, and amongst other things
as to how wealthy they were, and she answered him simply
as she could. He asked her also if they loved their bairns

and children well, and also if they had any custom there-about of casting any of their women-children forth, if it happened to be their fortune to have many daughters and little meat, and that especially when the years were bad. But thereat she cried out Haro! and said that such a deed was unheard of, and that when times were bad and there was lack, then hand helped foot and foot hand.

" 'Well,' says he, smiling, 'that failed Hamdir's Sons once, and may do others again.' Then he asked withal if it were not true that things had run short in the Dale this last season; and she answered, as was true of this west side of the Dale, where was no man called to war, that so it was. And again that talk dropped. But the carline, methought, looked keenly at him. After a while Anna asked the guest if he had will to go to bed, and he answered, No, he would wake the meat well into his belly. Then she bade me fare to bed, which I did, nought loth, for when all was said I scarce liked the looks of the man. As for my bed, it was a shut-bed, and opened not out of the chamber wherein we were, but out of an inner one, rather long than wide. There I lay down and went to sleep before long, but deemed I heard no little talk going on betwixt Anna and the guest ere I forgat all. And moreover Anna came to me and waved her hands over me before I went off sound.

"But when I woke again it seemed to me that I had slept long, but I slipped out of bed and laid hold of my smock to do it on, and even therewith I shrank aback, for there before me, naked in his shirt and holding the door of my shut-bed with one hand and his whittle in the other, was the stranger. But therewithal came Dame Anna and said: 'Heed him not, for as yet he is asleep though his eyes be open. Do on thy raiment speedily, my Elfhild, and come forth with me, and let him wake up by himself.' Even so I did, not rightly understanding her words. But when we were gotten into the garth and the mead Anna told me all, to wit, how that this wretch, after I had gone to sleep, had bidden her a price for me to bear me off safely and wholly with him. And that may easily be done, says he, as I see of thee that thou art wise in wizardry and canst throw the maiden into a sleep which she will not awake from till due time is; for, says he, I want two things, to have her in mine arms to do as I will with, and thereafter to bear her home with me, will she nill she. 'Now,' said Anna, 'I would not wholly gainsay him at once, for I would have my fox safe in the trap; so I hemmed and hawed, and said that he might belike rue his bargain unless he were full sure what it were worth; and to be short, I so egged him on and drew him back, and drew him back and egged him on, that at last he took off his outer raiment, gat his bare whittle in one hand and laid the other on the door. Now, my dear, I have long known thy door that I may so do that it will do my will in many matters; so when I saw the chapman's hand on the edge thereof, I spake a few words to it and went to bed myself, whereas I wotted that runagate could not move hand from door-board, or foot from floor-board, till the time which I had appointed to him; and thee also I had sent to sleep till the very time when thou didst awaken e'en now.' 'But what shall we do now?' said I. Said Anna: 'We will abide here in the shaw: there is meat on the board for the guest, and his raiment will not be hard to find, and he knows where are his horse and his gear and his saddle-bags. I doubt me he will not be eager to say farewell either to thee or to me; for he is not man enough to take his sword in his fist against even an old carline and a young maiden.' So into the shaw we gat us; as I have told thee, it is at the back of our houses but a furlong off. And there we lay till a little past noon, when we heard a horse going not far off. So we crept to the very edge of the wood and looked forth privily, and presently we saw our chapman riding off west with his saddle-bags and all, and his face was worn and doleful; at that Anna grinned spitefully, nor for my part might I altogether refrain my laughter. But thou dost not laugh, Osberne?" He sprang up and cried out fiercely: "I would I had been there to cleave his skull! Many a better man have I slain for less cause."

Then they were silent a while, and she sat looking on him fondly, till she spake at last: "Sweetheart, art thou angry with me for telling thee this tale?"

"Nay, nay," he said; "how might I live save thou told me everything that befel thee? Yet I must tell thee that I well-nigh wish I had not heard this one; for there thou dwellest, with none other to ward thee than a carline stricken in years; and though I wot well from all thou hast said of her, and this last tale in special, that she has mickle might in her, yet she cannot be always with thee, nor belike ever thinking of thee. God forbid, sweetheart, that I should speak to thee in the tongue of the courts and the great houses and lords' palaces, whenas for a fashion of talking they say of their lemans, and they not always nor often exceeding fair, that they be jewels beyond all price, whom an host of men were not enough to ward. But this I will say," and he blushed very red at the word, "that thou art so lovely and so dear that thy man, thy love, and the stout and good friends who love him, were not over many for thy guarding even in this lonely place. And with all that I can be of no more use thereto than if I were a wooden man."

She stood up also, and he saw that the tears ran over her cheeks, and he stretched out his arms to her; but she said: "Grieve not too much, my friend; and know, as thou saidst e'en now of thyself, that these tears are not wholly for sorrow of thy grief, but O! so much and so much for joy of thy kindness. And one thing I must tell thee, that if I am alone in my house I am at least alone with a friend, and one who loves me. And this shall come of it, that now every day I shall come down to the tryst, for the carline will hinder me in no way. But I know that oft thou wilt come to meet me: yet belike often thou wilt not, because I wot how thou hast work to do and things wherein folk call for thee to serve them. So any day if thou come not it shall be well, and if thou come it shall be better."

Now at last he seemed to be learning the full sweetness of her. But she held up her hand and said: "Now I bid thee tarry no longer, but fall to and tell me the tale of thy deeds; for soon shall the short autumn day be waning, and the moment of parting shall steal upon us ere we be ware." Even so he did now; but at first, to say sooth, he made but a poor minstrel, so much his mind was turned unto what she had been telling him; but after a while his scaldship quickened him, and he told her much in manner like life, so that she might as it were see the tidings going on before her. And he held her enwrapped in his tale till the dark and the dusk began to rise up over the earth, and then for that time they parted, and there was to be more of the war of Eastcheaping on the day after tomorrow.

So went Osberne home to Wethermel, and at first it seemed to him as if this first meeting after so long a while had scarce been so good as he had looked for; for both his longing to be close to his love, and the fear which had arisen in him as to the stealing of her, were somewhat of a weight on his heart. But after a little, when he had first been amongst folk and then alone, all that doubt and trouble melted away in the remembrance of her, as she had been really standing before his eyes, and there was now little pain and much sweetness in the longing wherewith he longed for her.

So on the said day appointed he went to meet her, smiling and happy and fresh as a rose; and she was of like mien, and when they faced each other she smote her palms together as in the old childish time, and cried out: "Ah! now the warrior is all ready and the minstrel is stuffed full of his tale, and happy shall be the hour." And even so it was.

XXXI

They Meet Through Autumn and Winter

So many a time they met that autumn, and Elfhild would ever be asking him some boon; as the next time after this, it was the gifts which he had brought for her from the Cheaping; for in thinking of her he had clean forgotten them. So then was the merry time in talking of them, and shooting and hurling of them over, and the donning of them, and the talking of them again. Another time she prayed him to come clad in that goodly armour of the spoils of Deepdale, and he could no less than yeasay her, and there he was on the trysting-day, striding by the river-bank in the sun, like an heap of glittering ice hurrying before the river when the thaw is warm and the sun shining bright at Candlemas. And over that also went many pretty plays, as taking the pieces off, and naming them, and doing them on again and the like.

So wore the days into winter, and yet the two saw each other full often even through the frost and snow and ill weather. And when the spring came, then it was dear to them indeed. And by that time had Osberne's fears about the stealing of Elfhild much worn off; though it is to be said that exceeding oft his heart was weary and sore with the longing to hold her in his arms. Yet the most of these times he kept his grief in his own heart; so much as Elfhild was moved when it brake forth from him, and she might, so to say, see the torments of him before her very eyes. Indeed on one time, when for a long while she might not comfort him, she told him that this was almost as bad as seeing him laid a-dying before her.

But kind and dear they were to each other, and there was nought in them that was not lovely in those first days of their manhood.

XXXII

Foemen Among the Westdalers

BUT when the spring was worn into April there fell new tidings: for on a morning early came Stephen the Eater hurrying into the hall at Wethermel and cried aloud: "Bows, bows! Come afield all ye of this hall, and thou chiefly, Osberne the Captain!"

Out then tumbled the stout men of Wethermel from shut-bed and hutch, and were presently armed, and Osberne was in his byrny and steel hood straightway, his bow in his hand and his quiver at his back.

They gathered about him and Stephen amidst of the hall, and then Osberne asks what is toward. "Great matter enough," says Stephen. "Yet how to help therein? There is unpeace in the Dale, but it has fallen on the Westerlings."

Quoth Osberne, short and sharp: "Ye, Otter, Simon, Long-

deer, Alison, take horse and ride straightway down the Dale
and round to every stead, and bid men gather to the side of
the Flood with bows and sling-spears and shot-weapons of all
kinds, and that they stand not in knots and clumps, but
drawn out in line, and space enough betwixt each shooter.
Bid them to leave not a shaft at home—we may speedily
make more—but not to loose once till they have marked their
man. Now hasten ye four! But ye others come after me at
once, for we will go afoot for the saving of time and the
steadying of the shooting."

So they went toward the water, a dozen men all told, and
all had bows and good store of shafts. And as they went,
Osberne spake to those about him and said: "Spread out, and
make little show of force, and show not your bows to the
foemen, so that they may contemn us and venture the nearer
to the bank. But shoot not till they defy us, lest we smite a
peaceful man." Now they were presently nigh enough to see
the going of men on the further shore, and they were all
riders. It was clear to see that they were aliens, men upon
big horses clad in outlandish armour with bright steel head-
pieces; they bore long spears with light shafts, and a many
of them had short horseman's bows and quivers at their backs
along with their targes.

Now as the men of Wethermel drew up to the water's edge,
a knot of the said aliens, about a score, came to them shouting and yelling, and there were within sight scattered about
the fields some two hundreds in all. When they reined up by
the Flood-side one of them, who seemed by the gold on his
armour and weapons to be a chief, hove his spear aloft and
brandished it, and fell to crying out in what seemed to be
words; but since they knew not his Latin they gat no mean-
ing from them, but he spake in a masterful and threatening
voice. Then by Osberne's bidding, Stephen, who stood anigh
him, drew a white clout from his scrip, made it fast to his
spear and held it aloft, to show that they would have parley.
But for all answer the chieftain and his brake out a-laughing;
and then the chieftain gat his spear by the midmost, and made
as if he would cast at them; but the Flood there was over-
wide for spear-shot. Then one of his folk unslung his short-
bow and nocked a shaft, and turned to the chief as if asking

leave, and the chief nodded him yeasay. Quoth Osberne hastily: "Stephen, cover thee! It will be thou. Then if he looses, we loose, for this is a foeman."

Even therewith the shaft flew, and Stephen turned it with his shield. Then the Wethermelers set up a shout and bent their bows, and Osberne loosed first, and the shaft smote the chieftain in the eye, and he fell dead off his horse: Stephen also put a shaft into the man who had shot at him, and three others of them fell withal at the first loose, besides three that were hurt. And the aliens liked the Wethermel breakfast so ill, that they turned their backs to the river at once and scuttled away into the field out of shot, yet not before they had lost two more men and three horses.

Osberne stayed his men there a little while to see if the foe would bring up others to go on with the game; but the aliens were over-wily for that, as it seemed; for they but gathered together, and turning all their heads down-dale fared on in one body.

As yet the Dalesmen had seen nought of any onset of their neighbours of the West, and sore troubled was Osberne when he fell to thinking that, as the robbers were wending, they must needs chop upon Hartshaw Knolls; so the best he could hope was that Elfhild might flee from her house to some other, or even, it might be, hide her in the wood, which she knew so inwardly.

Meanwhile he bade his men go quietly down-stream on the river's edge. Saith he: "If aught is to be done from this side, we shall presently have the folk from the lower steads drifting in to us, and we should make a good band were it not for yonder wet dyke which the thieves have gotten them for a defence."

So they fared on, and now and again some man of the lifters turned somewhat toward them to look on their demeanour, and whiles one would speed an arrow to them, but did no harm; at last, as they began to draw nigh the narrows above the Bight of the Cloven Knoll, a whole sort of the foemen came riverwards, but somewhat more than half held on the straight way down the Dale. Even therewith came to join the Wethermelers a many of the folk from the downward steads, stout fellows all, and well armed with shot-weapons.

And now there was nought for it but on both sides men were drifting toward the Bight of the Cloven Knoll, nor needeth words to tell of the anguish of Osberne's heart and the fierce wrath of his spirit. When the aliens, who were thronging to the river-bank, saw how narrow the stream was growing, they set up a whoop and drew closer to the Eastdalers, and the more part of them got off their horses and marched along foot by foot with them, and they were now within shot of each other, so that the foemen stayed at whiles and shot them a shaft; and now they hurt divers of the Dalesmen, but Osberne would not suffer them to shoot back as yet.

So came they within sight of the Dwarfs' cave, and there were not a few of the Dalesmen who feared the place even in the turmoil of battle; and some deemed it might be unlucky to them; but others said that most like Osberne's good luck would prevail over the evil will of the Dwarf-kind.

So when Osberne came to the trysting-place, he and his were fully two score men, and they of the stoutest; and he stood before them all on the very place where his feet had so often stayed for the comforting of his heart and the caressing of his love: there he stood, handling a heavy cast-spear.

Even therewith the aliens poured on to the ness, howling like dogs, and on to Elfhild's very standing-place. Before all his men came a chieftain of them, clad in armour wrought gaudily and decked all with gold and silver, and with a great red horse-tail streaming from his helm. He hove up his hand and poised a great spear, but in that nick of time Osberne cast his weapon suddenly, with a fierce shout, and all about him and behind him he heard the loose of the Dalesmen's bows. Sooth to say, as he cast, he almost looked to see all that turmoil clear away as a dream, and that he should see Elfhild falling with the spear in her breast. But nought it befel: the gold-decked chieftain took the spear under his arm, and he and his spear fell over clashing and clattering down into the gulfs of the green water, and many of the strong-thieves fell before the shaft-storm of the Dalesmen;

but therewith the foemen shot also, and some of the Dalesmen were slain and divers hurt, but that abated their hearts
no jot. But Osberne took twelve shafts from out his quiver
and nocked them one after the other, and every time he
loosed a man's life went away on the arrow-point; but bitter
was his wrath and his grief that he might not slay them all
and deliver his love. Many a shaft smote him, but the more
part of them fell off scatheless from the rings of Hardcastle's
loom. Now were many of the thieves slain; yet so fierce and
eager were they, that the more part would not draw aback,
nay, some were so hungry for that cruel slaughter of them
that they heeded not the sundering of the Flood, but rushed
on as if there were nought between them, and fell over into
the boil of waters and were lost in the bottomless depths.

So fared the battle, and the ranks of the Dalesmen began
to thin; but Osberne had no thought of going back a foot's
length, and his men were so valiant that they deemed
nought evil save the sundering of the Flood. Osberne was
hurt in three places, but not sorely; but Stephen bore a shaft
in his side, yet he stood upon his feet and shot no less valiantly than erst.

But now all of a sudden the raging throng before them
had some new goings-on in it and began to sidle landward,
and therewithal beyond them rose a great shout, and therein
the Eastdalers knew the voice of their kinsmen, and they
shouted all together in answer as they plied the bow, and
the strong-thieves turned about and ran yelling and cursing
toward the landward and the south-west, for the Westdalers
were upon them with spear and axe and sword.

That was the end of the shot-stour, and the aliens came
never again that tide under the shafts of the Eastdalers. But
betwixt the kenning of their dead and the tending of their
hurt folk, they stood gazing out anxiously over the field, if
they might but see how the battle of handy-strokes had gone,
and by seeming right hard had it been; but in a while they
saw the aliens thrust back and edging away towards their
horses, which they had left standing out of bow-shot not far
from the Bight of the Cloven Knoll. The Westdalers were
following on, smiting great strokes, but not so as to be
mingled up with them; nor did they seem as if they would

will to hinder them if they should get on their horses and ride away; and even so they did presently, and the Dalesmen saw them never again.

XXXIII

Osberne Seeks Tidings of Elfhild

Now when this stour was all over, and the men of the East Dale were still standing together (not very triumphantly, because of their slain) on the east side of the Cloven Knoll, the Westdalers came toward them treading the field of dead from which the Flood sundered them. As aforesaid, neither the East nor the West had heretofore been much wont to resort to that place because of their dread of the Dwarfs who dwelt in the cave above the whirlpool; but now the passion of battle, and the sorrow for the dead, and the perplexity of the harrying had swept all that out of their minds a while. So the chiefs of the Westdalers stood among the corpses of the aliens on the crown of the ness where Elfhild was wont to stand, and fell to talking with their brethren of the East; and the man who took up the word for them all was Wulfstan of Coldburne, a stead of the lower West Dale. And he fell to praising the good help which the Eastdalers had given them by cleaving so manfully to the shot-stour, which he said had been their deliverance; for delivered they looked to be. "Albeit," says he, "they whom ye dealt with so manfully, and whom ye have now put to the road, be not the whole host of them, whereas while one moiety turned aside to the shooting, the other went on down the Dale and somewhat away from the Flood; and we left our brethren marching against them, and must turn presently to their helping, lest they be outnumbered by the strong-thieves. Yea, and already we fear lest these devils have wasted certain of our steads which would lie on their road, before our folk might fall in with them. And now give us leave! But we pray that ye may live hale and happy for the help ye have given us; and thou in special, Osberne Wulfgrimsson, whom we know, and the tales of thee."

But as he was on the point of turning away, Osberne said in a loud shrill voice: "Abide, master, and tell me one thing, to wit, the names of the steads which the thieves have wasted." Said Wulfstan: "I may not, because I know not: hereabout it is thin of dwellings; 't is a five miles ere ye shall happen on a good homestead, Longryggs to wit: here is nought but a little stead, fallen to be a cot, wherein dwell none save two women, one old and one young. It is not like that the thieves would have stayed for so little a thing. Farewell; if the battle goes handily with us ye shall have tidings thereof tomorrow if ye will come down hither; or a little lower down maybe, lest the Dwarfs begrudge us."

And therewith he turned and went toward the place where they deemed they should find the battle. As for the Eastdalers, they might tarry no more in looking to their wounded folk; and a many were hurt so grievously, that they had to be borne home in the four corners; of whom was Stephen the Eater, and he lay long sick, but in the long last, and it was a two months, was healed as well as ever he was. A half score were sore hurt like to this; but of them who might carry their grief home on their own legs were at least a score and six; but thirteen were slain outright. And these it was deemed good, after due thought taken, to lay them in earth in the field but a little way from the Bight of the Cloven Knoll; and the place where they are laid, with plenteous earth heaped over them, has ever since been called Shooters' Knowe.

XXXIV

Osberne Sorrows for the Loss of Elfhild

Now some while before men were boun to depart to their own homes, the sound of fresh battle was borne to them on the south-west; so, saving those who must needs go tend the hurt on their way home, they might not tear themselves away from that field of deed; and in special Osberne, who had been busy enough in kenning the dead and wounded of his folk while need was, came back to the verge of the Flood, where so oft he had stood in love and joy, and stood there a long while, scarce moving, with a shaft in his fingers and his bended bow in his fist, his brows knit, his eyes staring out over the western field. It was two hours after noon when the Westdalers turned to stir up the battle again. And then was an hour ere the clamour of the fight came down thither, and two hours yet it endured and was in all men's ears; and then it died away, and the East men began to wander off from the watching-place, wending this way and that, and the autumn day fell to wane, and soon there were none left save Osberne and a half dozen of the men of Wethermel. And one or another of them plucked him by the sleeve and bade him come home with them, since the day was done, and the battle would not quicken again, and the Westdalers had overmuch on their hands to bear them any tidings till the morrow was a new day. At first he heeded them nought, but in the end he turned on them with an angry eye, yet spake mildly, and bade them get them home and eat and sleep. "But leave me here," quoth he, "that I may watch awhile lest aught of new befalleth; and I will come to Wethermel when my heart will suffer me." So they departed and left him; and there he stood, till himseemed he had been there a long, long time. Night grew black about him, and silence fell upon the cloven plain of the Dale, save that below him the speech of the eddies seemed to grow greater as other voices failed. Then arose the wind, and went through the long grass and talked in the crannies of the rock-wall of the Flood as the waters spake below; and none came anear, nor might he hearken any foot of man, only far-off voices from the steads of a barking dog or crowing cock or lowing cow.

At last, when the night was beginning to change amidst the depth of the darkness, himseemed he heard somewhat drawing anigh and coming up the bent on the western side, and he wotted not but it might be the unshod feet of men, and he lightly asked himself if the ghosts of the dead made any sound with their feet as they trod the puddled earth where a many had trodden before them: and so wild was his heart grown now, that he thought it no great marvel if those that they had laid to earth there should stand up and come before him in the night watches. Then he nocked an arrow on his bow-string and handled his weapon, but could not make up his mind to shoot lest the bow-draft should pierce the quiet and rouse up inextinguishable shrieks and moans; and even therewith, over those paddling feet, he seemed to hear a voice beginning to cry, and he thought within himself: Now, now it is on the way, and presently the air shall be full of it; and will it kindle fire in the air?

But at that point of time the voice sounded louder and was in two or three places, and even amidst its wildness the familiar sound smote to his heart, for it was but the bleating of sheep, and now all the bent over against him was alive with it. And of a sudden he was come to himself and wotted what it was, that it was Elfhild's sheep, and that they had been loosed or thrust out from their folds and had wandered up there in the dark where so oft she had led them before. And now the mere bitterness of grief took the place of his wildness, and he let his bow and arrow drop to earth, and cast himself down on to the trodden ground & buried his face in his hands and moaned, and speedily the images of his life to come and the sorrow he must face passed through his soul, for he knew that she was gone, and either slain or carried away to where he should never hear of her or see her again.

At last, that his grief and wanhope might not rend his heart and slay him then and there, and lest all the deeds whereto he was fated should be spoiled and undone, self-pity fell upon him with the sweet remembrance of his love, and loosed the well of his tears, and he wept and wept, and might not be satiated of his mourning a long while. But when the night was yet dark and no sign of dawn in the sky, and, might he have seen it, the south-west was driving the rack low adown along the earth, he rose up slowly and gat his bow and arrows into his hands, and weakly and stiffly, like a man who hath been long sick, he fell to going along the riverside toward Wethermel, and his feet knew the way though his eyes might see it not. And as he went, with the wind whistling about his ears and the picture of Wethermel before his eyes, he found that life was come again to him, and he was beginning to think about what he should be doing to win some way back to the love that had been rent from him. Ever and anon, forsooth, as he was amidst such thoughts, the tears brake out from his eyes again, but still now he could refrain them better and better after each outburst, and he had no more wildness as erst, as if he were out of the world and drifting he knew not whither or why; but now he knew which was himself, and which was grief and pain.

It was but just the grey of the morning when he crept into the hall at Wethermel, and found his bed and cast himself thereon, and, all undone by weariness, fell asleep at once.

He awoke with the house astir about him, and arose and sat down to eat with the others, and was no harsher of speech than his wont, albeit he looked stark and stern; and to some it seemed as if he had aged ten years since yestermorn, and they deemed that the death of the folk lay heavy on him, as was like to be, and they said as few words to him as might be, for his grief seemed aweful to them. But when they had eaten he bade three of his men come with him down the water to seek tidings of the Westdalers. So they went together, and a little below the Bight of the Cloven Knoll, out of earshot of the Dwarf-folk, they met with others from the lower steads come upon the same errand; and the Westdalers were just come to the water-side with Wulfstan for their spokesman, who forsooth had gotten some scratches from the war-beast, so that his head and his arm were bandaged. Now he spake: "Hail to you, stout-hearts of the East! Ye may deem that we prevailed in the second battle yesterday, or ye would scarce have seen us here this morn. Now the battle was foughten all about the garth and the houses of Longryggs, which the strong-thieves had fallen on to waste, but the women-folk of the stead had saved their lives by flight, and the carles thereof were in our company fighting valiantly. So whatever is lost was lost in open battle, wherein two score and six of our best men have changed their lives; but as for the strong-thieves, besides them who fell in your shot-stour, we have buried over seven score; and the rest are fled away, many of them grievously hurt. Wherefore, friends, we have won a great victory: God and his

hallows keep us from any more such!" And it seemed as if
the goodman were weeping-ripe, whereof none marvelled.
But Osberne spake, and the sound of his own voice seemed
strange unto him: "Tell me, goodman, have ye lost nought
by the murder of men whenas the strong-thieves fell on
some stead?"

"Nay," said Wulfstan, "the thieves have wasted no other
stead save Longryggs, whereas, as I said, the folks escaped the murder, and this little house which is hard hereby
of Hartshaw Knolls. There forsooth the two women be missing, but no slain body of carle or quean have we found,
nought of slaughter save the slaughter of kine and sheep.
And I must tell you that this morning our folk sought all
about heedfully, yea and looked into every thicket and nook
of the wood."

"Belike," quoth Osberne, "they will have carried off the
two women?" Said Wulfstan: "I fear me it may well be so."

Said Osberne: "Well, this loss of two women, whom maybe ye shall find again, is but little: but grievous is the man-
fall of the battles. Yet not soon meseem shall reivers fall
upon West Dale now they have learned the valour of the
folk thereof. Heried be the Lord God that the folk yet liveth
and shall live!"

He spake measuredly and in a loud voice, so that all
heard, and they cheered his speech with deep and strong
voice; but they who stood nighest unto Osberne say that his
face was stern and very pale as he spake; and it seemed to
them that had Boardcleaver been naked on the West side
in that stour yet more of the strong-thieves had fallen.

Now they parted, and Osberne and his Wethermelers went
home, and the other Eastdalers also, each to his place. But
as to the Westdalers, they fell to and drew away the slain
thieves from the field of deed, for that they feared the be-
grudging of the Dwarfs, and they laid them in earth hard by
where they had stood to have that converse with them of
the East; and they raised a great howe over them, and it is
called Thieves' Howe unto this day. And the tale of the said
thieves who were slain by the Eastdalers in the shot-stour is
three score and ten and seven.

XXXV

Osberne Seeks Counsel of Steelhead

WEAR the days hereafter into summer, and Osberne is at Wethermel, and doth what work cometh to hand no worser than heretofore; yet folk marvel that his sorrow over the man-fall of the Cloven battle seemeth to wear off him but little, though he is mild and kind in speech to all men. Much he sat talking with Stephen the Eater, who in these days was growing whole of his hurts, and it is thought he learned some hidden lore from him, for many deemed that Stephen was wise therein. Every third day he went all alone to the Bight of the Cloven Knoll, and sat there long through the day; but never had he any tidings of Elfhild, nor forsooth did he look for any such. He learned from over the water that there was no newcomer at Hartshaw Knolls, and that the house and garth lay waste, and so was like to abide.

Now when it lacked but three nights of Midsummer, Osberne, after he had spoken long with Stephen, set some victual in his scrip, and went afoot in the evening-tide up the bent and over it among the mountain-necks, and so into that same little dale where he had first met Steelhead. There he sat him down on the grass by the brook-side and ate his meat, and then, when it darkened so much as it would that June night, he laid him down and slept in all trust of safekeeping. He awoke at the end of dawn and washed him in the brook, and then clad him and sat down to abide sunrise. Then even as the sun arose it smote a beam of light from some bright thing overtopping the crown of the hillside before him, and Osberne knew that there was come his friend Steelhead, in such guise as he had first beheld him there: which was in sooth the very thing which he desired.

So Osberne stood up to greet him, and Steelhead came to him and put his arms about him and kissed and embraced him, and Osberne wept for pity and hope of his life. Then said Steelhead: "I know thee why thou art come to me; a while agone I laid my hands upon thee that I might make thy body stark for all adventure, and now thou wouldst have me do the like for the soul of thee. Herein will I do what I may, but first we will eat of the increase of Wethermel, that thou mayest see how much I love thee and the land that bred thee."

So Osberne bestirred him, and kindled the cooking-fire and made ready the meat, and they ate together in all content and friendliness. But when they were full Steelhead spake: "Now whether wouldst thou tell me all thy tale, or whether wouldst thou be silent thereof, knowing that I know it without words spoken?"

Quoth Osberne: "I would tell it."

"There is yet time," said Steelhead, smiling kindly on him, "so make no tarrying."

Then Osberne began straightway, and spared not words overmuch, but herein he used the most when he told of Elfhild, what she was like in those latter days, and how his heart enfolded her, and how sweet was her converse with him; and when he was done Steelhead said: "What is in thy mind concerning dwelling in the Dale amidst thine own folk?" Said Osberne: "My mind it is to live and die here, and do all that is due to the folk of my fathers." Said Steelhead: "Then must thou be healed of this trouble; that is, thou must forget thy love and thy longing, or at the least thou must think more of other matters than of this. For I will not have it that thou my fosterling shouldst be a kill-joy among men of the kindred; wherefore ill-luck will come of it."

Said Osberne, knitting his brows: "I will not be healed in this way. For do I not know that she also is wrapped in sorrow and tormented by longing. Shall I leave her, therefore, as the dastard leaves a wounded friend before the oncoming foeman?"

Steelhead smiled on him. Quoth he: "Thou wilt not be healed? So be it; then mayst thou not abide in the Dale amongst the kindred, but carry thy trouble to the lands of the aliens, where there is none to remember the joyous face of thee before the trouble was."

"This may I do," said Osberne, "and even so shall it be

since it is thy will. But hast thou nought else to say to en-hearten me in my travel?"

"This I have thereto," quoth Steelhead, "that though the world be wide there are many ways about it, and meseem-eth that there is somewhere a way whereon thy feet and Elfhild's may draw toward one another." Said Osberne: "May all good hap go with thee for thy word. Dost thou not see how my face is already gladdened thereby?"

Said Steelhead: "This is hope, my son, that flareth up swiftly and fadeth soon; but now this I shall give to thee, as I deem I may, that never shalt thou lack hope so long as thou hast deeds to do. Call to mind what thou thyself saidst unto Elfhild, that the only way to bridge the Sundering Flood is for one of you, or both, to wander wide in the world. But now tell me, what hast thou in thy mind to do in these days that pass?" Said Osberne: "I have been thinking of it, that when the Midsummer Feast is over I shall say farewell to my folk and ride to Eastcheaping to find Sir Medard; for meseems he is the man whom I know out in the world who will put me in the way of deeds." Said Steel-head: "And wilt thou go alone, or hast thou a mind to take any with thee? Suppose it were Stephen the Eater, who is a man of lore, and as I do thee to wit moreover, a friend of our own?" "Dost thou command me to have him with me, lord?" said Osberne. "Nay," said Steelhead, "I but ask thee of thy mind in the matter."

Said Osberne: "Then I shall tell thee that my mind is to go all birdalone. I would take no part of Wethermel with me, lest I soften towards the Dale, and turn back some fair day of summer and fall to nursing my sorrow therein. More-over I know of Stephen that he is both a wise man and a champion, and I deem it were well to leave such an one to uphold the good days of Wethermel; so that whether I do that which I would, and come back in joy and honour; or do it not, and die away from my place, not without honour it may be, I shall yet know of the thriving of my kindred and the pleasure of Wethermel, which shall yet be glorious on the earth, even as it were a very living creature and mine own true friend. Many a time shall I think of it, in good hap and in ill hap, in grief and in joy."

"Hail to thy word, son and stout-heart!" said Steelhead, "for herein thou thinkest of it as my very heart would that thou shouldst. Now I see that I have indeed sown the seed of hope in thee, and I call it the lack of fear."

And now he brought the talk on other matters, and was as kind and friendly as might be, and Osberne deemed it was a great thing for him that he had so won the love of this noble wight and great-heart. So in all pleasure the day sped, and when it was hard on sunset Steelhead spake: "Now must I get me back to my house and home of old time, and thou shalt go home to Wethermel the dear; and now I see of thee that thou shalt hold a cheerful countenance there, and depart when needs must in honour and well-liking of all men."

So they stood up, but ere Osberne turned his face to the west he said: "And when shall I see thee again, lord?"

"Who knows?" said Steelhead; "maybe when thou lookest least for me: on the lonely marsh maybe, or in the thick of the forest; or in the midst of the fierce battle, or on thy very death-bed; or it may be not at all in thine earthly life."

"And that house whereto thou art now going, shall I ever see thee there?" said Osberne.

"Surely I deem that thou shalt; and yet most surely not till thine earthly days are over. But now farewell, and my heart goes with thee." Therewith he turned and was gone, and Osberne went his ways to Wethermel without looking after him. And now it seemed to him as if he had been fain not to have gone back to that well-beloved stead, but to have gone on east at all adventure; and he looked toward the day when he must depart at last as a sad and sore time, when hope would be dimmed by mere sorrow and trouble.

XXXVI

The Staves which Osberne Taught to the Dalesmen

Now all folk at Wethermel when they looked upon Osberne's face deemed that he was bettering of the drearihood which had weighed on him ever since the battle with the strong-thieves, and of that bettering they were right glad, for they were wont to have much joy of his fellowship. Came on therewith the Midsummer Feast of the Cloven Mote, which, as aforesaid, was the greatest of all the feasts of the Dalesmen, and Osberne was there with a countenance of good cheer no worser than the best. Now at this feast not only did they do in the heedfullest and solemnest wise all that belonged to Midsummer, as the Trundling of the Fiery Wheel, and the Kindling of the Bale, and the Leaping through the Fire; but also before noon, and ere these plays were begun, was high mass sung in the goodliest fashion in each of the two churches of Allhallows for the good rest of them who had fallen manfully in battle with the thieves. And last of all, when the summer night was as dark as it would be before the dawn, and the folk of the two sides were all ranged each in a line on their own shore of the river, they sang these staves from side to side across the Sundering Flood, the Westdalers beginning and then the Eastdalers taking it up:

> Tis Summer and night,
> Little dusk and long light,
> Little loss and much gain
> When the day must needs wane,
> Little bitter, much sweet
> From the weed to the wheat;
> Little moan, mickle praise
> Of the Midsummer days,
> When the love of the sleeping sun lieth along
> And broodeth the acres abiding the song.

Were the spring to come o'er
And again as before,
What then would ye crave
From the summer to have?
Sweeter grass would ye pray,
And more lea-lading hay?
For more wheat would ye cry,
Thicker swathe of the rye?
Stouter sons would ye ask for, and daughters more dear?
Well-willers more trusty than them ye have here?

O the wheat is yet green
But full fair beseen,
And the rye groweth tall
By the turfen wall.
Thick and sweet was the hay
On the lealand that lay;
Dear daughters had we,
Sons goodly to see,
And of all the well-willers ere trusted for true
The least have ye failed us to deal and to do.

What then is this,
That the summer's bliss
Somewhat ye fail
In your treasure's tale?
What then have ye lost,
And what call ye the cost
Of the months of life
Since winter's strife?
For unseldom the summer sun curseth the Dale
With the tears thrust aback and the unuttered wail.

Forsooth o'er-well
The tale may we tell:
Tis the spear and the sword
And the House of the Sward.
The bright and the best
Have gone to their rest,
And our eyes are blind
Their eyes to find.
In mead and house wend we because they were stayed,
And we stand up because in the earth were they laid.

Would ye call them aback
Then, to look on your lack?

Nay, we would that their tale
From our hearts ne'er should fail.

This then maketh you sad,
That such dear death they had?

This night are we sad
For the joy that we had,
And their memory's beginning
Great grief must be winning.
But while weareth away,
And e'en woe waxeth gay.
In fair words is it told,
Weighed e'en as fine gold;
Sweet as wind of the south
Grows the speech in the mouth.
And from father to son speeds the tale of the true,
Of the brave that forbore that the brethren might do.

When this was sung then each man went home to his
house. But it is said that these staves were made by Osberne,
and that he taught them to the Western men as well as to
the Eastern.

XXXVII

Osberne Takes Leave of Wethermel

THE next day at even, when all the folk were gathered
before the porch of the hall at Wethermel, making the most
of that fair time, Osberne craved silence a while, and when
men were hushed he spake: "Kinsmen and friends, I make
it known to you that I must needs depart from you tomorrow
morning, though wheresoever I may be I shall ever hold in
my heart the hope of coming back to Wethermel; for it will

be well enough known to most of you that I love the Dale with great love, and this stead in especial. But now I may not abide here longer, to such a pass are things come with me.

"The story of the wherefore of this were long to tell if I had the heart to tell it, which I have not. But this much may I say, that I go to seek a life which will lead me back to Wethermel, it may be in joy, it may be in sorrow, but in either case with such a heart in me as I may live the rest of my days in the Dale, doing all that is due to the kindred and the folk. Now it will be of no avail for any to strive to put me from this mind, or to hinder me in my purpose, for go I must and will. But this even, as we sit amidst the summer, and our hearts are softened by beholding the peace and abundance of the Dale, and thinking of all days that have been, and our fathers that have lived and died here, I will ask you all and each one of you to say straightway if in any wise I have wronged or hurt you; and if I have, then will I make atonement to my power: so that since I may not bear away with me Wethermel and its folk, I may at least bear away the love of it."

When they heard these words of his they were mostly exceeding downcast, for in sooth to every one of them his fellowship seemed both a joy and a safeguard; and of the women, some were moved to tears, let alone his grandam and his foster-mother. Albeit he had told his mind beforehand to Stephen the Eater, who had dight him all things ready for departure.

Now there was neither carle nor quean amongst them all who had a word to say against him, or might call to mind aught but kindness at his hands; and one after another they all said so much. But when they were done, and there was silence again, Osberne spake: "Thou, grandsire, art the master of Wethermel, but of late years hast thou suffered me to share in thy mastership; nay, thou hast laid many charges on me which I have taken, and done with them according to my might. Now therefore meseemeth that thou wouldst scarce have it otherwise but that somewhat of my redes and my will and my might should be left after me when I am gone; but if I err in this my thought, I pray thee say as much, and I will leave the matter where it stands, and thou to be sole and only master of Wethermel whiles I am away."

Spake Nicholas thereat, and said that freely would he grant it that Osberne's redes and well-doing should still be felt at Wethermel, and that for his own part the governance of an house so great and lordly as Wethermel had now become was overmuch of a burden to him, and that gladly would he take to any man whom Osberne would put in his place; and in good sooth he deemed he wotted who it would be.

Then turned Osberne unto Stephen and said: "Thou, Stephen, art more in the heart of my redes than any man else, and thou art both a wise man as I deem, and a proven champion: so if I leave thee here in my skin, wilt thou do the best for me, and be debonnaire with Master Nicholas here and with my grandam, and kind to all the folk?" Said Stephen: "I will do my best thereto, and will pray this of the folk, that they will not hate me because I am not thou." At that word all they gave him a welcome cheer, whereas their hearts burned within them for love of Osberne and for praise of his words and for sorrow of losing him and hope of his return; so that at that point of time themseemed they might promise anything.

But Osberne said: "Stephen, my friend and fellow, reach out thine hand that I give thee hansel before all these of what mastership there is in me." Even so did Stephen, and they clasped hands thereon.

After this Osberne looked about him and said: "Lo friends, how the dusk has been creeping on us amidst all this talk. So now do ye women dight the board and light the candles within the hall, that we may eat and drink together this last time for a long while."

Even so it was done, and all folk sat to meat, and thereafter was the drink brought in, and they drank all a cup to Osberne, and he to them; and then was the cup filled for Wethermel, and then again for the Dale; and the last cup was for Osberne's luck.

Then came a word into his mouth, and he stood up and sang:

From the Wethermel reek
I set me to seek
The world-ways unkenned
And the first of the end.
For when out there I be
Each way unto me
Shall seem nought save it lead
Back to Wethermel's need,
And many a twilight twixt dawning and day
Shall the feet of the waker dream wending the way.

When the war-gale speeds
Point-bitter reeds,
And the edges flash
O'er the war-board's clash,
Through the battle's rent
Shall I see the bent,
And the gables' peace
Midst the Dale's increase,
And the victory-whooping shall seem to me oft
As the Dale shepherd's cry where the reek wends aloft.

When to right and left
The ranks are cleft,
And the edges wan
Mate master and man,
It shall be as the fall
Of a hindering wall
Twixt my blade and me
And the garth on the lea;
So shall day unto day tell the hope of the year,
And season on season shall draw the Dale near.

This they deemed kindly sung and well; and now so high
rose their hearts, that it was to them as if they saw the day
of his returning and the gladness of fellowship renewed.

XXXVIII

Osberne Parts from Stephen the Eater

THE next morning Osberne went his way riding on a good horse, and not without treasure in his scrip. He was girt to Boardcleaver and had the wonder-bow and shafts with him; but the byrny, Hardcastle's Loom, he left behind, and had but a white basnet on his head, for he deemed that his friend Sir Medard would purvey him of armour. All the household were without in the garth to see him off, but none went further with him save Stephen the Eater, who rode with him as far as the bent, and closely and lovingly they spake together on the way. But when they were come to the crown of the bent Osberne drew rein and said: "Now, my friend, shalt thou turn about and let me go my ways." And they turned about both and looked down on Wethermel, and Stephen cast his arm abroad and spake: "Best-beloved of all men, how long deemest thou it shall be ere thou seest this again?"

"I wot not," said Osberne; "I am in the hands of Weird, to wend as she will have me: but I will tell thee that I have hoped and prayed that it might be in no longer space than five years; then shall I be of twenty years and three, and she but a few weeks younger, and manhood and womanhood and due service of the kindred shall lie before us both if I find her alive; but if I find her dead, or have sure witness that so she is, that moment shall I turn my face and come back to you, to live and die with you as I may. There is the third thing left, to wit, that I may wander about the world and find her not till I am exceeding old; but even then shall I come back with her, or the memory of her. Now I will not say 'Remember me,' for therein I trust thee, but I will bid thee live hale and merry, that when I see thee again thy face may be as little changed as may be."

Therewith they parted, and Osberne looked not back again.

XXXIX

Osberne Gets Him a New Master

On the second day thereafter he rode through the gate of Eastcheaping, and so up the street to the Castle; and many of the townsmen knew him, and cried out good welcome unto him, but he stayed not for any, but came his ways to the Castle, and lighted down in the forecourt and asked for Sir Medard. Here also was he well known, and men were joyful of his coming, and asked him many things of his doings and his welfare; but he answered as shortly as he might and still asked for Sir Medard; and they said that he might see him straightway, for that he was sitting in the solar, and albeit he had a guest with him, they doubted not but that the good knight would be fain of seeing his fellow-in-arms.

So they led him in, and Sir Medard arose at once and greeted Osberne with great joy, and embraced and kissed him. Then he turned to the other man who was in the solar with him, and said: "Lo thou, Sir Godrick, here is a champion whom thou wilt be glad to talk to, meseemeth, when we have drunk a cup." Therewith he called for wine and spices, for it was the time of the morning bever. Sir Godrick hailed Osberne, who looked on him and saw that he was a tall man, long-armed and very strong-looking, a man swart of visage, long-nosed and long-chinned, with light grey eyes; he was somewhat sober of aspect, as if it would be hard to get a laugh or even a smile out of him; but though he was not goodly there was nought evil-looking in his face. He looked downright and hard at Osberne, and said: "If Sir Medard speaketh not by way of jest, thou hast begun early, young man, and I wish thee joy thereof." Osberne reddened and held his peace; but Medard said: "There be of our foemen no few, who if ever they jested at the lad have done with it now forever." Osberne reddened yet more if it might be, but the long man took him by the hand and spake kindly to him, and said: "Be not troubled at a light word of mine; at the first thou didst seem so young and fair that it was not easy to think of thee grim amongst the edges; but many a man lies hid within himself."

So now they were served of the wine, and Sir Medard spake to Osberne: "Well, Dalesman, thou art come amongst us again, grown in manliness, as was like to be. Now if thou be come but to see us and make us merry with thy fellowship, it is well; but if thou have an errand, and would ask something of us, it is better yet; since forsooth we deem that we owe thee somewhat." Said Osberne: "Well then, true it is that I have an errand and crave something, and that is soon told; for I would have thee put me in the way of deeds to do, since I have left the Dale and am seeking adventures."

"That will be the least of things to do for thee, my friend," said Medard; "and in good time comest thou hither; for though the good town is in all peace and lacks not men, yet here is Sir Godrick of Longshaw, who is here with me partly for the gathering of men. But good must they be who ride with him, and all without fear, whereas I shall tell thee that he is the hardiest knight and most fearless rider of these days. Now do ye two talk it over together."

Osberne looked Sir Godrick in the face, and ever the more he beheld him the better he liked the looks of his eyes and his visage. So now spake the Knight: "How sayest thou, young man? After all I have heard of thee I may well ask thee to be of mine. Only I must tell thee that the work may be both hard and rough; and though there may be somewhat to be won, yet on the other hand the pay may be little more than leave to do the work." Said Osberne: "So far as that goes, I am well willing to take my chance of it; but there is one thing which might stand in the way of service with thee." "What is that?" said Sir Godrick. Said Osberne: "It is in my mind that from henceforth for a while my days should pass in some land that is far hence, that is, from mine own place, and rather to the south than the north."

"Where dwelleth thy kindred then?" said Godrick. "In the Dale which is cleft by the Sundering Flood," said Osberne, "up under the great mountains; and I am of the East Dale, else scarce had I been here."

"Well," said the Knight, "my chiefest house, which hight Longshaw, lieth a long way south of this; but I shall tell thee that it is no great way from the Sundering Flood; but betwixt it and the Flood is a great waste and forest. As to the Flood, it is there, where it runs through this forest which is called the Masterless Wood, a mighty great river, whereon are barges and cutters and seagoing dromonds even, so that it sunders nought, but joins rather. Now besides my house of Longshaw, which is as it were the knop and ouch of my manors, I have other houses and strongholds, some of which be in the very forest itself, and none of them more than a little way thence. For, sooth to say, the said forest is a shield and a refuge to me, and I had been overcome long ago save for its warding. I must tell thee further, that the southernmost skirts of the said forest come down within a score of miles of the great city by the sea which men call the City of the Sundering Flood; and that the city-folk love the forest little, save they might master it and make it their own, wherein they have failed hitherto, praise be to Allhallows! For then were I their very outlaw; whereas now there be others of the knighthood who dwell anigh me who deem that I have the right of it in warding my lands and theirs from these king-ruled chapmen. More by token that the day may come when the folk of their own town, as the gilds of the Lesser Crafts and the husbandmen and simple mariners, may rise against them, deeming them, as the truth is, hard masters and tyrants; wherefore, despite all their mastership, when I will and have occasion thereto, I may ride their streets in safety, for they wot that if they laid a hand on me or mine, it would be 'Bills and bows! bills and bows!' up one street and down another. Wherefore they meddle not with me themselves, but set two or three of the barons who hold of them on the east side of the Wood Masterless to harry me from time to time. Lo thou, lad, now thou knowest not only whereabouts thou mayest go to serve me, but also some deal of the quarrel wherein thou shalt draw sword, if it come to that. How sayest thou?"

"Wait a while, Sir Knight," said Osberne, "and tell me first: if the King of the city overcome thee, will he take from thee that which is thine own of right, or that which thou hast taken from some other?"

"He will take nothing more than my life," said Sir Godrick; "but ye may add thereto some small matter of the remnants of houses and land which erst my fathers owned, well-beloved of all folk. Forsooth here and there I hold some tower or strength which I have taken from my foemen, who dared me thereto."

"Good is that," said Osberne; "now would I ask of another thing: when thou hast been so pushed to it that thou must needs burn men in their house, has it been the wont of thee and thine to let the old men and women and children come out safe, or to burn them in with the rest?"

The Knight looked grimly on him, and said: "Friend of the Dale, if thou comest to be my man, and thou dost such evil deeds as to burn in them that may make no defence, then if thou escapest hanging at my hands thou mayst call me thy dastard thenceforward."

Quoth Osberne: "One thing more I would ask yet: if those gilds of craft aforesaid should rise up against their King and the tyrants of the Porte, and they sent to thee for help, wouldst thou give them so much help as not to be against them, but let them fight it out and the mightiest to prevail? Or how much more wouldst thou give?"

Stood up Sir Godrick therewith and was very wroth. Said he: "If these good fellows of the Lesser Crafts rise against their lords and send to me, then if they have gotten to them so much as the littlest of the city gates, or if it be but a dromond on the river, then will I go to them with all mine and leave house and lands behind, that we may battle it out side by side to live or die together. Or if they may not do so much as that, yet if all or any of them may win out a-gates and turn their heads toward Longshaw, then will I ride to meet them with everything that may bear spear or axe, and I will have them home with me and arm them and clothe them and feed them and house them, and my lands shall be their lands, and bite and drop shall we share together, so long as it holds out: and a noble host shall we gather, and harry the King and his dastards till we prevail at last, and we will have a new rule of the City and a new Porte, and I will be the captain thereof if they will have it so: or else to die in the pain. Now I say this is the least that I shall do. And if any man be so bold as to tell me to my face that I will do less, I say that he lies in his throat; and that shall I prove on him, body to body."

Now Sir Medard fell a-laughing, and he said: "There, there! Here is no champion so hardy as to gainsay thee; for I know thee well, old friend, that thou art preux above all men. And as for the Dalesman, look on him and see how his eyes are glittering and his cheeks flushing. Trust me, thou shalt have a man after thine own heart, young though he be."

Sir Godrick sat down and passed his hand over his brow, and he smiled a little, and said: "Well, man of the East Dale, hast thou perchance yet another question to ask? for meseems for a man who would take wages of me thou hast already asked a few."

Quoth Osberne: "Lord, be not wroth, but one more question have I to ask. And as to my wages, let that be; for to ask these questions and to have them thus answered, is better than wages to me. But now this is verily my last question. That Masterless Wood which thou hast said is a shield and refuge to thee, is it not also a refuge for rufflers and runagates and strong-thieves? And what dost thou do in dealing with such ill-doers?"

Now Sir Godrick spake quietly and said: "My lad, true it is that there is a sort of folk who haunt the said wood, who live by taking from others. But thou shalt wot that they do but little harm to husbandmen and other poor folk, because such have little to be robbed of. And forsooth many of those from whom they rob are worthy to lose that which they have gotten from poor folk by fraud and covin, and may as duly be called thieves as those that waylay them. Nevertheless we suffer not the said runagates to live and rob wholly in peace; and if we take them, they have the choice of a high gallows or somewhat hard service under my captains. Nay, if it be proven of them that they have been murderous and cruel, they may not forego the dance in the air, even as I said afore. Now then, deemest thou me so evil a lord? Or dost thou deem thee meet for nought save the host of heaven and to be a sergeant of the blessed Michael himself? May he help and save us!"

Said Osberne: "That may come to pass, lord, one day, but meanwhile I pray thee receive me as thy man, and thou shalt find that I am not so ill at obeying a commandment as ye may deem."

And therewith he knelt before the Knight and put his hands between his hands, and swore by Allhallows to be true to him.

Sir Godrick was well pleased, and said to Sir Medard: "Hath he done aught hitherto for which I might dub him a knight?" "Many deeds," said Sir Medard, "hath he done whereby he might be made a knight; but he will not have it because his kindred are not and were not of the knighthood, albeit men of honour."

"Well," said Sir Godrick, "in these matters let each man go his own way, so let it be as it will; yet some name shall I give him that he may be known by it. And lo thou, he is clad all in red, and ruddy of countenance is he, and his sprouting beard shall be red when it hath grown greater, though his hair is yellow and shiny as glass. Wherefore now I shall call him the Red Lad; and by that name meseemeth he shall be known far and wide."

Then they laughed all three, and the two knights drank, both of them, to the Red Lad, and Osberne thanked them and pledged them in turn. And well content was he with the way that things had gone.

XL

Osberne Rides with Sir Godrick

OSBERNE tarried at Eastcheaping for half a month while Sir Godrick was doing his business, which was, in short, gathering good men for his fellowship; at the end of that time he had gotten him one score and five besides Osberne, of whom a half score were well known to Osberne from the war of Deepdale: and he was fain of them.

At last they departed, and Sir Medard took a kind leave of Osberne. And Sir Godrick rode oftenest beside the Red Lad and talked much with him. They had a let-pass through the lands of the Baron of Deepdale, but he would not suffer Sir Godrick to take any men from his country. So they came to Deepham, which was the Baron's chief town, in a very fair and fertile dale, well watered. And there was nought for it but the Baron would see the Red Lad, for Sir Godrick must needs speak of him to the lord; and it must be said that there was now no enmity between the Baron and Eastcheaping. So the Baron feasted them well amongst his folk in his great hall; and when he saw Osberne he knew him, and had been told as aforesaid that the Red Lad had been at the carrying him away from the midst of his warriors; but the Baron hailed him merrily, and cried out to Sir Godrick: "Sir Knight, if thou wouldst have any man-stealing done thou art in the luck of it, for this youngling is a past-master in the craft." And before the feast was over he sent for Osberne to talk to him, and asked many things concerning the war as Osberne saw it from his side; and he showed that he owed him no grudge for the stealing, for he gave Osberne gifts, a fair gown of crimson cloth of gold, and a ruby ring. So all went well: nevertheless Osberne was nought loth to leave Deepham, and thought it not ill that his life lay not over-nigh to the lord thereof.

Now when they had left the lands of Deepdale they turned away toward the south, and rode two days through a fair country and peaceful, of much tillage, besprinkled with goodly thorps, where they had entertainment for their money and none seemed to fear them; and there they saw no men-at-arms, and but few carles that bore any weapon save whittle or boar-spear. At the end of that land they came to a good town walled and warded; and there none hindered them, for the Knight had acquaintance with the captain of the Porte, who had gathered him a half dozen of stout carles, and there they rested three days. Thence they rode one day amidst the same fair country, and they entered a forest

through which was a way which led them a little west of
south. The said forest gave out in three days, and then they
came into a wide valley watered by a fair river running due
west. The said valley was more for pasture than tillage, so
that it was not thickly housed, albeit when they had crossed
the river they came on to a big stead of many houses (and it
was evening) much peopled, and the folk, who had seen
their riding, were standing with weapons outside the houses.

But when Sir Godrick had ridden forward alone and given
out his name and his errand, to wit, that he was riding to
Longshaw with some good fellows who were fain to be of
his folk, they all cried out a fair welcome to him and his;
for they knew of his deeds and his fame, and were well-willers to him, and were fain of seeing him this first time. Then
stood forth an old long-hoary man, but tall and stark, and
gave himself out for the master of the stead, which hight
Riverlease, and he named him David, and said: "Sir Knight, I
am father of ten of these men and the grandsire of one
score and five, and other good fellows I have with me to the
tale of ten score and ten, and all these thou wilt make merry
by thy presence here tonight."

So he brought the Knight and his into the hall, and fair
greeting he gave them; and to Osberne, though the land
were other and the houses far bigger, for this David was as
it were a king of the meadows, it was almost as if he were
back at Wethermel, so yeomanly and free seemed all about
him. And the folk were a fair folk, the women goodly and
the men free and bold. So all men were merry and thought
but little of the morrow. But ere the feast was over the old
David spake to the good Knight and said: "Sir Godrick,
meseems thou shalt have many a foeman on thy back these
coming seasons, wherefore if any of my grandsons or the
swains here have a longing to ride with thee and become thy
men, I will spare them to thee to the number of a half score.
How say ye, lads," cried he down the hall, "be there any
here who desire to see how the Lord of Longshaw arrayeth
his battles, and would bring back some fair stories to the
maidens' ears?"

Now it was soon seen that no few there were that would

be fain to ride with the Knight, who soon had his choice of ten tall men, stout, and deft in weapons, and the end of the feast was merrier than the beginning.

Next morning they were away early, and the old man led them out over his meadows, which were exceeding rich of neat and sheep; and at parting he said: "Fair Knight of Longshaw, I have gone as far as I may this day, and must turn again; but this I say to thee, If ever the world goes amiss with thee, as it yet may for all thy valiancy, or forsooth because of it, come hither to me, or if I be dead, to my sons and my grandsons, and abide here as merrily as thou mayst. And spare not to bring whomso of thine thou wilt, as maybe this goodly youngling here," laying his hand on Osberne's shoulder, "of whom some of thy men were telling tales to some of mine last night. And now I bid farewell to thee and thine."

So Sir Godrick and his went their ways, and the new fellows led them by the shortest road, when they knew whither Sir Godrick had will to wend. And when they were out of that valley they came up on to the down-country, which ran along the edge of the plain like a wall; and thereby they went due south for three days, seeing but few folk and no houses, save here and there the cot of a shepherd, and that often builded on a wain. The three days ended, they come on a dale in the downs where a little river cleft them, running about south-west, and by the rede of their shepherd-fellows they turned and followed it out of the down-country, and were presently in a land of mingled tillage and pasture, well builded, but more with single homesteads than thorps, though these were not lacking: albeit the folk of them were not very free with their guesting, but yet for money, and as if half compelled, they yielded up such good as the riders would have of them. The next day, riding the samelike country, they saw on a bent a fair town with white walls, and many goodly gables and slim spires rising above them. But when they drew nigh thereto, an hour before sunset, they found that the said walls were of other uses than to be looked at, to wit to keep them out of their night's lodging; for the gates were shut, and there were spears and basnets glittering over the battlements. So Sir Godrick rode forward toward the gate, taking Osberne and a trumpet with him, and there bade blow a point of peace and crave speech of the captain of the guard.

Then stood up a tall man on the gate, armed at all points in white armour, and by him were two or three men-at-arms and one with a cross-bow ready bent. Cried out the tall man: "Go ye, trumpet and all, and let us see the last of you! For we know you, outlaws of Longshaw. The better luck for you if we come not to your house speedily. Go ye, make ready for us!" Sir Godrick burst out a-laughing and turned his horse's head; but even therewith Osberne, who was exceeding keen-sighted, saw the cross-bowman raise his engine; but the Red Lad had his dwarf-wrought bow bended in his hand, so that ere the cross-bow stock came to the man's shoulder he fell clattering down with a shaft through his throat, and Osberne rode back speedily after his lord with a half dozen shafts and quarrels whistling about him, but none touched him, and great was the cry and the yell that came from the town gate.

Now when Osberne was with his captain again, that one spake to him and said: "Red Lad, Red Lad, a sharp shaft is somewhat of a fierce answer to a rough word. Next time let them shoot ere ye shoot."

"Nay, lord," said Osberne, "had I waited this time thou might'st have come by a knock from yonder carle's quarrel." And he told him what he had seen. Then said Sir Godrick: "Then am I wrong and thou right, and I thank thee for the shaft. I might have known that thou wouldst be wise."

So they fetched a compass about that surly town, and rode a two hours ere they took harbour in a little wood, and held good watch and ward all that night. But none meddled with them.

The day after, by the rede of the shepherd-folk, they turned up into the hills again, for they had no wish to raise the country against them; and to say sooth, Sir Godrick was somewhat pensive that he found enmity so far off his own land. So they rode the hills for five days, falling in with few folk, and going slowly because of the rough ways. Thereafter they needed victual, and had been fain of better lodging might they get it; and whereas they saw a fair plain well builded and tilled, with good roads through the same, and knew that this was the nighest way to the Wood Masterless, they turned down thither at all adventure, and found no evil haps there, but that the folk were well enough pleased to make their market of the riders, and had neither fear of them nor harboured enmity against them. Thus then they rode for two days, and at the end of the second day entered a good cheaping-town, unfenced save by timber pales. There they abode a whole day, yet warily, since, though there were no waged men-at-arms in the stead, there went about many stout carles, who all bore long whittles, and looked as if their bills and bows had not been far to seek. But no strife betid.

XLI

They Joust with the Knight of the Fish

THENCE they rode through the fields and the thorps two days, and on the third day in the morning they saw a fair white castle on a hill, and on the plain underneath a little plump of men-at-arms under a banner. So the Knight arrayed his folk and went forward warily, although that folk seemed to be not above a score; for he knew not what might be behind them; and they were hard on the baily of the said castle. But when they were come within half a bow-shot, and Osberne could see the banner that it bore two silver Fish addorsed on a blue ground, a herald pricked forth from the castle-folk, and when he drew nigh to Sir Godrick and his he said: "If I knew which were the captain of the riders I would give him the greeting of my lord, Sir Raynold Fisher of the Castle of the Fish." "Here then is the captain," said Sir Godrick; "what would Sir Raynold with him?"

"This," said the herald, "that whensoever my lord seeth the riding of any weaponed men over a half score by tale, they must tarry and joust with him, two of theirs against

two of his, and must run with sharp spears of war till one
side is overthrown or sorely hurt. This is the custom of the
Castle of the Fish, and hath been these hundred years.
Wherefore now declare thy name, Sir Knight."

"This is an evil custom," said Sir Godrick, "and sorts
but little with mine errand, for I have overmuch bitter
earnest on hand to play at battle. But since thy lord besetteth
the way I must needs defend myself against him, as I would
against any other ruffler or strong-thief. Go tell him that the
Knight of the Weary-Strife will come presently with a good
man of his and deliver him of his jousts." And Sir Godrick
was very wroth.

So when the herald was gone Sir Godrick turned to Osberne and said: "How sayest thou, Red Lad, is this any of
thy business?" "All of my business, lord," said Osberne,
"albeit I am none so wroth as thou art." Said the Knight,
looking on him kindly: "Thou art not bound to run, Red
Lad; the sharp spear is an unhappy beast, and these men are
doubtless of the deftest." Said Osberne: "It all comes in the
day's work, lord; I pray thee turn me not back."

"Well, do we on our basnets and make we speedy end of
it," quoth Sir Godrick; "a wise man must ever wait upon
a fool's pleasure."

So the two of them went forth, and found the others
ready over against them, the Knight of the Fish against Sir
Godrick, and a very tall, stark man-at-arms against Osberne.
Short is the story of this course; for Sir Godrick and the
Fish brake their spears, but in such wise that the Castle-
knight lost his stirrups, and it went but a little but that he fell
to field. As for Osberne, he played so warily that he set his
spear-point in the default of the long man's defence just
where arm joins shoulder, and the spear went through and
through him, and he fell to the earth most grievously hurt.
Therewith Osberne, who must needs let his spear fall, took a
short axe from his saddle-bow (for he would not draw
Boardcleaver) and abode what was to do. But the Knight of
the Fish cried out for fresh spears for him and Sir Godrick,
and must needs run again, and this time the knight's spear
brake on Sir Godrick, whose shaft held that he drave the

Knight of the Fish clean over the arson of his saddle, and but for the goodness of his shield and double jazerant the spear-head had been in his breast withal.

Then Sir Godrick cast up his spear-head, and lifted the visor of his basnet and looked around, and saw Osberne sitting still upon his horse and the long man in the arms of his fellows, and he cried out: "Now this comes of fools! Here is our journey tarried, and one man or two, who be not of our foes, slain or sore hurt, and all for naught. Ho ye! give my man his spear. And thou, Red Lad, come up before they make us do more hurt."

But therewith the Knight of the Fish sat up and had come to his wit, and laughed and said: "Here is a surly one! Why, thou might'st complain more if ye had come to the ways as we have. Come now, all the sort of you, into my house, and drink a cup with us for the washing away of all grudge against the honourable custom of the Fish." Sir Godrick shook his head, but the wrath ran off him and he said: "Sir Knight, thou art debonnaire in thy folly, and I thank thee; this thy bidding might we have taken with a good will hadst thou not compelled us to waste our time in knocking you off your horses. And I am sorry we have hurt thy champion, and well I hope that he will be clean healed."

"Dost thou?" said he of the Fish; "now I will tell thee that if he be healed, I will send him on to thee to be thy man, that is if he will go. For well I know thee that thou art the Lord of Longshaw: and as to my champion, he will suit thee to a turn, for he is well-nigh as surly as thou, and as stiff in stour as may be."

Hereat all laughed, and they bade each other farewell, and so departed with good will. So they rode on, and nought more befel that day, and they guested in a fair thorp in good enough welcome.

XLII

They Deliver the Thorp-Dwellers from the Black Skinners

Now they rode that fair well-peopled land, and nought befel them to tell of till the fourth day thence, and then, as they were riding a good highway with a somewhat steep bank or little hill on their left hands, as they turned about the said hill and had all the plain to their right hands before them, they saw new tidings, and it was just about high noon. For there lay in their road, a mile and a half a-head, a thorp so big that it was well-nigh a little town, but quite unfenced, though many of the houses were goodly and great as for such a place. But now all was going ill there, for they saw smoke and flames coming forth from the windows and roofs of many of the houses, and a confused crying and shrieking came down the wind to them, and Osberne the keen-eyed deemed he could see folk, some a-horseback, fleeing down the highway toward them. Then Sir Godrick cried out: "Prick on, good men of mine! This is no case for tarrying, these be the Black Skinners, and if we make not the more haste all will be under fire and steel."

And he spurred withal, and Osberne after him. But now as they drew nigher there was no naysaying but that folk were fleeing desperately along the highway, and some with their hands spread out to the newcomers as if praying for help, young men and old, women and children; and after them came howling and smiting men-at-arms in wild armour, and though they were not in all ways like to those with whom the Dalesmen had fought by the Sundering Flood, yet somehow they called those wretches to Osberne's remembrance, and he knew at once what had befallen, and wrath flamed up in his heart, for it well-nigh seemed to him as if Elfhild must have been borne off again. And he unknit the peace-strings from about Boardcleaver, and drew him forth so that a clear humming noise went forth into the sunlit air, and spurred on so hard that he outwent every man there.

But when the Skinners saw those riders coming on, they stayed the chase, and some few tarried while they shot from their short-bows, which did but little harm, and so they hustled back into the thorp; and some few, the first of them, gat through and off into the fields; but the fleers drew aside to the right hand and the left, calling blessings on the good Knight and his, and, when the torrent of them was past, followed after timidly towards their wasted dwelling. And as Sir Godrick and his were within the thorp they found a many of the Skinners there (two hundreds of their carcases were buried afterwards) and all about by the houses lay mangled bodies of the country-folk, some few with weapons in their hands, but more of women and children. But when Godrick and his had slain the first plump that they had driven in from the road, the Knight cried out: "Ye thorp-dwellers, look to quenching the fires, while we slay you these wolf-swine." Thereon the countrymen began to run together with buckets wherever the riders were before them. And there was a pretty stream running down the mid-most of the street, and though it were dyed with blood that day, it was no worse for the quenching of the flames. Meanwhile Sir Godrick and his set themselves to the work, and it was not right perilous, for the thieves were all about scattermeal in twos and threes, and most afoot robbing and murdering and fire-raising, so that they made but such defence, when they made any, as the rat makes to the terrier. Shortly to say it, in half an hour there was not one of them left alive, save some few who gat to their horses and fled, having cast away their weapons and armour. Then the riders turned to help the thorp-dwellers in quenching their fires, and in some two hours they had got all under wherein was any hope, and the rest they must let burn away.

Then would Sir Godrick have gone his ways, but the poor folk of the thorp prayed him so piteously to abide till the morrow that he had no heart to naysay them. So they brought him and his what things they might get together after the ravage, and begrudged them nought. Moreover in the morning five stout fellows of the younger sort prayed him to take them with him to serve him in war, since they knew not now how to live; so he yeasaid them, nothing loth, and horsed them on the Skinners' way-beasts, which were good, and armed them with such of their armour as was not too filthy for decent men to use. The rest of the horses and gear they left to the thorp-abiders, to better their hard case withal.

So they departed, and that same day they came on two other thorps, but not so big as this, which had been utterly ravaged, so that there was neither dog nor cat therein, save in one house two little men-children of two and three years old, whom they brought away with them for pity's sake.

The next day they came to a cheaping-town, walled and defensible, whose gates were shut for fear of the Skinners. But when Sir Godrick had spoken to the captain of the guard at the gate, and had told him how they had fared of late, and of the slaughter of the Skinners, they opened to them joyfully, and made them kindly welcome, and there they rested a three days, of which rest their way-beasts had great need.

XLIII

They Come to the Edge of the Wood Masterless

Now when they went on thence, they came within two days into a country all broken up into little hills and ridges, and beset with scraggy shaws, wherein were but few men and fewer dwellings, and the men either hunters or herders of neat, well-nigh wild, and this lasted them for three days more; but they knew hereof beforehand, and had made provision therefor at that last cheaping.

But at the end of the three days they came to a place where was a narrow stretch of green mead and a few acres in the wilderness, and a little river ran through all that, and above it on a height, steep and wellnigh sheer on all sides save one, was a castle high and strong, and as they drew nigh thereto Osberne saw a banner thrust out from the highest tower, and the Knight said to him: "Red Lad, whose banner is that?"

"I wot not," said Osberne.

"Canst thou see the blazon of it?" said Sir Godrick.

"Yea," said the other; "it hath a White Hart collared and chained with gold and emparked on a green ground."

"Sooth is that," said Sir Godrick. "Now look behind thee over thy shoulder." Even so did Osberne, and saw a banner borne by one of theirs, and the selfsame blazon on it; and now he called to mind that never erst had he seen Sir Godrick's banner displayed. And he laughed and wondered, and was some little deal abashed, and he said: "Lord, is this Longshaw?" Laughed the Knight in his turn, and said: "What, thou deemest this no very lordly castle for him who hath to withstand barons and portes and kings? Nay, lad, look again, and tell me if thou seest the Long Shaw; this is called Woodneb, and therein is a captain of mine who hight Edward the Brown, and therein shall we rest a while ere we enter the Wood Masterless. And hence onward to the Long Shaw is a twelve days' journey if all go well."

Now when Osberne heard that he was the better content, for in good sooth that desert-hold seemed all too strait to keep within its walls the valiancy of Sir Godrick and his host.

So presently the gates were thrown open, and folk gaily clad and armed came forth to meet their lord and his new men, and before them went Edward the Brown, a short thick man, but very sturdy-looking, his hair cut short to his head; small brown eyes [had he] and short nose, so that he looked somewhat like to a bear; but a valiant man he was, and a trusty.

There then they had good entertainment, as men who were at home again, and they abode there seven days or they departed, and had good disport of hunting and hawking; and there was much minstrelsy and tale-telling in the hall a-nights: and there must Osberne tell what stories he knew of the war of Eastcheaping and the matters of the Dale, both the tidings of his own day and of the days of his fathers; and therewith were men well content, for a good tale-teller he was.

No little also he talked with Sir Godrick, and especially on one matter: for his mind dwelt much on those same Skinners whom they had overthrown, and he kept weighing them against those evil aliens with whom he had fought across the Sundering Flood, and who, he deemed full surely, had borne away Elfhild. And on a day he asked Sir Godrick concerning it, and if these two sorts of wretches had aught to do with it; and he told him all the story of that battle, and what like his foemen were in body and array, and of their horses and armour and weapons, and of their shrieks and the gibbering of their Latin.

Then said Sir Godrick: "I will tell thee what meseemeth of thy foemen of that day, that they be of the kindred of these Black Skinners, though of another tribe, so that men call them the Red Skinners, though ye shall know that neither the Red nor the Black call themselves Skinners, which is but a name of terror which the country-folk have fixed on them for their evil deeds. Now further, although the Red Skinners be worse than any men else, they are not so bad as the Black. That is, they are more like men and less like wolves standing upright: to wit, they waste not and destroy not everything forthright, but keep it to make some gain thereof. As for example, they slay not and rip not up all their captives whatsoever they may be, but keep such as they may deem likely to sell to the thrall-cheapers. Now as to thy foes being of this ill folk, I deem it more like the more I think thereof, for not only hast thou given me a true picture of their aspect, but it is mostly the other side of the Sundering Flood which they haunt, though whiles we meet them about the borders of the Wood Masterless nigh unto the Flood. Withal I must tell thee, that though I speak of both the Black and the Red Skinners as of nations or tribes, I say not but they be mingled with runagates of divers folks; for whatever is worst or evillest or cruellest will drift toward them; and I wot not but that these men be worse than they of the blood, having in them more malice and grudging. But this I know for sure, that these are they who set them to work on such a business, and spy for them, and sell them their plunder, as they may well do since they are of aspect like other folk and know their tongues—But what aileth thee, Red Lad, to look so wan and so perturbed of countenance? Hast thou aught on thine heart which thou wouldst tell me?"

"That have I," said Osberne: and so as shortly as he might

he told his lord the whole tale of his dealings with Elfhild, and how she had vanished away before hand might [touch] hand, or face face; and how he deemed that she had been borne off by these same Red Skinners. And when he had done Sir Godrick said: "Poor lad, and this was the cause then that made thee so eager to take service along with me! Well, thou hast done wisely; for first, thou hast got thee a faithful friend; and next, if thou never amendest it nor settest eyes on the maiden again, yet surely the doing of deeds shall ease thy sorrow, till at last it shall be scarce a sorrow to thee, but a tale of the past. And moreover, in coming to my house thou shalt have come to the only place where thou mayst perchance happen on tidings of her; since with these men we have to do, and also at whiles with those who deal with them by way of chaffer. And if we fall in with any of the Red ones, thou shalt make what captives thou wilt, and for the saving of their lives they may tell thee somewhat to further thy search. Hold up thine head then! For surely even now thou art doing all that thou mayst in the matter."

Herewith must Osberne be content perforce, and in sooth his heart was the lighter that he had told his trouble to so good a friend as was Sir Godrick.

XLIV

They Reach Longshaw and Osberne Gets Him a New Name

BUT the seven days over, they departed on their ways to the house of Longshaw, which well they knew; and they rode first for two days through rough land pretty much as it had been before Woodneb, and they saw all that way but three little houses of hunters or fowlers; and this, they told Osberne, right on from Woodneb was the beginning of the Wood Masterless. Thereafter they came amongst great timber-trees with wood lawns betwixt, and but little underwood, and a goodly piece of the world that seemed unto Osberne. Three days it held so, and then came broken ground, whiles with much tangled thicket and whiles treeless, and this was a two days' ride; and many were the wild deer therein so that their cheer was greatly amended. Thereafter was the wood thinner and more plain, and there was a clear road through it; and on the first day of their riding this way they came upon a sort of folk who were sitting on the greensward eating their dinner. They were fifteen all told, all of them with weapons, but Sir Godrick and his came upon them so suddenly that they had no time to rise and flee, so sat still abiding haps. They had a good few of sumpter-horses with them, and it was soon clear to see that, though they were weaponed, they were not men-at-arms, but chapmen. Sir Godrick entreated them courteously, and asked them whence and whither, and prayed them of tidings. They said they were come from the City of the Sundering Flood, and had ridden the Wood instead of taking ship on the river, which was far safer, because they were bound for some of the cheaping-towns to which Sir Godrick and his had given the go-by. They said that all was at peace in the City and the Frank thereof, and there was little of strife anywhere anigh. In the end they bade the Knight and his men sit with them and share their feast under the green-wood tree. Sir Godrick yea-said that with a good will, and they were presently all very merry. Sooth to say, though they made as if they knew him not, and never named his name, they knew him well enough, and were a little afeard of him, and only too well content if he named himself not, for they were of the gilds who were scarce good friends with Longshaw: so that it had been little more than a fair deed of war if he had made them unbuckle and open.

When dinner was over and they were drinking a cup, he called three of the wisest of them apart along with Osberne, and asked them straightway if they knew of any fair maid who had been bought of late by any chapman from the Red Skinners, and he bade Osberne tell closely what like was Elfhild: even so he did, sore abashed the while. But when he was done, the chapmen laid their heads together, and asked one or two others of their company, but could give no tidings of any such.

So therewith they parted, and Sir Godrick and his rode

the wood, which was diverse of kind, for six days more; and at last, on a bright sunny afternoon, when after riding a plain not much be-timbered they had made their way through a thick and close wood for some five hours, they came out of the said wood on to a plain of greensward cleft by a fair river, which winded about the foot of a long low ridge where were orchards and gardens a many, and all above them so many buildings and towers and walls of stone, that to Osberne it seemed as if they had before them a very fair town. But even therewith all the company by Sir Godrick's bidding stayed, and drew up in a line, and the banner of the Hart impaled was displayed; and Sir Godrick spake to Osberne and said: "Lo, Red Lad, my House of Longshaw, and this is the Shaw which we have come through: now how likest thou the house?"

"Well, and exceeding well," said Osberne; "it is as a town."

"Yea," said Sir Godrick; "and therefore if I can but keep it well victualled, and have with me a host big enough of stout men, it shall never be taken."

Now Osberne looked again, and he saw that midmost of the towers and walls was a very great hall exceeding fair, with lovely pinnacles and spires and windows like to carven ivory, and beside it a church fairer yet; and then before it and lower down the hill and on either side were huge towers, stern and stout, all without fretwork or ornament; and there were many of these and one to help the other, all about the hill, and down by the river-side a baily such as never was a stronger or a wiser. And Sir Godrick said: "See thou, lad, those fair and beauteous buildings in the midst, they were the work of peace, when we sat well beloved on our own lands: it is an hundred of years ago since they were done. Then came the beginning of strife, and needs must we build yonder stark and grim towers and walls in little leisure by the labour of many hands. Now may peace come again, and give us time to cast wreaths and garlands of fretwork round the sternness of the war-walls, or let them abide and crumble in their due time. But little avails to talk of peace as now. Come thou, Red Lad, and join the host of war that dwelleth within those walls even as peaceful craftsmen and chapmen dwell in a good town. Lo thou, they fling abroad the White Hart from the topmost tower: Blow, music, and salute it."

Then all their horns blew up, and they set forward toward the baily of the castle. And it is said indeed that five thousand men-at-arms, besides the women and other folk that waited on them, dwelt for the most part in the House of Longshaw.

So that even was high feast holden in the great hall of Longshaw, where by Osberne's deeming all was fairer and daintier within even than without. There was the Red Lad shown to a good place and all honour done to him, and his lord looked to it that the tales of his valiancy should be known, so that all thought well of him.

There was but little doing in those months which followed the home-coming of Sir Godrick, as he was at peace with his neighbours so to say. But he made Osberne captain over a band of good men, and sent him on divers errands wherein was some little peril; and in all of these he did wisely and sped well. Amongst others he went with ten tens of men through the Wood and right down to a certain haven on the Sundering Flood, with the errand of warding chapmen and others who were bringing many loads of wares for the service of the house. There then he beheld the great water for the first time since he had left the Dale, and wondered at its hugeness and majesty; and the sorrow of his heart stirred within him when he thought how far they two had come from the Bight of the Cloven Knoll, he and the Sundering Flood. But he had no leisure to grieve overmuch, and his grief was but as the pain of a hurt which a man feels even amidst of his deep sleep. Of those chapmen and others he asked much concerning Elfhild; and they could tell him many tales of the Red Skinners and their misdeeds, but nought that seemed to have aught to do with his love. On the way back with the train of goods, which was great and long-spun-out, a band of the waylayers laid an ambushment against it, hearing that the leader of its guard was but a young man new to war. But they were best to have left it alone, for Osberne was well ware of them; and to be short, he so ambushed the ambushers that he had them in the trap, and slew them every one: small harm it was of the death of them. Now this was the first time in his warfare that his men fell on with the name of him in their mouths, and cried, The Red Lad! the Red Lad! Terrible indeed became that cry in no very long time.

XLV

The Red Lad Scatters the Host of the Barons

So wore the seasons into winter, and all was tidingless at Longshaw.

Long were it indeed to tell the whole tale of the warfare of the House of Longshaw, even for those years while Osberne abode with Sir Godrick. For the Knight was not only a fearless heart in the field and of all deftness in the handling of weapons, but he was also the wisest of host-leaders of his day and his land, so that with him to lead them an hundred was as good as five hundred, take one time with another. But of all this warfare must only so much be told as is needful to understand the story of Osberne and his friend of the west side of the Sundering Flood.

But first it must be said that Osberne throughout that autumn and winter spared not to question every wight whom he deemed anywise likely to have heard aught of Elfhild; and heavy and grievous became the words of his questioning, and ever his heart sickened before the answer came. But of one man he gat an answer that was not mere naysay, to wit, that months ago (and it must have been when Osberne first met Sir Godrick at Eastcheaping) he and two fellows were journeying on the other side of the Sundering Flood, but much higher up, and they came across a thrall-cheapener who said that he had a choice piece of goods if he could but get a price for it, and thereon showed them a damsel as fair as an image, and she was like to what Osberne had told of her. And the thrall-cheapener said that he had bought her of the Red Skinners, who had borne her off from a country-side far and far away, but somewhere anigh the Sundering Flood. That man said that they bought her not of the carle, whereas the price was high and it was not much in their way of business.

Now this story was told a little after Yule, and the chapman who told it was going back again presently through the Wood and across the Flood, since the season was mild; and Osberne asked would he take him with him, in case he might hit upon anything in those parts. The chapman was nought loth, as may be deemed, to have such a doughty champion to his fellow farer; so Osberne asked leave of his lord, who would not gainsay him since nought was stirring, but bade him take three good men of his friends with him. So they went, and crossed the Flood a few days before Candlemass; and when they were on the other side they fell to asking questions at the houses of religion and of the chapmen whom they met there. Also they gat them into castles and great houses where many servants are wont to be, and not a few bought at a price; and there they used both tongue and eyes. Thus fared they a twenty days' journey up the water, keeping ever somewhat nigh; but woe worth, if they gat them no great scathe (though they had some rough passages forsooth, which time suffereth us not to tell of), yet also they gat no good, and were no nearer to hearing a true word of Elfhild than ever.

So back comes Osberne, cast down and somewhat moody, but straightway finds tidings that drive all other things out of his head for a while. It was a little after Marymass that he comes home to Longshaw, and hears tell how war, and big war, has arisen. For the Barons who lay mostly to the east and north of Longshaw (though some help they had from the west and the south) both hated Sir Godrick sorely because he withheld them from the worst deeds of tyranny, and also, though they owed not service to the King of the Great City or the Porte thereof, yet were they somewhat under their power; at least each one of them was. These then had met together and made a great league, and had sworn the undoing of Sir Godrick and the House of Longshaw for ever. And all the world knew that they were but the catspaw of the King of the City and the tyrannous Porte, though neither of these would let themselves be seen therein.

Now Godrick sends for Osberne, and talks long with him,

and the end of that talk is that he sends him on the errand to
go seek the hosting of them of the Barons' League who dwelt
furthest north, and to fall on them as fast and as fierce as he
may, so as to break up the said hosting, so that he may not
have these men on his flank when he marches against the
main host, which he will do with all speed. All of which he
deems may be done, because he wotteth that the Barons
deem of him that he will abide their coming to Longshaw,
and that when they have shut him up there, they shall then
have the open help of all the strength of the King and the
Porte.

Now Osberne heard and understood all, and the men are
all ready for him, a thousand and three hundred by tale; so
he makes no delay and leads them by ways unkenned so
diligently that he breaks forth on them before they be duly
ordered, though they be all out in the fields drawing together. Shortly to say it, his thirteen hundred men are more
by a great deal than their six thousand, and they scatter
them to the winds so that they can never come together
again, and all their munitions of war and matters for feeding
and wending are destroyed. Then turns the Red Lad and
wendeth, not back again to Longshaw, but thither whereas
he wots the great battle shall be, and on the very eve thereof
he rideth into Sir Godrick's camp; and such an outcry of joy
there was when he bears in the taken banners and such spoil
as was not over-heavy to ride with, as that no man there was
of Sir Godrick's but he knew full surely that the victory
would be theirs on the morrow. As for Osberne, all men
praised him, and the good Knight embraced him before all
the host and the leaders thereof, and said, "Here is one shall
lead you when I am slain."

Even so it went. Of a sooth stiff was the stour, for the
Barons and theirs were hardy men and of great prowess,
and were three to Sir Godrick's one. But they knew that
they should not have the help they looked for, for they had
seen, ere the battle was joined, those taken banners, and
the others had mocked them and bade them come across to
serve under such and such a banner. So it was not long ere a
many of them fell a-thinking: What do we to perish here,
when at our backs are those so mighty castles and strengths

of ours? Let us draw away little by little and get behind our walls, and there gather force again little by little. But soon they found that they would have no such leave to depart but as broken men fleeing at all adventure, for their foemen had entered too far in to them, and had cleft their array in many places. And their banners were thrown down and their captains unheeded, and at last there was no face of them against the foe; nought but heaps of huddled men, who knew not where to turn or whom to smite at: and the overthrow might be no greater, for at noon-tide there was no host left that at matins had been as great and goodly an host as ever was seen in those parts.

And now was the purpose of the King and the Porte broken, and they must sit still and do nothing; nay, have got to be well content if the Small Crafts take not the occasion to rise against them. But to say sooth these knew their own opportunity and took it, as ye shall find hereafter.

That great battle was foughten on the first of May, and ere a half month was fully worn the Barons' League sent a herald to Longshaw praying for peace; but Sir Godrick straightway sent back answer that he would grant the Barons peace when they had delivered up all their strengths into his hands, then and not before. Such answer the herald bore back. But their proud stomachs had not yet come down so far, and they but sent back their defiance renewed: for they thought that, though they were not strong enough to meet Longshaw in the field, yet they might hold their strengths in despite of it, and so dally out the time until the King and the Porte were strong enough to come to their help. Now was this put to the test; for straightway, when Sir Godrick had their answer, he rose up and led a host against the castle of the greatest of those Barons, and took it in ten days, after much loss of his men. Then went he against the next greatest, and took that, with less pain. And meanwhile the Red Lad to the north, and another captain to the south, had the business of riding here and there and making nought of any gathering if they heard of the beginnings thereof. And this they did, with much labour and no little battle; but thoroughly they did it, so as Sir Godrick might carry on his sieges of the strongholds without let or hindrance, so that before the winter came he had all he wanted, and most of the Barons captive at Longshaw. As to the strongholds, into some he put his own men, and some he threw down.

So noble Yule they kept at Longshaw that year, with all those great men feasting at the table. But a day or two after Yule came a herald riding through the snow (for that season was hard), on behalf of the Barons' League, what was left of it, craving for peace, and Sir Godrick said that peace they might have if they would, or not as they would, but the terms were that he should keep what he had got, but ransom his captives duly; or else they might dwell at Longshaw all their lives long if they would. Now there was no help for it but such terms they must take, and be glad that it was no worse.

So peace was made, and all was quiet till after Marymass. Osberne had somewhat of a mind to get him into the Wood, and seek through the strengths and other houses that were scattered about in the Wood itself, and the edge thereof toward the Sundering Flood; but partly he was sick at heart of for ever asking questions to which came evermore but one answer, and partly there was very much work come to his hand that he might scarce turn over to another, of visiting the captured strongholds, and seeing to the men-at-arms therein and their captains, and suchlike matters; for now he was closer to the rede and mind of Sir Godrick than any other.

XLVI

Osberne Enters the City of the Sundering Flood

So, as aforesaid, the time wore till Marymass was over, and then came fresh tidings, to wit that the men of the Small Crafts and the lesser commons were risen against the Porte and the King, and had gotten to them the North Gate of the City, and were holding it against their foemen, together with that quarter of the city which lay round about it. The news hereof was sure, for it was brought to Longshaw one night by three of the weavers who had ridden on the spur to tell it to Sir Godrick, and these three men he knew well, and that they were trusty.

Now so it was both that it had been not easy at any time that war should find Longshaw not duly prepared, and also that at this time there was no tidings which Sir Godrick looked for more than this. Speedy therefore was his rede. For he gave into Osberne's hand fifteen hundreds of his best men, and bade him ride to the City and the North Gate and see what the fields without the City looked like; and the very next morning the Red Lad and his rode out of Longshaw, having with them two of the said weaver-carles, but the third abode with Sir Godrick.

Now so good were the Red Lad's wayleaders and knew all the passages and roads so inly, and so diligent was the Red Lad himself and his men so good and trusty, that by the second day about sunset he was but five miles from the North Gate, and he and his covered by some scattering woodland that lay thereabout.

Straightway Osberne sends a half score of spies to get them to the City and see what was toward, and come back, they that were not slain, and tell him thereof. Straightway they went, and had such hap that all they came back unscathed, and this was their story: That the men of the Small Crafts were not by seeming hard pressed, for still their banners hung out from the North Gate and the wall and towers thereabout; but that both within the City had been bitter battle against them all day long, and also an host of men of their foes had come out from the East Gate, and were now lying round the North Gate in no very good order, because they looked for no peril save from them within the North Gate, and deemed that as for them they had enough on their hands to keep them within their walls, and least of all things did they look for any onfall from without.

Thereon the Red Lad called to him his captains and hostleaders and asked them of rede, and to be short therewith. Some said one thing, some another, as to send back news hereof to Sir Godrick, or to array them in the best wise to fall on these men on the morrow. Nay, some were for hanging about till they should have news of Sir Godrick.

But when they were done, spake the Red Lad: "Sirs, many of these things are good to be done, and some not; for sure am I that we be not sent hither to do nothing. But now if ye will, hearken my rede: it is now well-nigh dark, and in two hours or somewhat more it will be pit-mirk, and these men outside the walls will be going to their rest with no watch and ward set outward toward the upland. Wherefore I say, let us leave our horses here and do off so much of our armour as we may go afoot lightly; for if we win we shall soon get other horses and gear, and if we lose we shall need them not. But meseemeth if we do deftly and swiftly, all these men we shall have at our will."

Now they all saw that it would do; so there was no more said, but they fell to arraying their men on foot, and in an hour they were on the way; and going wisely and with little noise, in two hours thence they were amidst the foe and doing their will upon them; and when they were well entered in amongst them and had slain many, they fell to the blowing of horns and crying out, The Red Lad! the Red Lad! Longshaw for the Small Crafts! Then both there was no aid to come to the men of the Porte, whereas they were far away from the East Gate, and also they of the North Gate heard the horns and the cries, and guessed what was toward; so they issued out with torches and cressets and fell upon the foe crying their cries, and so it befel that none of that host of the Porte escaped save they who might make the night their cloak. Then was the gate thrown open, and the Red Lad and his entered, and ye may think whether the townsmen were joyous and made much of them. But when the tale of his men was told, Osberne found that but three of his were missing. And so soon as it was light he sent back a band of his men to bring on their horses and armour. Thuswise first came Osberne into the City of the Sundering Flood.

XLVII

The Battle in the Square

ON the morrow's morn the leaders of the town met Osberne and his captains in council, and their rede was that they should do warily and not throw the helve after the hatchet. This they deemed best, that they should now, while they might, make strong with mound and wall their quarter of the town, since, until Sir Godrick was come to them, they might even now look to it to have much might against them. This rede the Red Lad nowise gainsaid, knowing well how valiant and stout these men would be behind walls; but he said: "Yet, my masters, the more leisure ye may have for this spade and mattock work, the better it shall be for you and the work. Wherefore my rede is that some of your chosen men go with the best of mine, and that we issue out of our quarter and fall upon the others, and make a good space clear of foes of the streets and carfaxes that march unto your quarter, which forsooth shall serve you as an outwork to your castle until Sir Godrick comes with a great host and fills up all that and more. And, sooth to say, now at once is the best time to do this, while the foe is all astonied at what befel last night."

That seemed good to one and all; so when they had eaten and were duly arrayed they issued forth into the streets, and at first indeed wended those that were truly of their quarter, only on the day before they deemed them not big enough to hold all that; but now it was their mind to bring it within their defences. So the Red Lad and his rode on warily, taking heed that they should not be cut off by any at their backs. So at last they came unto a great carfax with a wide square round about it. There they drew up their folk in a long line with a wide face to the foe, well furnished of bows and other shot-weapons; for the townsmen were archers exceeding good.

There was nought in the square or on the carfax at first but themselves; but after a little there entered by the east way and the west a rout of archers, and fell to shooting at Osberne's, and they back again. The archers of the Porte did not dare to show much face to the Red Lad, but were gathered together in plumps at each incoming into the square. Said the Red Lad to himself: Let us make an end of this folly. And he bade his men leave shooting, and then gave the word, and they rode at the carles right and left with spear and sword. Straightway the archers ran all they might, yet not so fast but that the Red Lad and his captains got amidst them ere they could take to the narrow byways, so that a many were slain. And this was a matter of but ten minutes. But when the horsemen had been along with the bowmen a little while, they heard great horns blowing from the south, and therewith great noise of horse, and presently a great rout of men-at-arms in the best of armour began to come in by the southern road, and the Red Lad's men were all agog to fall on them straightway, but he made them forbear till they had filled the square over-full. They were not long about it, but meanwhile the townsmen shot all they might; and so nigh they were that, despite their armour, not a few fell, both of men and horses; yet did they fall not on till the square was full of them, so that it looked far bigger than might have been deemed. Then they thrust on, but so close that they might scarce handle their arms, and the Red Lad and his cried their cry, The Red Lad for Longshaw! and rushed forward, smiting and thrusting, till the front of the foemen began to try to turn about if they might; but scarce they could, though if they might not flee they might not fall. And they behind strove to get forward to smite, for they said they were many more than the others; but they could get but little done, for their forward men who had been overthrown were hindering them. Now also the carle-archers of the town laid aside their bows and entered among them with short swords and axes, and hewed and slew and took none to mercy, and it seemed hard to know how that would end, save by all those men-at-arms falling in the place.

Now, as ye may deem, Osberne was more thrust forward

than any other, and somewhat of a space he had cleared before him, and his yellow hair came down from under his basnet, and his long red surcoat streamed all rent and tattered in the wind, and Boardcleaver was bare and bloody in his fist, and his face was stern but not exceeding fierce; for he would the slaughter of the day were over. Now he hove up Boardcleaver, and before him was a tall man in gilded armour and a gay yellow surcoat of silk, and his armour was little rent and his sword unscathed in his hand; a stark man he was of aspect, but terror was come into his soul because of the slaughter of the press and that there was no escape therefrom. So when he saw Boardcleaver arising he cried out, "O Red Lad, Red Lad, O thou seeker, let me live, that I may tell thee what thou wouldst give many lives to know!"

Then Osberne restrained Boardcleaver and let him fall to his wrist, and stretched out his hand to the gilded man. But even therewith his hand was thrust aside, for many a man there was mad and drunk with the slaying: and a short, dark, long-armed man of the weavers' craft, armed with nought else save a heavy short-sword cutting on the inner edge, drew him on to the gilded man's horse, and brought his sword back-handed across his face and neck, and fell with him as he fell, and mangled him that he was more than dead, and then got up again amidst the horses and fell to work again. Then Osberne, when he saw the tale was done, groaned aloud; but none heeded him, for it was to them but as a cry of the wounded. Then he uphove Boardcleaver again and cried out shrilly: "The Red Lad, the Red Lad for Longshaw and the Crafts! On, on at them!" And that all heard, both his and theirs. And now they of the foemen began to cease pressing forward, and many fled without a stroke stricken, till there was somewhat more room for the rest to flee, but little leave, for even so was more room for the pursuers, and soon was the square clear of all but dead and sore hurt; and the chase endured all up and along the carfax, and mad-fierce it was, and that mostly at the hands of the townsmen, who deemed that they had much to pay back to the men of the King and the Porte.

Now after this Osberne and his drew not back from the

carfax, but by the rede of him the townsmen made trenches and walls to strengthen them right up to the said carfax. And for three days the King's men durst not fall upon them there, save that they tried a little arrow-shot from afar, but did not much hurt thereby.

But the next day thereafter comes Sir Godrick with his host to the help of the townsmen, and rides into the North Gate amidst the joy of all men. And the next day they push on to their outworks and fall on. Three days of battle they have thereafter, wherein Sir Godrick will not suffer the Red Lad to deal: "For," saith he, "it is thou that hath won, and now we have little to do, but as it were the woodwright's and the carpenter's work. Wherefore now I bid thee to rest." Laughed Osberne, and tarried in the North quarter, while Sir Godrick and his with all deliberation set to work on clearing all the quarters on that side of the river; and they were four days about the business albeit the men of the Porte and the King were scarce so stubborn and enduring as they looked to find them.

But Osberne did all he might to keep good order and good heart amongst his men, and they made their strongholds strong to the letter, and looked to it that all their forward places should be ready for battle at a moment's notice.

XLVIII

Sir Godrick Is Chosen Burgreve of the City

BUT on the third of those four days came a man to Osberne early in the morning, and told him that the foe were holding the East Gate somewhat heedlessly, and that they had lost many men in those last battles. Wherefore Osberne looked to it, and gat three hundreds of picked men, and passing through byways of the streets came to the townward end of the said gate but a little after sunrise, and without more ado made at the doors of the gate, which were but half shut. There they drave the few guards in, and followed on them pell-mell; and to make a long story short, they presently won the gate utterly with but little loss, and all those inside, who were scarce three hundreds, slain or taken. Now you may judge if this were good news for Sir Godrick, when with mickle labour and not a little loss he had won the town on the east side of the Sundering Flood.

But now, when they had won so much, they had yet to carry the war into the west side of the Flood, where was forsooth the chief strength of the King and the Porte. For there was the King's palace and the great gildhall, both whereof were buildings defensible, and moreover they had full command of all the haven and the ships therein, for they had all the quays and landing-places and warehouses; so that both the sea and the river was under their wielding. Two bridges, made of great barges linked together, crossed the Flood, one near to the haven, the other a good way higher up; nor had the King and his thought it good to break either of them down. Both had fair and great castles to guard them at either side.

So now when Sir Godrick and the Council of the Lesser Crafts had met in divers motes with Osberne and other captains of the Longshaw host, it yet seemed a great matter that they had to deal with; and that if they had won many victories, they had yet to win the great one. And all men saw what would have befallen if the Barons' League had not been so utterly broken up the year before. But now the greatest gain which Sir Godrick and the Lesser Crafts had was that they by no means lacked men, and those of the best; and though they were shut out from chaffer with the merchants of the City, yet whereas the whole countryside was open to them because of the riders of Longshaw, they were not like to fall short of victuals. Though true it is that the King's men set swift keels on the Sundering Flood stuffed of men-at-arms, and these would land on the eastern bank so far as a twenty or thirty miles up, and plunder and ravage the country-folk, or whiles would come upon trains of victuals and suchlike wending towards the eastern city; and many fierce deeds they did, which made them no better beloved, so that men got to saying that the King's men were but little better than the very Skinners themselves. Moreover, it is not to be said but that often these reivers and lifters were met by the riders of Longshaw or the weaponed men of the country-side, and put to the worse by them, and such as were taken at these times had nought for it save the noose on the tree.

Thus then these two hosts looked across the Sundering Flood on each other; and surely, unless the Craftsmen had been valiant and stubborn beyond most, they had lost heart, whereas war was not their mystery. Skirmishes there were a many. Whiles Sir Godrick would gather such boats and barges as they had, and thrust over into the haven, and lay hold of some good ship and strive to have her over to their side. Whiles they might do nought therein, and whiles they prevailed; but even then the King's men contrived to set fire aboard the craft and spoil their play. Again, from time to time the King's men would set certain ships and barges across the Flood, and strive to land and skirmish on the east side. But herein they but seldom gained aught, but they in turn would have their ships burned and their men slain or taken. Thus then it went on, and now one now the other came to their above; but neither might make an end of it.

At last, on a day when September was well worn, the King's folk came to the midmost of the upper bridge with a white shield aloft and a herald, and craved safe conduct for three of theirs, an old knight to wit, and two aldermen of the Porte; this was granted, and they came all to the North Gate, and the council-chamber of the Lesser Crafts therein. There they set forth their errand, which was in short that they would have peace if it might be had on such terms as were better than war and destruction. The men of the Small Crafts took their errand well, and asked them how long they might tarry, so that they might bear back conditions of peace. The messengers said that they were not looked for back that day, and the others said that by the next day at noon they would be all ready to send three of theirs back across the water with the terms of peace. Then were the messengers handed over to the guest-masters and made much of, and the masters of the Crafts fell to close council with Sir Godrick and his captains.

Now whatever other terms they bade need not be told, but the heart of the matter was this: First, that so many of the masters of the Small Crafts should sit on the Great Council of the City, and that enough to make them of due weight in the Council. This they doubted not to gain since the war had gone with them. But the other was a harder matter, to wit that a Burgreve should be appointed to govern the City, and that he should be of might to hold a good guard, and eke it at his will and the will of the Great Council; the said Burgreve to be chosen by all the Gilds of Craft, voting one with another, and not by the Great Council; which, as things went, would give the naming of him into the hands of the Lesser Crafts, who were more than the great ones, though far less rich and mighty. This indeed seemed like to be hard to swallow, whereas it was much like putting the King out of his place. Yet some said that belike by this time the Porte was grown mightier than the King, and if they would have it so, then would he have to give way. Herein they were doubtless right; but another thing had happened of which they knew nought, which was driving the King and Porte both toward peace, to wit that a king from over-sea had sent heralds defying the King, and that his host was to be looked for in no long while, and the King and the Porte well knew that they might make no head against him, so divided as they of the City then were. Wherefore when on the next day the three King's men bore back the terms of peace, they tarried but a little while, and came back in two hours with safe conduct for as many as Sir Godrick and the Small Crafts would send. Whereon Sir Godrick and two of the Crafts were chosen, and went back across the water straightway, and without any tarrying fell to council with the King and the Porte. There they soon found what had befallen, and that their matter was like to be carried through with a wet finger, for the others were in hot haste both to make peace and to get the swords of Longshaw on their side against the Outland men. Nor did they gainsay any one condition which the Small Crafts had put forward, but added only this one thing, that the host of Longshaw should join with them in defending the city against the Outland men. Hereto Sir God-

rick accorded well, for he had no mind that all his battle
for the Small Crafts of the City should have been of no
avail, as it would be if Outlanders were to conquer the city
and play the tyrant there.

The very next day then was peace signed and sealed on
the terms abovesaid. And three days thereafter the Porte
and the Crafts went about the choosing of the Burgreve. As
none doubted it would be, Sir Godrick was chosen, and,
which had scarce been looked for, none else was named;
both big crafts and little would have none but he.

XLIX

Of the City King and the Outland King

Now then was great feast and glee in the City of the Sundering Flood. The gates were thrown open, the bridges made
free, the country-folk flocked in, and the markets were
thronged and gay; neighbour held merry converse with neighbour, and there was marrying and giving in marriage. Of the
Outland foe none thought, save it were the King and one
or two of his councillors; for all men trusted in Sir Godrick
that he would look to the safe-guarding of the city. But as
for Sir Godrick, like a wise man of war he set to work
looking to all points of defence, both the castles of the town
and especially the ships in the haven, that they were as defensible as might be.

And after all the Outland king came not all that year,
whereas he had fallen sick when he was just at point to
take ship with his host; so that all was put off till the next
spring, and there was time and to spare for Sir Godrick to
do all he would in strengthening the defences of the city.
But none the more for that was he sluggish, but did so
much that he made the City of the Sundering Flood exceeding strong, so that it might scarce be stronger; and all things
flourished there: old foes became new friends, and all men

were well content, save it were the King and his faitours, who rued it now that they had sold themselves so cheap.

Amidst all this, Osberne was somewhat more at Longshaw and the borders of the Wood Masterless than in the city. Of numberless folk did he ask his old questions, and gat ever the same answer, that they knew nought of it; and indeed now it was less and less like that they should know aught as time wore. So that at last he began to get ungleeful at whiles and few-spoken with men.

Came the spring, and therewith the mighty Outland conqueror; but the shortest tale to tell of him is, that there he conquered nothing, but was held aloof at all points, save here and there he was suffered to break through to his great scathe. But his host was so big, that he hung about till the autumn. He gat but one gain, such as it was, that ere he brake up his host the King of the City fled to him and became his friend. And they two took rede together as to what they should do the next year to fall upon the land which was his, as he said.

Meantime, his back being turned upon his once subjects, many men began to think that belike they might do without him once and for all, when they cast up the use he had been to them in times past. And this imagination grew, until at last a great Mote was called, and there it was put forward, that since the City had a Porte and a Great Council, and a Burgreve under these, the office of King was little needed there. So first with one accord they escheated their runaway, who they well knew would henceforth be their foe, and gave out that all they who had held of him should now hold of the Porte; and next, with little gainsaying, they did away with the office of King altogether, and most men felt the lighter-hearted therefor. And the City throve as well as ever it had done. So wore that year to an ending.

The next year the two Kings did in very sooth bring a great host against that folk; but fell not on the city itself, but gat a-land some twenty miles to the east thereof; and this they did easily, because Sir Godrick, with the rede of the Great Council, let them do so much, whereas he deemed it were well if he might be done with them once and for all.

So he gat the very pick of his folk together, of whom was the Red Lad in high place, much dreaded of all his foemen.

Then Sir Godrick by his wisdom chose time and place for the battle, whereas the others must fight when and where he would. Such an overthrow they gat, that they might not draw to a head again. The old City King, fighting desperately, was slain by the Red Lad in the beginning of the rout; but the other King escaped by sharp spurring and the care and valour of his best knights, who rode about him in a plump. He stayed not till he came to his ships, where he gat aboard and sailed away to his own land, whence he came back again never to trouble the City of the Sundering Flood.

L

The Red Lad Speaks Privily with Sir Godrick

THIS befel in April, and toward the latter days of it Osberne came before Sir Godrick and would talk with him apart, and Sir Godrick received him with all kindness, and spake to him privily, and asked him what he would. Said Osberne: "Lord and dear friend, thou art now become a mighty lord far greater than most kings. So busy have our two lives been with deeds that might not be set aside, that now for a long time we two have had but little converse together such as friends desire. Yet nevertheless through it all I have felt thy love unto me, as mine unto thee, wherefore this word that I must say irks me sorely, to wit that now at last we must presently part."

Said Sir Godrick: "If I am become a mighty ruler, thou hast become a warrior such that I well think the world holds none other so mighty; and true it is that I love thee no worse for all the hard and troublous days. And hard and troublous have they been forsooth; so that oft have I bethought me of that old man the king of the kine, and his welcome and his bidding, in the wide green valley by the river whereby we passed when we were wending to Longshaw that first time, though well I wot that earth has no such refuge for me. I say thou art great, and I love thee; wherefore thou hast a right to make thy choice, and least of all would I balk thee in thy desire. Belike we may meet again. Now wilt thou tell me what thou wilt do?" Said Osberne: "With a good will. For this is true, lord, that having been now five years amongst all sorts of folk, and some of them being such as might tell me some tidings of what I seek, I have had no tidings, and now needs must I say that lost is lost. But first, before I give all up, I will go to Longshaw and abide there, and hang about the Wood for one month, to give me one last chance; and then if nought befal, I shall ride straight to my folk in the Dale beside the Sundering Flood, and there shall I live and die in such content as I may. And I do thee to wit, my friend, that the picture of the grey bents and the long houses, and the sheep and beasts going to and fro, and the few folk of the stead, and the hall within with its shining black timbers, all this comes before me and softens my heart. For hast thou not noted how bitter and surly I have grown in these latter days?"

"I have seen thee sad," said Sir Godrick.

"Nay," said Osberne, "it is worse than that; but let it be. Well, now I shall tell thee another thing that hath got hold of me, and thou wilt think it wild folly belike. But this it is: When I am in my own Dale again, then the first morning when I arise I shall hie me straight to that old trysting-place, and look across the Sundering Flood; and then it may be that a miracle of God shall betide, and that I shall see my maiden there in her old place, and then shall we be no more utterly disunited, as though each for each we were neither of us in the world."

Said Sir Godrick: "This is a hope of no great things, nor is it like to come about. Were it well for this to leave thy fellows and thy friends and all the fame of thine that shall be?"

Osberne laughed. "Ah yes," he said, "some deal I know it now, that fame; when we draw together before the foemen, and our men cry out, 'The Red Lad! the Red Lad!' in no faltering voice, and even therewith the foeman's ranks quaver, as the trees of the wood when the wind comes up from the ground amongst them; and then I ride forward with Boardcleaver in my fist, and the arrows fly away about me for fear, and the array opens before me, and we plunge in and find nought there, and the rout goes down the green meadows. Yea, so it is, and many deem it fair. But then comes the quiet of the night, and my comrades are as though they were dead, and my praisers are voiceless, and I am alone; and then meseems it is I that have been overthrown and thwarted, and not thine enemies and mine, my friend. Nay, let me go back to my folk, and the land that I know and that endures before me when others have faded out. There will I abide whatso may come to me." Then he said: "Moreover there is this last month at Longshaw; who knows what may there betide? I shall keep my eyes and ears open I promise thee."

"Ah!" said Sir Godrick, "but beware, Red Lad, beware! Thou knowest how much hatred thou hast drawn upon thee for thy dealings with the rascaile of the Wood. Be sure that traps will be laid for thee, and look to it that thou walk not into one! And now I will say to thee farewell! It may be many a long day ere I see thy face again; and yet methinks I shall. And now I tell thee, that hitherto I have had more than enough gain out of thee, and scarce enough of joy. Maybe in days to come it shall be otherwise."

So they kissed and departed each from each. And Osberne made no farewells to anyone else, and said that he was for Longshaw, and should abide there a month or so. And thus he rode his ways.

LI

Osberne Is Beguiled by Felons

Now he took up his abode there; and presently he took to going day after day along a certain path, which was just well within the borders of the Wood. And there he would walk well-nigh all day, sometimes going further, sometimes stopping short and going to and fro, and this became known to all men; and such times he was unarmed, save that he was girt with Bordcleaver under his gown.

Now on the thirteenth day of his sojourn he walked this path, and had gone somewhat further than usual, and was beginning to think of turning back, when there came a man toward him from the Wood and hailed him, and he took his greeting. The man was clad in black, and had a buckler at his back and sword and dagger by his side, a white sallet on his head: a long-nosed, dark-haired man, beardless and thin-lipped, whose eyes came somewhat too near to each other each side of his head. He looked as if he might be some chapman's servant.

Osberne looked for him to pass by him, and stood a little aside; but the man stopped and said: "O famous warrior, might a carle of no worth speak with thee a few words this noon?"

"Why not?" said Osberne smiling, for never might he bring himself to the fashion of great men to be rough and short with common folk. Said the newcomer: "Thou art far from the host today, and hast no angry look on thee, wherefore I shall risk thy wrath by saying that thou lookest somewhat less than gleeful, great warrior." Said Osberne: "I have a trouble on me, and I have been forced to let many men know thereof."

"Wilt thou tell me thereof?" said the newcomer; "maybe I shall be the last to whom thou shalt tell it."

Osberne looked on him a while doubtfully and anxiously; at last he said: "This it is. Five years ago a maiden was stolen from me, and I have sought her since in many places, and have heard no word concerning her of any avail." Said the carle: "Dost thou remember the battle in the square by the carfax of the great City, and how there was a man before thy mighty hand who cried out to spare his life, for that he could tell thee of the said maiden; and thereon thou wert about to give him peace, but ere thou couldest take him to thy mercy he was slain by one of the carle-weavers?"

"Yea," said Osberne, "I remember it."

"Now," said the carle, "I shall make no mystery of it, but

shall tell thee at once that that same man was the brother of the master whom now I serve. And I have an errand from him unto thee, and he saith that what his brother knew, he knows, and somewhat more; and thy maiden is yet alive, and that he can tell thee how to find her surely if thou wilt. And he is not far hence."

Osberne looked somewhat wildly, and he caught the carle by the hand and cried out: "Good fellow, bring me to him at once and I will well reward thee." "Nay," said the carle, "but there comes something before that: my master is a chapman, and liveth by selling, not by giving; and he will take of thee two hundred nobles before thou hast his tale. Thou and I may call that weregild for the slaying of his brother." "Yea," said Osberne, "but I carry not two hundred nobles in my pouch."

"Well then," said the carle, "I will be here tomorrow or the day after, if thou wilt." "O nay, nay," said Osberne, "but abide thou here, and I will go up to the castle and fetch the gold." "So be it," said the carle; and he sat him down by the way-side, and pulled out victuals and wine from his scrip and fell to dining.

But Osberne put forth all his swiftness of foot, and was speedily in his lodging, and came to his treasury and took forth the gold and set it in a bag, and hastened back again, and found the carle where he had left him. "Thou art swift-foot indeed," said the carle, "but belike thou shalt not often again run so fast as thou hast e'en now. But thou art breathed; wilt thou not sit down a while till thou come round?" "No," said Osberne shortly, "I will on at once." "Well then," said the carle with a grin, "suffer me to carry thy bag." "Take it," said Osberne, and reached it out to him. The carle handled the bag and said: "Plump are the nobles, lord, if there be but two hundred herein." "There is more in it," said Osberne, "for there is the gift for thee. But lead thou on straightway." So the carle led on, and they went by divers woodland paths for some two hours, and then they heard the sound of a little water falling. Quoth the carle: "It is down in this ghyll that my master promised to abide me." And therewith he began to go down the side of a ghyll well bushed and treed, and somewhat steep, and Osberne followed him. When they got to the bottom there was a fair space of flat greensward underneath a little force of the water; but no man awaited them.

"Where is thy master, good fellow?" said Osberne. "He will scarce be far," said the carle; "I will call him." And therewith he set two fingers to his mouth and whistled shrilly.

Now Osberne was all beswinked with his run to and fro the castle and his two hours' walk thereafter, and he was sore athirst, so he went down on his knees to drink of the clear little pool beneath the force. And now, what with the failing day and the tall trees well-nigh meeting overhead, it was dusk in the ghyll; and moreover as Osberne drank (and he was in no hurry about it) with his face to the force and his back to the length of the ghyll, the tinkling and splashing of the force deafened his ears to any sound but a somewhat big one. So he drank and thought no evil; but of a sudden he felt a sharp pain in his left side, and ere he could say that he knew he had been smitten, another and another, and he rolled over on the greensward and lay still, and there stood above him three men, the carle-messenger to wit and another of like sort, and a third clad in white armour.

"The end of the Red Lad!" quoth the messenger. "Nay," said the other carle, "draw thy sword and smite the head from him, lord; make sure of him." The knight half-drew his sword from the scabbard; but then stayed his hand and said in a quavering voice: "Nay, nay! let us begone! Dost thou not see? There is one sitting by him!" "It is a bush in the dusk," said the other; "give me thy sword." But the knight for all answer ran swiftly down the ghyll, and they two that were left shrank and trembled, for there verily sat one by the wounded man in a scarlet kirtle, as they deemed, and a bright steel basnet. So they ran also after their master, and all three fell to climbing the side of the ghyll.

Now about a mile thence was a certain hermitage in a clearing of the wood, and when the night was growing dark the door was smitten on, and when the hermit opened, there was before him a tall noble-looking man in scarlet kirtle and bright steel basnet, bearing in his arms another man dead or grievously hurt. And the tall man said: "Canst thou leechdom?"

"Yea," said the hermit, "therein have I been well learned."

"See here then, here is a man grievously hurt, but he is not dead. Now I have done all I might for him, for by my craft I have staunched his blood; but I wot that he needeth long leechdom to be made whole. Now I may not come under thy roof, so take him of me, and lay him on thy bed and look to him, and do thy best: for if thou heal him thou shalt thrive, and if thou heal him not thou shalt dwindle." "Fair sir," said the hermit, "I need neither promise nor threat, for God's love and Allhallows' I will heal him if it may be."

So he took Osberne from Steelhead's arms, and being a stark and big man got him on to the bed and did off his raiment. Then he searched his grievous hurts according to leechcraft, and presently looked up from the wounded man and said: "Since this man is not yet dead, I deem not his hurts deadly, and I think to heal him with the help of the Holy Saints." Said Steelhead: "Thou hast in thy mouth, my friend, a deal of holiness that I know nought of. But I thank thee, and if thou heal my friend verily I will call thee Holy. Now shall I depart, but tomorrow forenoon I shall come here again and learn tidings of him."

"Go in peace, and God and Allhallows keep thee," said the hermit.

"Well, well," said Steelhead, "we will not contend about it, but I look to it to keep myself." And therewith he strode off into the night.

There then lay Osberne between life and death a long while; but after a time he began to mend, and came to his right mind, and remembered the felon-strokes in the ghyll; but of Steelhead's being there he knew nothing, for Steelhead had charged the hermit to say no word of it to Osberne. The hermit was a good and kind man and a well-learned leech, and after a while Osberne began to mend speedily. And he would have amended speedier, but he was sick at heart that his sudden hope had so failed him, and said within himself that now all hope was gone. Albeit the Dale and Wethermel drew him to them without ceasing.

LII

The Meeting of Osberne and Elfhild

AT last, when it was some six weeks from the time of that felony, and Osberne was on his legs again, and had gone to and fro in the wood nigh to the hermit's cell, now he began to think he must get him home to the House of Longshaw, and thence away to the Dale with a trusty guide; and the hermit would not say him nay, whereas his strength was but just come back to him.

On a time he went abroad from the cell, and was girt to Boardcleaver lest he should come across aught ill; he went somewhat further than he had been wont, till the day was beginning to draw toward sunset. It was now the latter end of May, and the leafy boughs were at their fairest; the sky was bright and blue, and the birds were singing in heavenly choir, and he scarce thought it good to go back speedily to the dark cell. So he went on a little further and a little further, till he was ware in the glade before him [of one] whom, as she drew nigher to him, he saw to be a seemly dame as for her years, straight and tall; neither was she clad in rags, but in a comely black gown and white coif. Nevertheless, as 't is said, Once bit, twice shy, so it was with him, and he was for giving her the go-by. But she would not have it so, and she greeted him and said: "Hail to thee, noble; whence art thou last?" Her voice was clear and good, and now as he looked in her face he deemed he saw no evil in it, but good-will rather. But he said: "Hail to thee, dame; I am last from a sick-bed where guile and felony had laid me."

"Well," said she, "but there is something else than guile and felony in the world, is there not?"

"I know not," said he shortly.

"I have seen somewhat else, if only once," she said. "I have seen truth and good-faith and constancy, and hope without reward; and five years have worn no whit of that away."

"Hah," said he; "was it a man, a warrior? Meseems I know one such, were it not for the hope."

"Nay," said she, "it is a woman."

"And what like is she to look on?" said he. She answered: "If thou wilt come with me, she is no great way hence abiding my home-coming." Said Osberne: "But what or who is it she is true to? Or for whom doth she long, hoping against hope? Is it father, brother, son, sister, or what?" Said the carline: "It is her troth-plight man; and verily I, as well as she, deem that he is worthy of it; or was when last she saw him."

Osberne laughed, and said: "Good dame, if this be so, what profit were it to me to see her? I am not her troth-plight man, and if it be as thou sayest, I shall be unto her as one of the trees of the wood." "There will be this profit," said the carline, "that thou wilt set eyes on one of the fairest creatures that God ever made." "Small profit therein," said Osberne, laughing again, "if I set eyes on her beauty and am ensnared thereby; then maybe shall be another tale for this woodland. For belike thou deemest me old, but I am a young man, only I am haggard with the battle between life and death as I lay wounded yonder." Therewith he pulled aback his hood, and the carline came close up to him and looked him hard in the face, but said nothing. Then he said: "Dame, to be short with thee, I have walked into the trap once, and will not again, if I may help it. Now I know not what thou art; for all I know thou mayst be a bait of my foes, or even a sending from evil things. Nor hast thou yet said any word why specially I should come with thee."

She was still standing close to him, and now she laid her hand on his breast and said: "This I say as a last word, and thou must take it how thou wilt. If thou dost not come with me now, thou shalt rue it only once, to wit, all thy life long."

He looked on her and knit his brows, and said at last: "Well, it is little to throw away the end of my life, and there may be some tidings or tracks of tidings to be found. I will go with thee, dame. Only this time," he muttered, "let there be no coming to life again."

"Thou art wise," said the carline; "let us lose no time." So they set off, and up and down by rough and smooth, till the wood was quite dark, and the stars were overhead when they came to a clearing, and sweet was the peace of the May night. At last they saw before them a glimmer of light, which as they wound about became presently a little window, yellow-litten, and casting its light upon a space of greensward and a little tinkling brook.

So came they to a little cot, seemly enough thatched with reed from the woodland meres. Osberne made up toward the door, but the carline put forth her hand and thrust him back, and said: "Not yet; abide where thou art a minute;" and straightway fell to going withershins round the house. This she did three times, while Osberne gat his anlace bare in his hand.

At last the carline came to him, and spake softly to him in his ear: "All is free now, Dalesman, come thou!" And she took him by the hand and opened the door, and lo, a little hall like many another cot, but clean and sweet and comely. Now Osberne had pulled his hood about his face again, and looked round; for as often happens when one enters a chamber, the child of Adam therein is the last thing one sees. Then he drew back a little, and stood there trembling. For what was in the chamber besides the simple plenishing was a maiden who stood up to receive them; tall she was and slender, clad in a dark blue gown; her hair dark red and plenteous, her eyes grey, her chin round and lovely, her cheeks a little hollow, and in the hollow of them entreaty and all enticement: she stood looking shyly at the newcomer, of whose face she might see but little. The carline seemed to note neither her nor Osberne, but cried out in a cheerful voice: "Now, child, if I be somewhat later than I was looked for, yet I have brought the gift of a guest, seest thou; a good knight who hath of late been brought to death's door by felon's deed, but is now grown whole and fight-worthy again. So let us bestir us to get him meat and drink and all that he needeth."

So they fell to, while Osberne stood where he had first

come in; and he scarce knew where he was, but looked down on the floor, as though the Sundering Flood of the Dales rolled betwixt him and the maiden; for indeed when his eyes first fell upon her he knew that it was Elfhild. Now the two women had not been long at dighting the supper ere there came a rough knock on the door, and straightway the latch was lifted and in strode three men-at-arms; two in jack and sallet with bucklers and sword and dagger, the third a knight clad in white armour with a white surcoat. This stirred Osberne out of his dream, and he sat down on a stool nearer in than he had been. The Knight cried out: "Ho, dame, I see thou hast one guest, and now here be three more for thee; we have stabled our horses in thy shed already, so thou hast nought to do save getting us our supper: dispatch I bid thee. And now who is this tall carle sitting there?"

Osberne knew them at once as they came in, that they were the three felons who had smitten him in the ghyll. He answered nought, and kept his hood about his face. "Roger," quoth the Knight, "and thou, Simon, cannot ye get an answer from the lither loon?" Roger lifted up his foot and kicked Osberne roughly, and Simon laid hold of his hood to pull it off him, but found it held tight enough; and Osberne spake in gruff and hollow voice: "I am a living man; ye were best to let me be."

Then had there been battle at once, but even therewith comes in Elfhild bearing a pewter measure of wine and beakers withal, and the newcomers stood staring at her beauty, silent for a minute. Then the Knight did off his basnet and spake in a loose, licorous voice: "The liquor we hoped for, but not the cup-bearer; and so it is, that I would liefer have the cup-bearer than the cup. Fair maid, will not a kiss go before the pouring out? Or never shall I have heart to drink." And he rose up and went toward the maiden, who stood confused and trembling, and turned pale. But Osberne had risen also, and with a quick turn had thrust between the White Knight and Elfhild, and now stood with his back to her, facing the felons.

"What, cur!" cried the White Knight; "shall we have thee out and flay thy back with our stirrup-leather?" Said Osberne, speaking slowly: "That is the third question too much thou

hast asked in these last few minutes. Lo thou!" And he
shook his hood from his face and had Boardcleaver bare in
his hand straightway. Then those three set up a quavering
cry of, The Red Lad! the Red Lad! and ran bundling out of
the cot; but Boardcleaver was swifter than they. One of the
serving-men lost his head just outside the threshold; the
Knight stumbled at the brook and fell, and never rose
again. The messenger strove hard for the thicket, but the
moon was up now, and it was but a few strides of the
swift runner of the Dale ere Boardcleaver had taken his life.

The two women stood looking toward the open door the
while, and the maiden said faintly and in a quavering voice:
"Mother, what is it? What has befallen? Tell me, what am I
to do?" "Hush, my dear," said the carline, "hush; it is but
a minute's waiting after all these years." Even therewith
came a firm footstep to the door, and Osberne stepped quietly over the threshold, bareheaded now, and went straight to
Elfhild; and she looked on him and the scared look went
out of her face, and nought but the sweetness of joyful love
was there. And he cried out: "O my sweet, where is now the
Sundering Flood?" And there they were in each other's arms,
as though the long years had never been.

LIII

Strangers Come to Wethermel

Now turns the tale to Wethermel, and tells how that on the
morrow of Midsummer, five years to the day since Osberne
had bidden them farewell, the folk once more sat without-
doors about the porch in the cool of the evening; neither
was there any missing of the settled folk of those to whom
he had said farewell. For all had thriven there that while.
There sat the goodman, more chieftain-like than of old; there
sat the goodwife, as kind as ever, and scarce could she be
kinder; there sat Bridget, not much aged in the five years;
for ever she deemed it a certain thing that her nursling would

come back to her. Lastly, there sat Stephen the Eater, wise of aspect and thoughtful, as if he were awaiting something that should happen which should change much in him; and there were the carles and the queans (with some few children amongst them who had not been there five years ago) who had been familiar to Osberne ere he left the Dale for warfare. It was growing late now, and the twilight was creeping up under a cloudless sky, when those folk saw newcomers wending the lane betwixt the outbowers, and making straight for the house-porch. They were but three, and as they drew nigh it could be seen that they were hooded and cloaked despite the warm night; and one was tall and seemed a stalwarth man, and another was jimp and went daintily, as if it were a young woman, and the third, who forsooth had her face but little hidden, seemed a carline of some three score years and ten.

None of the folk stirred save Stephen the Eater, who rose up as if to welcome the guests; and the tall man spake in a strange high voice that seemed as if it came from the back of his head: "May we three wayfarers be here tonight? For we saw this stead from afar, and it seemed a plenteous house, and we deem it guest-kind." Quoth Stephen: "A free and fair welcome to you; ye shall eat of our dish, and drink of our cup, and lie as the best of us do. Ho, ye folk! now were we best within doors; for our guests shall be both weary and hungry belike."

So into the hall they wended, and the three were shown to a good place amidmost thereof, so that all might see them; and there they sat, the tall man innermost, nighest to the dais, the young woman by him and the carline outermost. Then came in the meat, which was both plenteous and good, and when all were fulfilled the drink was brought in, and the tall man arose and called a health on Wethermel, and that it might thrive ever. But some men thought that, as he lifted his hand to put the cup to his lips, a gleam of something bright came from under his wayfarer's cloak. And Stephen the Eater called a health on the wayfarers; and then one drank to one thing, one to another, and men waxed merry and gleeful.

But at last rose up Stephen the Eater and spake: "Meat

and drink and lodging is free without price to every comer
to Wethermel, and most oft, as here it is, our good will goes
with it; yet meseemeth that since these friends of ours come
belike from the outlands and countries where is more tidings
than mostly befalleth here, it might please them to make us
their debtors by saying us some lay, or telling us some tale;
for we be not bustled to drink the voidee cup now, these
nights of Midsummer, when night and day hold each other's
hands throughout all the twenty-four hours."

Then rose up the tall, high-voiced man and said: "It is
my will that each one of we three should say something, be
it long or short, to make the folk of Wethermel glad. For
they have treated us wayfarers as though we were lords and
kings, and their words go to our hearts. Now I will that thou,
mother, begin, and that I make an end of this saying."

Then he sat down, and the carline said: "I am all the
more willing to this, as meseemeth I can tell you a tale such
as ye have never heard the like of, and which will move
every heart of you. And yet I must pray your patience, as
belike it may be somewhat long for a tale of one night's hall-
glee: and on this night must the tale be begun and ended.
Hearken then!

LIV

The Carline Beginneth Her Tale

THERE was an old woman, yet no cripple, who dwelt in a
stead beside a great river, which none might cross, either by
bridge or ford or ferry. But she dwelt not alone, neither
was the house her own: for with her abode a damsel young
of years, who was the owner of the said house, but had no
kindred, for father and mother and all else had passed away
from her. Therefore it is like that the Carline came to dwell
with her because she loved the Maiden, and would serve her
and do good to her. And no wonder was that, for not only
was the Maiden now grown so beauteous that she was the

pearl of all beauty, but also she was merry and kind, and loving as might be. So that none that saw her but must love her if they had any good in them.

Now ye will ask, since so it was with her, was there no young man who was drawn into the net of her love. But I must tell you that the stead where these twain dwelt was lonely, and there was but little recourse of folk thither. Yet I say not but that there was more than one young man of the dwellers thereby who thought it better than good to come to the house and sit and talk with her, and would have kissed and caressed her had they durst. But they durst not, for not one of them touched her heart; and though she was kind and friendly with every one of them, there was nought in her words or her mien by which they might anywise deem that she would suffer the toys of love from them. Sooth to say, the Maiden had a love, a fair youth and stalwarth, and a glorious man, and many were the words they had spoken together, but never had her hand touched his hand, nor his lips her lips; because betwixt these two was a river such as are few upon the earth, unbridged, unfordable, unferryable. And few might think that it was anywise like to betide that ever their two bodies should touch each the other; but the Carline, who was somewhat wise in lore, had an inkling that, despite this terrible hedge of water, the twain should one day meet.

Now it is to be said that oftenest the Maiden was patient, and abode the sundering will no ill cheer. But whiles her trouble was over heavy for her, and she would wander forth into the wood or the field, and go weeping and lamenting there; or she would sit in the chamber with the Carline, and cry out aloud on her love to come to her, and on all things on the earth and in the heavens, yea, the Great God himself sitting amongst the Cherubim, to help her, that for once, if once only before she died, she might feel her love's arms about her and his face laid to hers.

Or again, she would, as it were, tell stories of how it would betide that at last they should meet, both grown old, and kiss once, and so walk hand in hand into the Paradise of the Blessed, there to grow young again amidst the undying spring, in the land where weariness is come to nought; and there would she sit and weep, as if there were no ending to the well of her tears.

At such times was the Carline sore grieved for her, and would strive to comfort her by giving her some little inkling of the hope which she, the old woman, had conceived in her heart, that the meeting of those two should come about whiles they were yet young and lovely; more than that she might not tell the Maiden, lest the might should ebb from her. Thus wore the days between patience and despair, betwixt cheer and lamentation.

At last, when the Maiden was of some eighteen summers, great matters befel that country-side; for on a day came the alien reivers, such as are called the Red Skinners, with intent to rob and carry off all that was not too hot or too heavy for them, and to lay waste and destroy all that they might not bear away. But the folk of the land met them valiantly, and their friends on the other side of the fierce river aforesaid helped them what they might with the shot-battle; and great and grim was the murder, and the stour of the hardest.

Now there were the Maiden and the Carline at their house, and nought easy was the rede for them. The Maiden bade flee to the next stead, which was some four miles thence, but the Carline bade abide, lest they be caught upon the way, which forsooth she deemed was most like to betide if they left the house, and that rede they took at the last. So they sat expecting what should befal them.

For a long while none of the aliens came anear them; but at last, when the battle was at its fiercest, rode up three men leading two unbacked horses, and they were of the mien and in the gear of the Red Skinners; and the Carline stood in the door to meet them, and she spake to them and said: "What will ye warriors? Why are ye not in the battle with your fellows?" Said one: "Because our errand is here and not there: neither are those men our fellows. We be the servants of that goodly merchant who guested here a while ago, and would have bought the maiden within there in all honour, and ye rewarded his good will with scorn, and mocks and japes and scurvy dealing. Wherefore he hath set these reivers on your folk, and hath sent us along with them to look to you. And two-fold is our errand, to bear away the maiden without a price, and to slay thee. Hah! dost thou like it?"

Now the Carline remembered the coming of the said merchant, and how he had cast his love on the Maiden unhonestly and lustfully, and would have lain by her against her will had it not been for the lore of the said Carline, who letted him of his evil will and sent him away shamed.

But now she muttered something under her breath, and looked on those men, and made signs with her fingers, and then spake aloud: "Slay me speedily then, whiles ye are about it; for I take no great keep of life." The men handled their weapons, but nothing came of it, and they sat in their saddles staring on the Carline as if they were mazed. And even therewith ran the Maiden forth from the house, and cast her arms about the Carline, and cried out: "Nay, nay! but ye shall not slay her! For as my mother hath she been, and none other have I had save her. But as for me, I will go with you without more words. But I pray you by your salvation to take this my mother with you, for I cannot do to be without her; and if I miss her, then shall I be of little use, miserable and forlorn, to that lord of yours that ye tell of so goodly."

The old woman kissed her and embraced her, and then turned to those men and laughed in their faces; and they seemed presently as if awaking out of slumber, and one said: "Well, this may be; I see not why we should not slay thee there as well as here; and since the damsel would have it so, we will have thee along with us, and let the maiden settle it with our lord whether he will be wheedled by her or not. But come, to horse both of you! For time presses."

So the two women were set a-horseback, and the men rode with a good pace out of the Dale toward the fells at the back thereof; and if at any time the women thought of turning rein and riding off, they had but to look on the men, how they were horsed, for their way-beasts were mighty strong steeds of good race, but the women were set on everyday nags, such as be seen on any highway.

After a while they came on to the broken ground at the foot of the fells, and all must needs ride slower; and then the Carline came sidling up to the Maiden, and saw how wan and woebegone was her face, and asked what ailed her; and she answered faintly at first, and then clearer and louder: "It is because I am thinking of him and his woe; and I wot well that now, so soon as the battle is over, there shall he stand yet and look over the Flood on to the field of deed, as if he were seeking after me dead amongst the corpses of the foe. And tomorrow he shall come down to the water's edge while the dead yet lie there, and stand looking to see if I be not coming to meet him, as now I have been wont so many years. And the morrow of that morrow will he come, yea, and many a morrow, till his heart shall be outworn with longing and grief, and he will go away out of the Dale to escape from his sorrow, and shall nowise escape it. Ah, and how shall I know whither he will wend, or the place of the shifting dwelling of his wanderings? And I, and I, I wend away from him."

Sore grieved was the Carline at her grief, and she said: "O my child, I pray thee keep up a good heart within thee, lest thou die of sorrow, and endure not the chances of the meeting. Who knows whether thou be wending away from him? Nay, to my mind thou art wending toward him, and he to thee; for never had ye come together hadst thou abided in thine old home and he in his."

But the Maiden wept. But therewith rode along by them one of the men, and smote the Carline on the shoulders with his spear-staff, and bade her hold her peace, and not go on like a crazy hen.

So they rode their ways till they had passed the straiter part of the pass that led through the fells, and there night began to fall on them (it was April-tide in those days); so the men-at-arms chose a place where was grass and water and three thick thorn-bushes, and made their harbour there. They took some pains to dight a shelter for the Maiden by speading cloths betwixt a thorn and their spears stuck into the ground, but to the Carline, as was like, they gave no heed. But she laid her down peaceably within call of her dear fosterling, muttering as her head fell back: Here at any rate it is over-soon; let us get out of the mountains first. So they slept, yea, even the Maiden amidst her grief, so weary as she was. And when morning was they fared on, after a short tarrying for breakfast, whereof they gave of the best they had to the Maiden, but nought at all to the Carline. Nevertheless, when her fosterling fed her kindly from her abundance they naysaid it not.

This day is nought to tell of: toward sunset they came out of the mountains into a very fair green plain, wherein were neat and sheep a many; but though there were not a few houses of the herdsmen about, they made not for any of them, but took harbour in a little copse by a stream-side, and supped of such meat as they had; save that two of them rode out into the plain and drove back with them a milch-cow, which they milked then and there for the Maiden's behoof.

The next day they rode across the plain, and here and there fell in with some of the herdsmen by the way; but small greeting passed betwixt them, and the country-folk seemed well pleased that the men-at-arms had little to say to them. Before evening was they rode off the plain and into a land of little hills and streams, with green meadows for the most part, but here and there a little tillage, and a good many houses, yet these but the cots of the husbandmen. This day they rode long and late, yea, till it had been dark night but for the rising of the moon upon them. At last said one of the men to another: "We shall not do it tonight; let us rest, and come in fresh a morning-tide." So again that night they had the shelter of the trees and the fields, but on the morrow betimes they were up and rode forward.

LV

The Blue Knight Buys the Maiden of the Chapman

THEY had ridden scarce a three hours ere they came through a cleft in the hills which here were grown somewhat higher and straiter, on to a very fair little valley, well-grassed, and with a stream of clear water running through it; and amidst of the said valley a fair white pavilion pitched, but no coat-armour done thereon. Then quoth one of the men to the Carline: "Lo, dame, how likest thou the sight of our master's journey-house? Meseems in an hour's time thou shalt be well on thy journey to hell." The other men laughed, but the Carline answered them nought.

So down they went, and as they drew nigher they saw a tall black-bearded man standing before the tent-door, and presently knew him for the chapman who had been such an ill guest to them at their own house. And the Maiden quaked and turned pale at the sight of him. But the Carline spake to her under her breath and said: "Fear not, we shall not abide long with this one." Now he came forward to meet them; but when he saw the Carline he cried out wrathfully to his men and said: "Why have ye brought this accursed hag with you over all these many miles of way? Now must she be hewn down here, and her carcase will lie stinking at our door." The men said nought, but sat in their saddles staring stupidly at him. But the Carline looked him hard in the face, and again made that muttering and the passing of her hands to and fro. The chapman said nought for a while, and then he spoke in a lower voice, wherein his pride seemed abated, and said: "Well, after all, the damsel must needs have some woman to wait upon her, and this one shall serve our turn for the present. Ho ye! Come and take these women off their horses, and take them into the inner tent and give them to eat, and then let them rest." Then came forward two serving-men, who bore short-swords by their sides, and led the Carline and the Maiden through the big tent into the lesser one, and there brought water for their hands, and then victual and drink, and waited on them with honour; and the Carline laughed and said: "Lo my dear, here am I an honoured guest instead of a stinking corpse. Seest thou, the old woman is still good for some-thing, and always to serve thee and help thee, my dear." Then the Maiden kissed the Carline and caressed her, not without tears, and presently, being very weary with the way and the sorrow, laid her down on the bed and fell asleep. But the Carline sat watching heedfully all that went on, set-ting her eye to the defaults between the cloths of the tent, so that she could see all that was toward in the big tent, and somewhat the goings-on without.

Now it must be said the chapman, for as eager as had been his lust after the Maiden when he saw her at her house, found it somewhat abated when he saw her lighted down from her nag at his tent door. Forsooth she was worn with the travel, and yet more with the overmuch sorrow, so that she looked wan and haggard, and he said to himself that of all her beauty there was nought but the eyes of her left. But he thought: Let her rest a little, and be by herself if she will, and have good and pleasant meat and drink, and not be worried and troubled; and I will withhold the heat of my longing, and then in a day or two it will all come back again. So he bade his varlets deal with her as ye have heard, and suffered her to have the fellowship of the Carline her friend.

After this it befel that about noon the chapman and his men saw the riding of folk; so they looked to their weapons, and presently came riding up to the tent a Knight in bright armour, and two men-at-arms, and all of them right well arrayed. The Knight bore on his coat-armour wavy of blue and white, and he looked like to be a proper man of his hands.

Now when he had drawn rein at the tent door, and saw the men standing to their arms thereby, he seemed to be not thinking of battle with them, but he said: "The sele of the day to the men. Which of you is the master?" Then came forward the chapman, and sheathed his sword and said: "That am I, Sir Knight; and to make a long story short, I am no warrior or fighting man, but a merchant seeking gain from town to town and house to house. And I have some pretty things amongst my packs. Might I ask of your valour what thou wouldst have of me?"

The Knight, who by this time was off his horse, laughed and said: "Well, first we three would have meat and drink of you, and some horse-meat also, for we have ridden far this morning; and next, meseems, after what thou hast said, that it would help the victual down if I were to turn over some of those dear-bought and far-fetched wares of thine, even if I have to pay for peeping."

Who then was full of smiles and soft words save the chapman; he bade the Knight into his tent most sweetly, and set his folk to dighting a noble dinner. The Knight entered and did off his basnet, and showed a well-looked face, with good grey eyes like a hawk, and dark hair curling close to his head; there was nought cruel or base to be seen in his visage, though it had the fierceness of the warrior. So they sat down to meat, and talked the while of their eating; and a good deal of their talk was concerning the Knight of Longshaw, Sir Godrick, and his uprising, and what his chances might be of his outfacing all his foes, who, said the chapman, were many and great, and more belike than Sir Godrick wotted of. Quoth he: "And glad shall I be if he be overborne: for what should a knight do, to set him up against great and noble men, and wage all kinds of rascaile on behoof of a set of villeins and handicraftsmen!" And he looked on his guest as if he deemed he should please him by that word; but the other shook his head and said: "So should I not be glad; for Sir Godrick is both fearless and wise, and of good heart to such as need help. Yet I doubt me that he will be overthrown at last, such might as is arrayed against him. Forsooth could he get to him two or three like to himself, yea, or were it only one, then might he endure; but where shall he find such an one?"

Quoth the chapman: "If ye bear the man such love and honour, mightest not thou thyself give thyself to him and be such an one to him as thou tellest of?" The Knight laughed: "Chapman," said he, "of such mere skull-splitters as I be hath he enough amongst his men-at-arms, who, I must tell thee, be nowise rascaile, but valiant and well-ordered warriors. What he needeth is one fulfilled of the wisdom of war; yea, and of peace also, so as to know when to hold fast and when to let go, when to press hard on the foe and when to cast the golden bridge before them. Of such wisdom have I nought, and know little but of hard hitting and how to keep the face to the foe in the stour. Moreover, though in a way I wish him goodhap, yet is it such goodhap as one wishes a man who must needs be a foe. For I must tell thee that I am of the Barons' company and against Sir Godrick. Yet this I know, that if he fall at the last it shall not be till after he hath put us to the worse more than once or twice."

Herewith their talk turned else-whither; but all this the Carline heard, and stored it up in her breast, and thought that she might hereafter get more tidings of Sir Godrick, and belike piece one thing to another till she had got somewhat which should be to her purpose.

So when they had done dinner the chapman opened some of his packs before the Knight (who is here called the Blue Knight), and the Knight cheapened here an ouch and there a finger-ring or a gold chain, and a piece of Saracen silk, and so forth; and all these he paid for down on the nail in pennies good and true, for he had with him a big pouch of money. Said he, "Thou seest I am rich in spending-silver, for I have been paid the ransom of three knights whom I took in sharp stour last autumn."

But now as he was sitting turning over his fairings, a tidings befel. For the Carline, having well considered the looks of the Knight and having hearkened heedfully his speech, deemed that deliverance might come of him from the sordid wretch who had stolen the Maiden. So while the two were yet at table she roused her fosterling, and dight her attire as seemly as she might, and tired her hair and made it smooth and sleek; and just as the Blue Knight was about doing his marketings together, she brought the Maiden to the entry between the two tents and bade her stand there, and then drew the hangings apart to right and left and let the Maiden stand there as in a picture. The Knight looked up and saw it, and stared astonished, and was wordless a while; the chapman scowled, but durst not say aught, for he knew not how the Knight would take it; and as for the Knight, he leaned across to the chapman and spake to him softly, not taking his eyes off the Maiden the while: "Chapman, wilt thou tell me what this is, this wonder of women? Whether is it a queen of some far country, or an image made by wizardry?" The chapman, taken at unawares, had no lie handy, so he said: "This is my war-taken thrall, and she hath been with me but some three hours." Said the Knight, still speaking softly: "Thy thrall! Then mayst do with her what thou wilt. Tell me wilt thou not sell her, and to me?"

The chapman was somewhat slow to answer, for he feared the Knight, and durst not buy the slaking of his lust with the peril of death. And moreover he deemed it a thing to be looked for that, if he sold her not, the bold Knight would take her from him perforce, so that he should lose both wealth and woman. Again, it came into his mind that if he sold her he might yet take an occasion to steal her again; so he said in a surly voice: "I took her not to sell her again, but to keep her and make her one of my household."

"Yea," said the Knight, "and wilt thou bring her to the church and wed her before the priest with ring and book?"

The chapman answered nought, and the Knight held his peace a while; but presently he spake to the Maiden kindly, and said: "Sweet maiden, wouldst thou draw nigher to me, for I would speak with thee?" Then she left the fold of the tent and came and stood before him with no fear in her eyes.

Said the Blue Knight: "Tell me, fair damsel, is it true what this man says, that thou art his war-taken thrall?" Said she: "Three days ago I was stolen from mine own home by this man's servants while the stout men of my folk were in battle with a sort of reivers who had fallen on our land. How might we defend us, two weak women against three weaponed men?"

"Wert thou thrall or free before that day, damsel?" said the Knight. She flushed red, and said: "Never has there been an unfree man of our blood for generation after generation." Said the Knight: "Now thou art here in this man's tent, wilt thou go with him freely and of thine own will, if he swear to thee to take thee into his household and deal honestly by thee?" She reddened again: "But he will not deal honestly by me, lord," she said, "and never will I go with him uncompelled." "How knowest thou that he is not a true man?" said the Knight. "Fair sir," she said, "hast thou looked in the face of him? Look now with what eyes he is beholding me!"

The Blue Knight was silent a while; then he said, but halted in his speech: "And with me—wouldst thou go with me of thine own free will, if I swore to deal with thee in all honour?"

"Yea," she said, "or without the swearing if thou make me the same offer after I have said a word to thee; to wit, that there is a young and goodly man whom I love, and he me again. And now I have lost him, and know not how to come to him; but I will seek him the world over till I find him, and he me: and if I find him not, then never shall I come into any man's arms in this world. What sayest thou now?"

The Knight rose up and walked to and fro a while, casting a look on the chapman every now and then. At last he came to the Maiden, and said to her in a low voice: "I make thee the same offer, and will swear to thee on my father's sword, which here is." She looked on him, and the tears came into her eyes: nor forsooth were they very far from his. But she said: "This goes with it, that thou take along with thee my foster-mother, who is hereby, and suffer her to be ever with me if I will." "That is soon yeasaid," quoth he. Then he set her down in his chair, and said: "Fear nothing, I will see to this matter straightway."

Then he turned to the chapman, who sat scowling on the Maiden, and said: "Now, chapman, wilt thou sell me thy thrall as thou hast sold me those pretty things?" The other answered him not a while, and the Knight said: "Nay, it avails nought to draw faces at me; one way or the other the thing can soon be settled. For look to it, that thy war-taken thrall may be mine by the same title. There are weapons enough hereby, and ye are five and we three; and thou shalt arm thee, or I will unarm me to my kirtle and sword, and then let us out on to the green and fight for the Maiden." The chapman said: "I see thou wilt take her perforce; so give me her price: but take heed that I sell her not uncompelled. And thou who hast eaten and drunk with me!"

"I would I might vomit up thy victuals," said the Knight angrily; "for then I knew not that it was thy wont to carry off free women from their houses while other folk were fighting. But I will have no more words with thee, save this, that thou shalt sell me also two of thy nags, that we may all ride and be away hence the speedier. Ho Robert, go thou and take two fresh horses of the chapman and saddle them straightway."

Now the chapman named his price, and it was a big one indeed, no less than an earl's ransom; but the Blue Knight but nodded his head in token of yeasay, and the chapman said: "I suppose thou wilt not have all that gold in thy scrip; but thou mayst take thy bargain away, for as violently and strifefully as thou hast dealt with me, if thou wilt send the money in one month's frist to the hostelry of the Wool-pack in the good town of Westcheaping hard by here, and let thy bearer ask for Gregory Haslock to give him quittance. But for thine ill-dealings with me I shall give thee no quittance, but shall watch my turn to do thee a service."

The Knight said all shortly: "I shall send thy money as thou biddest;" and then turned away from him, and took the Maiden by the hand and led her out of the tent, and the Carline followed them. So they gat to horse and rode their ways. But so it was that the Carline rode the last of them; and when they were gone but a few yards the chapman ran to the tent door with a bent bow in his hand and an arrow notched to the string, and drew on the said Carline, who was but some ten yards from him by then. But, whether it were the caitiff's evil shooting or the Carline's wizardry, ye must choose between the two, the arrow flew wide of the mark, and the Carline laughed merrily as she rode along. Thus were those two quit of this felon for that time.

LVI

The Blue Knight Talks with the Maiden by the Way

The Blue Knight rode beside the Maiden, and it could be seen that in all ways he would take care of her and give her honour; but he was few-spoken at first, nor for a while had she much mind to speak. But after a little she looked on him aside, and seemed to think that he would be fain were she to cast a word to him. And she herself was grown of good cheer now, for she deemed herself delivered from captivity; and, however it were, she trusted in this man's good faith and kindness. So she asked him some simple question about the way, and he started when he heard her voice, but turned and answered her frankly, and seemed as if he had liked it better if he might have made more of it. Then she said: "Fair sir, thou hast not yet told me whither we be going."

"Nay," he said, "that is true, and heedless it was of me, and I pray thee pardon me. We be boun for the Castle of Brookside, which is my chiefest manor house, though no great things. But we shall not be there tonight, nor for many nights. Now if thou ask me what we shall find there, I shall tell thee that beside the serving-men and a few men-at-arms and sergeants, and three squires, thou shalt find little save my mother there, for I am unwedded as yet."

At that word the Maiden fell silent again, for she was wondering what like would be the Knight's mother, and what days she was like to make for her. But presently she set that all aside, and fell to ask the Knight of other matters, such as the fashion of the country-side and the ways of the folk round about his castle, and freely he answered to everything; and so at last began to ask her concerning her land and folk, and her way of life, and she told him of all freely. But no word did she say to him of the man whom she loved; nay, when the talk seemed drawing near to such a point that it seemed he must be told of presently, she would break off and hold her peace straightway; neither did the Knight say aught, nor ask her wherefore she went not on with her tale, but let speech be till the spring thereof began to run again of its own will.

Thus then they wore the day, riding through a fair country of husbandry, not very thickly housed. None meddled with them, till at sunset they came to a goodly grange walled and moated; and the Blue Knight said: "If we take not harbour here we shall have to lie out in the field, for we shall fall in with no other house till the night is well deep." Therewith he rode up to the door and lighted down, and so did they all; and there came forth a tall and somewhat goodly man of some fifty winters and bade Welcome, Sir Mark! And without more ado they entered the hall, which was fair and big and well-plenished. There presently they were feasted by the goodman and his sons and his folk, for Sir

Mark the Blue Knight was well known to the said goodman. In due time withal the Maiden was shown to a fair chamber well hung and with a good bed therein, wherein she slept sweet without dreams. So was the ending of that day better than the beginning. They took to their road betimes on the morrow, and two of the goodman's sons and three of his men rode with them, well armed; for though this was a peopled part, yet whiles reivers rode therein. But on the way the Blue Knight excused him to the Maiden for suffering this eking of his army, and he said: "Seest thou, lady, were I with my two lads here, or even were I riding birdalone, I would have bidden these five good fellows abide at home; but I fear for thee, lest the fewness of our company should draw on this rascaile to come within smiting distance, and then who knows what might betide? For a chance stroke might do all the scathe at once, and make me an unhappy man till the end of my days."

She smiled on him friendly and said: "Sir Knight, there is no need to excuse thee; trust me I am nowise greedy of battle, and thank thee heartily for thinking of me."

The Knight made as if he would have said something which would not come forth of his mouth, and he turned very red, and so rode, but presently drew rein, and bade the others ride on and he would catch up with them. So they went on, and the Maiden would have ridden on also, but he said: "I beseech thee to abide with me, for I have a word or two to say to thee before we get on with this day's journey." She looked on him wonderingly, and was somewhat abashed, but turned to hearken to him, and he said, not speaking very glibly: "Thou thankest me for thinking of thee, but meseems I have nowise thought of thee enough. I have told thee that we be riding to my house of Brookside, but now I will ask thee if thou hast will to go thither?"

"Why not?" she said; "I deem not by thy looks and thy speech that thou wilt be hard or cruel with me, or do me wrong in any wise, or suffer others so to do."

"Nay, by Allhallows," said he; "but this I ask. Tell me right out if thou hast any will to go back to thine old home in the Dale. I beseech thee to tell me thy mind hereon; and if thou longest to go back, then will we turn bridle at once and seek to the stead where thou wert born and bred, and there will I say farewell to thee. For what! It may not be for ever; I shall ride to see thee once and again, I promise thee."

Now the Maiden flushed red and the tears gathered in her eyes, and she looked piteous-kind on him; but she said: "Thou art kind indeed; but that farewell in the Dale needeth not to be, for I have no will to go back home. Such an errand is laid on me that hath made me homeless now; for I must go seeking that which is lost, it may be, wide over the world; and if thou wilt shelter me a while in Brookside Castle I shall thank thee and bless thee as scarce a man hath yet been thanked since earth was new."

The Knight hung down his head, but presently he raised it, and heaved a sigh as if a weight were lifted from his heart, and he said: "Let each of us take what content may be in the passing days." Then he shook his rein, and they both sped on together till they caught up with their company.

That night they harboured at a husbandman's cot, where was no room save for the two women, and the men lay out under the bare heaven, but all was done that might be for the easement of the Maiden. The franklin's folk rode on with them on the morrow, and whereas they must needs wend a somewhat thick wood the more part of the day, they rode close, and had the Maiden in their midst, while the Blue Knight went the foremost of their company, and was as wary as might be. So whatever strong-thieves might have been lurking under cover of the thicket, they adventured them not against so stout and well-ordered a company, and they all came safely through the wood into a fair grassy valley some little time before sunset. But though the pasture was good there and the land well watered, there were no houses within sight, for it was over-nigh to the wood for folk to venture their goods, yea and their lives, by dwelling in neighbourhood to such ill men as haunted the thickets of the forest. Wherefore this night all the company, women as well as men, must needs forego lying under rafters: albeit they dight some kind of a tent with what cloths they had for the Maiden and her fosterer.

The fourth day, as they rode the fair grassy valley, as it was noon, they saw somewhat aloof the riding of another company, which they deemed to be more than they. So they looked to their weapons and rode on steadily, but without haste, lest the others might deem they were fleeing them. So the others, when they had well espied their demeanour, passed on without meddling with them; and well-nigh the whole valley could be ridden, so there was nought to drive them to meet side by side in a strait road, wherefore they came not very nigh, but yet nigh enough to know the newcomers for such as would be evil way-fellows to any whom they feared not. As it was, the Blue Knight and his drew rein and turned a little toward them as they went by, to show that they feared them not, and Sir Mark rode forward before his folk and abode them with sword in fist. But the newcomers did nought but set up a yelling and jeering, and rode on their way not over slowly.

Three hours thereafter they saw, a little mile aloof, a fair white house garnished with towers on a knoll, round about which ran a little river; so the Maiden, who was now again riding close beside the Blue Knight, asked him if that were Brookside, and he smiled and said: "Nay, my house is still five days' ride away, but this house, which hight Warding Knowe, is the house of a friend, and there shall we have good guesting, whereof I rejoice for thy sake." Then he was silent a while, and said thereafter: "Tell me, lady, dost thou wish those five days over?"

"Nay," she said, "it is little matter to me where I am, and to say sooth, this riding through the fair land likes me well."

He sighed and said, yet slowly: "Well, for my part I would that the five days were fifty." "Why?" she said heedlessly. He reddened and said: "I must needs tell thee since thou askest me. It is because I have got used to seeing these men and thy Carline about thee; neither does it irk me to see the folk that give us guesting gazing on thee or speaking to thee. But when we come to Brookside it will be all other than that; for there will be the folk all about, and some belike will make friends with thee; and there will be my mother. And look you, all and each of these folk shall have as much part and lot in thee as I shall have. Now, art thou angry that I have said this?"

"Nay," she said, and knew not what more to say. And

she looked at him covertly and saw grief and torment in him, and she was sorry for him. But within herself she said, Woe's me! And how long it shall be belike ere I meet my beloved!

LVII

They Come to Brookside

THEY were not long ere they were before the gate of Warding Knowe, and the master thereof standing over against them, bidding them a free and fair welcome. He was well on in years, more than grizzled, but a stout and stark knight: he hight Sir Alwyn. He embraced Sir Mark as he got off his horse, for they were dear friends, and then looked keenly on the Maiden, and took her by the hand and led her in and treated her with all honour. Thereafter, before supper, while she was under the hands of the tire-women, the said lord took occasion to ask the Blue Knight if he had done well, so doing, or whether he should have given her less honour; and the Blue Knight said that he had done right well, and that he thanked him for it, for of all honour was she worthy.

Now the Maiden sat at table beside the lord and Sir Mark, and hearkened their talk, which at one time ran much upon that great captain of war whom they called Sir Godrick of Longshaw. And she might see of both of them that they thought much of his wisdom, and not little of his luck, and feared him what he would to do them of the Barons' League, whereof were both those knights. And Sir Alwyn furthermore told the Blue Knight concerning tidings in the City of the Sundering Flood, and said that the King thereof was of little account before such a man as was Sir Godrick, for though he were well enough in a fray, if the sword were put into his hand and the horse were between his knees, yet was he feathered-headed, stubborn in wrong, and hard-hearted. Said Sir Alwyn, that save the said King was in all things according with the best men of the City, as the Porte and the masters of the Great Crafts, he was undone. Then he said again: "Yea, and there is talk also how that the Small Crafts have in their hearts to rise against both Porte and King, and certes if they may have Sir Godrick on their side, which is not wholly unlike, they will perchance come to their above; and then again is the King's cake but dough."

Said Sir Mark, and smiled withal: "One thing we have to our comfort, that there may not lightly be found two Sir Godricks, and though his men be fell fighters, there where he is only shall his luck prevail to the full."

"Yea," said the house lord; "but I can see in the eye of my mind another well-nigh as good as he, if he might but hit upon him. Yea and one who should be even better than his double, filling up what little lacks there may be in him; one who should cheer the heart of his host as much even as the captain, and yet should be liker to the men themselves, and a part of them in all wise."

Said Sir Mark: "Even so much as this I said a day or two ago. Yet scarce is such an one found by seeking." "Sooth is that," said Sir Alwyn, "but such-like haps drift toward the lucky."

So the talk thereof dropped down in a while; but the Carline, who had been shown to a good seat not far off, heard all this, and said to herself: I wonder if this old knight is somewhat wise of foresight, for surely along the same road wendeth my mind. And afterwards, the next morning, when as it happed the Carline was standing close to the lord, and they two alone, she said to him: "Lord, might an old and feeble woman ask of thy wisdom without rebuke if thou hast any inkling of what thine end shall be?" He looked hard on her and said: "Dame, I note of thee that thou hast some foresight of things to come, and thou art old as I am, therefore to thee will I tell it, as I would to none other, that I shall fall in battle, and in that said battle our backs shall be turned toward the foe and our faces toward the world beyond; and this shall be ere the earth is eighteen months older." So she thanked him, and they parted.

But as for the Maiden, she also had hearkened heedfully to the talk of the two knights, and something went to her heart as they talked about a meet fellow for this great captain, and she said to herself, Ah! and where shall such a man be on the earth, if it be not he whom no man friendly may see without his heart being drawn to him, whom no foe may see without casting aside hope of victory, the wise one, while yet a boy, of the war of Eastcheaping, the frank and the fair, and mine own love who is seeking me?

When the morning was they departed with all good wishes from Warding Knowe, and the franklin's men turned back home; for Sir Alwyn's stronghold was as a bar against the strong-thieves of the forest and thereabout. But the others went forward toward Brookside, nor is there much to tell of their journey; for the most part they guested at the houses of the husbandmen, or whiles at a franklin's or yeoman's house, and none begrudged them the harbour and victual; but the poor folk Sir Mark paid largely therefor.

At last, on the ninth day as it grew toward dusk, and they had been riding a land of little hills, with no little woodland betwixt the meadows so that they might see no great way ahead, they saw but a half mile aloof a hill nowise high, and before it a little river bridged with a goodly stone bridge; and on the said hill was a long house, defensible by reason of its towers and walls, yet no mere stronghold, but a goodly dwelling. Then Sir Mark raised his hand and pointed to it, and said to the Maiden: "Lady, yonder is Brookside, my poor house, where I would have thee dwell so long as it pleases thee." Then he drew forth his horn and said: "We will sing a little to them, for it will be in their minds to ride out some of them to meet us, and I would not balk their good will." Therewith he set his horn to his mouth and blew a long and loud blast, wherein were strange changes and quirks, so that it might be known for his music; and then they rode on slowly, and presently a banner of the blue and white waves came out from a high tower, and therewithal from out the Castle-gate came forth a score of folk a-horseback and rode swiftly down to the bridge.

Then Sir Mark said: "Now light we down and meet the rest on this pleasant greensward, for they will like it better to come on us thus, so that they may have the better and the nigher sight of us; and though there be little shade of trees here, yet this cool hour before the twilight all green places be pleasant this fair day."

Even as he bade so did they, and it was a nigh to the bridge, so that it was but a few minutes ere that folk were riding over toward them, and the Maiden could see at once of them that they were merry-faced and gay-clad. The two that rode first were young men, and one slim and very goodly, with the hair of his head plenteous and waving and brown, and little hair upon his pleasant, happy young face. He threw himself off his horse at once and ran straight up to the Blue Knight, and made obeisance to him, and took his hand and kissed it; but the Knight laid his hands on to his shoulders and shook him and rolled him about, looking kindly in his face the while, and then he cried out: "Ha, Roland! By St. Christopher but thou art glad to see me, lad! Is all well up there?"

"All is well, Sir Mark," said the youngling, "and I am like to be glad to see thee back safe and sound, when who knows what folly thou wilt have been mixed up with, so that thou mayst well be brought home any day between the four corners: and all is well up yonder."

"Hark to the prudence of the sage and the grey-beard," said Sir Mark, laughing. "Yet I must tell thee, and all of you, that I have had an adventure. But here is James and his greeting." Now this was the other young man, who got off his horse in less haste and came up slower to his lord, and as he went cast an eye on the Maiden, who had risen up to meet the newcomers and was standing there simply and somewhat shyly; and as the young man beheld her he blushed red and cast his eyes down. He was not so fair a youth as the other, tall and stark, red-haired, the hair cut short to his head, yet no ill-looked man neither, grey-eyed and firm-lipped. The Knight took him kindly by the hands and greeted him, and then he turned to the Maiden and took each of the young men by a hand and led them before her, and said: "Fair lady, these two, who will ere long be knights, are my squires-of-arms, who love me wholly and are good men and true, and perilous in the stour to them that love me not. Now I pray thee be as kind to them as thou wilt, yet as I am, to wit, ruling them well, and making them run

and return for thee, and giving them but little of their will."
And he laughed therewith.

So James knelt down before her, and would have kissed
her hand but she reached it not to him. But if James were
abashed when he first cast eyes on her, how was it now with
Roland? He turned red indeed, and made no obeisance to
her, but stood staring at her with all his eyes.

But the other folk gathered round them to get the Blue
Knight's greeting, and also, sooth to say, to gaze upon the
Maiden. And when the Knight had taken the welcome of
them with many kind words, he said in a loud voice so that
all could hear: "Squires and sergeants and men-at-arms, this
is the adventure that I have had: that I came upon this
lady in the hands of a caitiff who had set his men to steal her
while others held her kinsmen and folk in battle, and now
called her his war-taken thrall. And whereas he was a craven
and would not fight for her, I must needs buy her of him,
though I bade him battle in all honour; and fain am I that he
took it not, for the slaying of such dogs is but dirty work.
But hearken, though I have bought this lady at a price, it
was to make her her own and not mine, and of her own will
has she come hither to my house. But I think on the way
thither she has become somewhat my friend in all kindness
and honour, and I deem that to you also she will be a friend
while she dwells with us, and if ye be less than friendly with
her, then are ye hewn out of far other wood than I be. But
all this I have told you that there may be no slander or back-
biting, or deeming of evil whereas none is; yea, and no
deeming of guile or mystery in the tale, but all may be plain
and outspoken."

They gave forth a murmur of yeasay and welcome when
he had done, and the Maiden deemed that they looked as if
they loved and trusted the Knight. But therewith one and
all of them came before her and knelt to her and did her
obeisance, and she looked full kindly on them, for she
deemed all this good and happy. And yet she said to herself,
If it could be that I could forget him or the search for him,
how should I one day awaken when all was lost and curse
myself! But she heard the Blue Knight say: "James and
Roland, I would have you prevent us and go up to the

Castle, and go to my Lady-mother in her chamber and tell
her hereof, how I have come home, and all that ye have seen
and heard." But the Maiden wondered somewhat, for looking now on Sir Mark she saw that his face had reddened and
his brows were knit.

But the two squires got to their horses and rode briskly
up to the Castle as silent as might be, and all the others followed at a foot's pace.

Now they were soon under the gate of the Castle, and
came into the forecourt, and the buildings round about it
were goodly and great, but not very new. There were a many
weaponed men in the said court, all come together to welcome their lord and his fellowship, and they clattered their
spears on their shields, and tossed their swords aloft and
shouted, so that the Maiden's eyes glittered and her heart
beat quick.

But when they were off their horses, straightway Sir Mark
took the Maiden by the hand and led her into the great
hall, and all that folk followed flock-meal. Long was the
said hall and great, but not very high, and its pillars thick
and big, and its arches beetling; and that the folk loved
better than flower-fair building, for very ancient it was and of
all honour. Ancient withal were its adornments, and its hall-
ing was of the story of Troy, and stern and solemn looked out
from it the stark woven warriors and kings, as they wended
betwixt sword and shield on the highway of Fate.

LVIII

Peaceful Days in the Castle of Brookside

Now the Knight led the Maiden up to the dais, and thereon
were squires and priests and ladies; for Sir Mark's mother
was there, sitting on a very goodly chair beside his seat of
honour, and when those two came on to the dais the said
lady stood up to meet them, and put her arms about the
knight's neck and kissed him. Then she turned to the Maiden

and said: "Thou also art welcome, and thy follower the old woman, since my son hath bidden you to the house which is his own. But look to it that thou be obedient to him, and take more heed of his honour and his welfare than thine own welfare. Then shall I give thee what honour thou art worthy of, and thou shalt find in me a well-willer."

So the Maiden knelt before her and kissed her hand, but the Lady looked no more on her, but on her son. She was a tall and goodly woman of some five and fifty winters; hawk-nosed and hawk-eyed, dark-haired, and her hair waved as the coat-armour of the house. She spoke in no very soft or kind voice, not even to her son, and the Maiden had feared her that while, had it not been that even therewith her heart turned toward the man she loved and whom she sought, and all these that were round about her, even the valiant and generous Knight, had become for the time to her but images that had no part in her life.

But now the tire-woman came to her and led her into a chamber apart, and bathed her and clad her in fair raiment and led her back into the hall, for so had the Blue Knight commanded.

As for the Carline, she was shown to a good place, and sat there heedfully, and had ears for everything that was said and eyes for all that was done. And she said to herself that they should not abide there very long ere she would find out something of the way her bird must follow if she were to have a happy life thenceforth.

But the next morning the Lady-mother took her son into a window of the hall and fell to talking with him. And the Carline was not far off, and heard a good part of all that they said: for she was fine-eared, and had brought lore to bear upon the hearkening.

Now spake the Lady: "Well, son, so thou hast brought home a woman of the husbandmen, a churl's daughter, to dwell with us. What wilt thou do with her? Wilt thou wed her with priest and ring?" "Nay, mother," said Sir Mark; "but thou needest not call her of churl's blood. I wot of these folk of the dales under the mountains, that they are both proud and warrior-like, as if they were earls' kindred." "Is it so?" said the Lady." "But she is neither of the baronage nor the knighthood. I say, wilt thou wed her?" "I shall not," said Sir Mark, reddening and knitting his brows. "What wilt thou do with her then?" said the Lady. Said he: "She shall abide here in all honour and kindness so long as she will." "Even such shall she have from me then," said the Lady, "since it is thy will, so long as thy will is steadfast herein; but when it changes, then must we seek other rede." So the talk between them dropped for that time.

Here then began new days for the Maiden, nor is it to be said that there was aught evil in them, save the abiding on hope deferred; for there was none in the house that looked not kindly on this lovely one, save it were the Lady, the mother of Sir Mark. But then, to say sooth, she looked not kindly on any, scarce even on her son, though in her heart she loved him strongly. And no wrong she did to the Maiden, or put any tasks upon her, nor said nor did aught covertly to make her heart bleed, as belike she might have done had she willed it. The two young squires, Roland and James, did all they might to be with her and have speech of her, and she suffered them frankly, seeing no harm therein. For to her they were but bright and fair youths whose lives had nought to do with hers, but who should find friends and loves and deeds with other folk whom she had never heard of, and in lands far away from the grey Dale where she was born and bred.

As to Sir Mark, it was somewhat different, for such thanks she owed him for her deliverance and for his kindness that never wore thin, and for the faithful love that looked for no reward, nay not even for pity of the love, for ever he bore him frank and merry, and had such kind good-will to all folk worthy who were about him, that none had deemed of him but that he was heart-whole, and bore about no pain that fretted his life. So much she owed him, I say, yea and was glad to owe him, and so fain she was to hear and see this friend, that scarce might she think of her life on the earth and he not a part of it in some way.

So wore the spring and summer, and all seemed at peace about Brookside: and many merry days did the Maiden and the Carline share in, as riding in the meadows and woods with hawk and hound, and feasts in the fair land further aloof; and the Midsummer and Michaelmas markets, which were held in the meadow betwixt the Castle and the township of Brookside; and a riding more than two or three to the cheaping-town of that country-side, which was some five leagues distant and was a good and plenteous town. Withal a many folk came a-guesting to the Castle, knowing it to be a guest-kind house, as pilgrims and chapmen, and knights and men-at-arms riding hither and thither on their errands, so that it was no unlikely place to hear tidings of the countries and kingdoms.

LIX

Tidings of Longshaw and of the Hosting of the Barons' League

But when the aforesaid Michaelmas market was, great recourse was there of far-travelled and wise men, and the Carline set herself diligently to learn all she might of suchlike folk. And she had wherewithal to buy wares of likely chapmen, and to treat men-at-arms and others to wine and banquet. For she had brought away with her a marvellous collar of gems, which the Maiden owned, and which, as she said, was the gift of the Dwarfs; and the Maiden consenting thereto, the Carline had sold three gems from the said collar, so that they lacked not money.

Now as to the tidings the Carline heard of, they had for the most part to do with the deeds and uprising of Sir Godrick of Longshaw, and how that the Barons of the lands that lay about would not endure his ways and his pride, and were levying war against him; and they said they knew for certain that, when spring came next year, they would be on him, and that they had made a League into which they looked to draw the King of the City of the Sundering Flood, and that meanwhile the League was already most mightily manned, and so far-reaching that it was a sure thing that the Lord of Brookside had come into it, yea and even others further west and north than he. Now all were in one tale about this;

but one man there was with whom the Carline spoke, and he neither the youngest nor least wise, who said: "And yet, dame, I look for it that the Knight of Longshaw will yet give this League a troublous hank to unwind, so wise a man as he is, and so well accompanied by wise and lucky men; and now hath he gotten a new captain, a young man from far away up-country; and though there has since his coming been no great war afoot, yet hath this newcomer been one of certain adventures, wherein he hath proved himself. And by all I could see and hear, for I was dwelling seven days at Longshaw, he will be the right hand of Sir Godrick, and that means that the Knight deems of him as no mere man-at-arms, but a wise man also. Moreover I myself have seen the young man, and this I seem to see in him, that he has the lucky look in his eyes; and I am deemed cunning in the judging of men." All this and more did the Carline hear tell of, and she weighed it heedfully, and thought that a change of days was coming.

A month after this, and ere the winter had set in, came riding to Brookside a knight and two squires, and had a special message to the Blue Knight, who received them with all honour and kindness and heard what they had to say, and prayed them to abide with him a while, since they had ridden far from the south and the east; but they would not tarry but one night, for they had further to go. When they were departed Sir Mark made no secret of their message, which was that the hosting of the Barons' League would be in such place, east of the water and far to the south, a month before Marymass of next year; and they prayed him to be leal and true to the League, and gather to him what force he might, as well armed and formed in all ways as could be done. But he answered that he was all ready thereto, and should do his devoir to the uttermost of his power.

When the Maiden heard this she was troubled, and asked him what he deemed of the chances of the war, and he said: "Lady, this is what we were talking of with the Lord of Warding Knowe that other day; and I must tell thee, though I shall go to the hosting merrily and expend me there to the utmost, yet I deem that they be the luckiest who may keep them out of this strife, as I may not." "Yet," said she, "be they not mighty men, these Barons? And all men say that their League is well knit together; so that at the worst, if they overwhelm not the Knight of Longshaw, they may hold them well again him."

"Lady," said he, "by my deeming, if we crush not this valiant man utterly he will scatter us; he is not such a man as, if he have any force left, may be held aloof, as a man will hold a fierce sheep-dog with a staff till the shepherd come. To end it, since I am saying this to none but thee, I see myself so bestead that I shall deem me a lucky man if I bring back a whole skin from this war."

"It will be evil days for all of us," said she, "if thou come not back hale and sound."

"It gladdens my heart that thou shouldst say so," quoth he; "and yet I would have thee look to it, that if we overthrow this wise man and good knight, and I say again that must be utterly or not at all, there will be more moan made over him than over a dozen such as I; and that is no otherwise than it should be." Said she: "I would thou wert with him and not against him." The Knight said kindly: "Dear maiden, thou must not say such words to me, for thou knowest that my part is chosen by my own will."

She said nought, but nodded and looked on him as one who understood and thought well of him; and he began again: "So it is that yonder knight-messenger told me, amidst of his talk, that he had been but the other day to Longshaw under safe-conduct, and that there it was told him by one of the loose-tongued and grudging kind, as I deem, that Sir Godrick of Longshaw had gotten to him these latter days a new captain, a man very young, and as it were a David to look on in the days before he slew the Philistine. Furthermore, said this grudger, that though the said youth was a tall lad of his inches, and strong and well-knit, he was all untried, and yet was he shoving aside older and well-proven men in the favour of the Knight of Longshaw. In short, the said grudger went on with his tale as though there were some big grievance against his master brewing in Longshaw, and our knight deemed that so it was, and that they would hold together the looser, and that thereby we should have the cheaper bargain of them. All of which

I trow nowise, but deem, on the contrary, that I see in this glorious young man even the one sent from heaven for the helping of our enemy, of whom I dreaded that he would come ere long time was worn. But now let all things be as they will that be not under my hand."

The Maiden still kept silence, but she flushed very red and her eyes glittered; for her heart was smitten by this tale of the young champion, and the thought sprang up suddenly, Who then can this be save mine own beloved? But the talk between them fell.

LX

The Blue Knight Gathers Men and Departs from Brookside

Wore the days then till the winter came upon them, and though the season was not hard, yet was there but little coming and going about the country-side, that is to say for long journeys; but even so the Blue Knight had his hands full of business in seeing to the gathering of men and stuff for the hosting of the Barons' League. But when March was at hand, and the roads were dry, there was no need of further message to him, and he let it be known to all and several that on the very first day of the month he would depart before sunrise. And this he told to the Maiden specially, and by this time she had got to look upon it as a thing already done, so that the news thereof took not much from her cheer, which, to say sooth, was but little.

Mighty was the hubbub and toil of their getting ready; but when the morning was come all was in good order, and the men and their wains and what not were all drawn up in array down on the little plain before the bridge, and they looked as if nothing might overthrow them, so stalwarth they were each man, and so well learned to move as though they were one. The sun was not yet up ere there came a knock on the Maiden's door, and she, who was fully clad, and had been looking out of her window (whence she could see all the array) for a good while, went to the door and opened, and lo! it was Sir Mark, fully armed save his head. She put out her hands to him and said: "Thou hast come to say farewell to me. See, I have saved thee the pain of saying that word; soon may it be that I shall have to say Welcome back!"

He took her hands and kissed her face many times, and she suffered him. Then he said: "O my thanks to thee! Yet hearken: If I come not back at all, when it is known for sure here that I am dead, then I rede thee make as little delay as thou mayest, but get thee gone at once, thou and thy nurse, from the pleasant house of Brookside, and go straight to the house of the Grey Sisters, which thou hast seen from without many a time, and which lieth betwixt wood and water a seven miles down the river, and tell them that I have sent you and bid them to cherish you; then will they see to thy matters in the best way they know. Much more might I say, and I know that thou wouldst hearken me, but I must forbear, lest I soften my heart overmuch for this day and this hour."

Then he turned and went, but came back in a twinkling while she still stood at the door, and said to her: "I tell thee it needeth but a little but that I should do off this weed of war and abide at home while my men wend to battle." Then he turned again and was gone.

But the Maiden went to the window weeping thus to lose her friend, and the Carline came to her there, and they looked forth, and beheld the Knight ride down to his men. And then all the array shook and clashed, as they shouted for joy that their captain was come amongst them; and there were the two young squires, gay and bright in their broidered surcoats, and they fell into their places beside the lord, and Roland bore the wavy banner. Then arose the sun, and Sir Mark drew forth his sword and waved it aloft, and Roland shook the banner loose and displayed it in the clear air. The horns blew up, and the whole band of them got on to the bridge and went their ways toward the place where the road to the south and the east turned off from the northern road. Even so departed that glorious piece of ordered might; and when they were quite gone those two turned away from the window, and the days which were next to come seemed empty and dull.

But the Maiden told the Carline all that the Blue Knight had said to her about fleeing straightway to the Grey Sisters if he himself should fall in the war; and the two looked at each other a while, and each knew the thoughts which were in the other's heart, and which each left unspoken; to wit that Sir Mark feared his mother's pride and malice, what she might do if he were no longer there to refrain it; yea, and she seeking some outlet to her grief and solace for it in wrath and cruelty.

LXI

The Maiden and the Carline Flee to the Grey Sisters

Now wore away the days of March, and all was peaceable, but no tidings came from Sir Mark, nor forsooth was any looked for so early. The Blue Knight had left but three score of men-at-arms at Brookside, under an ancient knight who had won his spurs with hard fighting and was as wise of war as may be, but whose strength was worn away somewhat. But this seemed of little import, as none looked for any war, save it might be the riding of a band of strong-thieves, who would scarce try the tall ramparts of Brook-side, or had been speedily thrust aside had they so done. Yet did the seneschal look well to his gates, which were shut save for a few hours midmost of the day, and kept good watch and ward day-long and night-long. And few people were suffered to enter the Castle, save the neighbours who were well known, or now and again a wandering chap-man; but such an one was ever put out a-gates before sun-set: and no one of these even made a show of giving any news of the country of the war. But midmost of April came some news, such as it was, to wit that the Barons' League had driven him of Longshaw out of the field by the mere terror of their host and the wind of its banners, and he had shut himself up in Longshaw, whereto they were drawing speedily, and that the King of the City of the Sundering Flood had brought his host into the field to help the Barons. But when the Castle-folk heard this they doubted not but that the Lord of Longshaw was undone, and they were exceeding joyous thereof. But the Maiden, though she might hope the more to see her friend come back whole and sound, was unmerry at the tidings, she could scarce tell for why; neither did the Carline blame her therefore.

But again, almost in the face of May, chapmen more than two or three brought tidings, to wit that all was done: Longshaw taken and ruined, the warriors thereof slain or scattered, and Sir Godrick brought to the heading-block in the King's City. Now great indeed was the joy in Brookside, and great joy and feast they made; and the Lady of the Castle sat at the high-table, clad in golden garments, at a glorious banquet which was held every night of the octave of the day when they had first heard these good tidings. But when the Carline saw the sadness of the Maiden because of it, she said to her: "Nay, nay, my child, put on a good countenance and up with thine heart. For every tale is good till the next one is told; and I must tell thee that these last two who had this one in their mouths, the chapman and the canon to wit, I questioned them closely, first the two together, and then each one by himself, and methought I could see that they knew little more about it than we do, and were but carrying about empty hearsay, ever making the most of what they deemed we and they would like the best to hear. I would rather they had told us once more of the Aunturs of King Arthur and Sir Gawain."

The Maiden smiled at her word, and her heart was lightened, for it pleased her nought to think that this good Knight, Sir Godrick, whom her friend had so bepraised to her, should have been overcome and led to death by his foemen. Now after this they gat no tidings of any account till May was well on; and then none at all a long while, till at last June was come, and folk about the Castle were getting fearful, lest something untoward had befallen.

At last, on a hot and dry afternoon of June, when the Carline and the Maiden were together and had gotten leave to be without the gate, they saw a horseman come riding from the wood on the other side of the gate, with his head turned toward the Castle, and then another, and then two more. And as they drew nigher they could see that these were gaunt and tattered and in evil array, and they rode very slowly. And those two beheld them, and saw that no more came, and they wondered what they were. But at last, when they were close on the bridge, they saw only too well by the rags of their array and by the faces of two of them, whom they knew, that these were men-at-arms of Brookside. And the women stood still astonied and wist not what to do; and the men also drew up to them and then abode, and one, he whom they knew the best, spake to them in a harsh voice and said: "God knows we have striven hard to save our lives this long while past, that there might be one or two left to tell the tale; but now it is not so sure but that up there they will slay us for coming home alive. But we heed not, for we be foul like beasts and hungry like beasts and weary like beasts. Let the beasts pass who were once men of Brookside!"

"Poor men," said the Maiden kindly, "ye need not wound your lips by telling me the tale, for I know it, to wit the others are all slain and perished, and that your lord fell with all valiance in the very heat of the battle. O woe is me for my friend!" And she wept.

But the man stared at her wildly, as if he were astonied to hear the unused sweetness of her voice. But she said: "Come now, and let me lead thee to thy fellows; maybe they will be astir now." So she put her hand on his bridle to lead him, and he followed without naysay, and the others after him. And they passed in under the gate; and by this time there were a score or more folk in the court, for they had seen the riding of men from the walls or windows. But lo, now the Maiden, when she looked about for the Carline, might see her nowhere. But even therewith came one man and another thronging about those runaways, and some crying out, Tell all, tell at once! and blubbering outright, bearded men though they were; and some standing stock-still and staring straight before them in the extremity of their overthrow. And amidst of all this the Maiden was shoved aside and swept out of the way, till presently she felt a hand laid on her shoulder, and found it was the Carline, who spake: "Come out now amidst all this hubbub ere some one think of it to shut the gates. Come speedily." And they came outside the gate, and found none there, but two horses, and saddle-bags and a pack upon each. And the Carline said: "Mount now, and we will go as thy dead friend bade us; for none may stay us now, and these horses are our very own. Now will we ride away, tonight it may be as far as the Grey Sisters, but tomorrow further."

LXII

They Fall in with Three Chapmen

Now when the next day was, the Lady of Brookside sent a half score of men-at-arms to the House of the Grey Sisters, and bade them give up to them the Carline and the Maiden, if they had them there. But the Sisters said that they had come to them indeed the night before and had slept in their house, but had gone on early in the morning; and when the men asked what road they had taken, they said that they had gone north, and were minded for the uplands and the mountains. So the men-at-arms made no delay, but turned and rode the northern [way] diligently, and put their horses to it all they might; and they rode all that day and part of the next; but rode they fast or rode they slow, it was all one, for they came across neither hide nor hair of those twain, and so must needs come back empty-handed to Brookside. And when they told the Lady hereof, she fell into a cold rage, and cursed those twain for their folly and thankless-ness, and said that now they had missed all the good which she had in her heart to do them, since they had been such close friends to her dear son, late murdered. But however that might be, the Carline and the Maiden never saw Brook-side again.

Sooth to say, it was by no means north that those twain

rode, but as near south as might be. The Sisters were good
to them, and gave them each a gown such as their lay-sisters
wore, for they said that so arrayed they would be the less
meddled with. Therewithal the Prioress gave them a writing under her seal, praying all religious houses to help them
wheresoever they came, whereas they were holy women and
of good life. And the twain thanked them and blessed them,
and made an oblation, each one of them, of a fine ruby from
off that necklace of gems aforesaid.

Now they rode through a peaceable country, not ill-peopled,
for two weeks or more, and gat good guesting, whiles at
some houses of nuns, whiles at a good yeoman's, and ever
were folk good to them; and nought befel them to tell of,
save that once they were chased by riders, but overwent
them and came under the shelter of a good old knight's
castle, who drave off the thieves, and gave them good guesting, but was of somewhat heavy cheer, whereas his son, who
had gone to the wars, had been taken captive by the Lord
oᶠ Longshaw, and was not yet come back again.

After this they came into worser lands, rocky and barren,
but made their way through somehow, whereas the Carline
was deft at snaring small deer, as coneys and the like, and so
they lived and got forward on their way.

But on a day toward sunset, as they had just turned about
a corner of the road, they came upon a fellowship of a half
score men who were at their supper on the green grass just
before them. Two of these gat straight to their horses and
rode toward the dames, who, seeing that their horses were
well-nigh spent, and not knowing which side to turn to, stood
still and abode the newcomers, who were nought but cour-
teous to them, and bade them to eat with them. The
twain yeasaid it perforce, and were well treated by the travel-
lers, who said they were merchants on the road to the peopled
parts that lay beyond the mountains; and even so it seemed
by their packs and bundles of goods. Albeit, ere they lay
down to sleep, the Maiden whispered to the Carline: "Mother,
I fear me that we be fallen amongst thieves: and this seems
like the tale of the felons who first stole me, with no kind
and dear knight at hand to buy me out of servitude." "Yea,
my sweet," said the Carline, "the hay smelleth of that weed;

but fear thou not, for I will deliver thee if so it be." So when the morning was, and the day was bright, those merchants drew about the Carline and the Maiden; and there were three masters there, and two of them young men not ill-liking.

Now the Carline speaks to the elder of the three, and thanks him for the meat and drink and company, and says withal that they will now be gone, as time presses them. Says the chapman: "Nay, Carline, not so fast; how shall ye go safer than with us, ten weaponed men to wit? And safe thou shouldst go, dame, whereas thou bearest with thee so great a treasure." Said the third and youngest of the chapmen: "Go with us ye needs must till we have seen thy damsel safely set in good hands: or what do ye with her?" Said the Maiden: "O my masters, this is my fostermother, and to say sooth the only mother that I have known; it is with all my will that I go where she leadeth. I pray you let her do her will." And she was sore moved, and wept.

"Let-a-be, child," said the Carline, caressing her; "if these lords are fain to be our guides and guards, let us thank them kindly for it and go with them joyfully." The chapmen looked keenly on her, but could see nought amiss in her way of speech; so they trowed in her, and went about their matters arraying them for departure, and right joyous they seemed of the adventure. As for the Maiden, she yet wept; and when the Carline got to talk to her apart, as was easy amidst all the bustle, the sweetling said amidst her tears: "O my mother, I know not how to bear it, that now after all is done I am to be a thrall, and sold to someone, I know not who. And I shall be hidden away from the quest and the quest from me, so that I shall never see my love again. And even now who knows how sorely he longeth for me!"

"Nay, my sweetling," said the Carline, "hold up thine heart; no thraldom shall befal thee from these men, for I shall most surely deliver thee; but let them first bring us safe toward the edge of the mountains, and [we will] take their false guesting the while for what it is worth, and trust me I shall watch them all the while." So the Maiden stayed her weeping, but was shy and timid these days, and her loathing of these thieves of folk's bodies and souls made her downcast.

Two nights after, when they were resting at the day's end, the Carline (she hidden in the brake) came across the three men contending together in speech, and the words of the elder ending his talk she just caught: "Two thousand nobles at the least would the Lord James pay down for her; he hath none like her in the house." "Nor will have ever," said the second man. "And for my part I will not give her up for my share of a two thousand nobles." Spake the third thereon, and he was the stoutest-built and the gallantest-looked of the three: "Thou wilt not, thou! What sayest thou to me then? The beginning and the end of it is that I will take her to myself alone and sell her to none." "Yea, yea," said the elder, jeering, "and what shall we do?" "Thou shalt give her to me for a price," said the youngest. "Nay, but to me," said the second: "every one of thy pieces can I cover with a piece." "Now," said the elder, "we get on swimmingly; since, forsooth, I know not where either thou or he shall get all that gold from. Wherefore now the best thing ye two may do at this present is to fall both upon me, and slay me; and after that ye two can try it out betwixt yourselves, and he who is left can go back to our carles, who will straightway slay him when they have found the other two corpses. How say ye, my masters, is this a good game to play?"

They sat looking surlily on him, but said nought. Then he said: "Since this is come above ground, which to say sooth I looked for, as ye are two such brisk lads, and the woman such a pearl of beauty, I bid you this way to take: let us bring her down into the peopled parts in peace and good fellowship, and then go all three before a priest and take God's Body at his hands, and pray may it choke us and rot us if we take not her straight to the Lord James and sell her unto him for the best penny we may, and share all alike, even as the honest and merry merchants we be. Ha, what say ye now?" Belike they saw that there was nothing else to be said, but as moody they were as moody might be. And to say sooth the Carline deemed that, had it not been for the serving-men that would be left over, she might well leave them to slay themselves. But now they went back to their folk, and the Carline followed them in a little while.

LXIII

They Escape from the Chapmen by the Carline's Wizardry

THE next night after, they were come to but a little way from the end of the mountains, and could see the tilled and peopled lands lying down before them, and this had been no very long day's journey. The three merchant masters had ridden much apart from each other all day, and there was little feasting between them at even, and all men laid them down early to sleep. The Carline had spoken a word to the Maiden as they were a-riding, so that none might hear: "Sweetling," she said, "the thing thou hast to do tonight is to give heed to my least word or beckoning, and obey it, and then will all be well." So they two lay down somewhat away from the carle-folk. Amidst of the night then, awoke the Maiden, and the moon was high and very bright, and looking to her left side she saw the Carline was not there where she ought to have been; but nought scared was she thereat, since she wotted well that something would betide. But moving as little as she might, she let her eyes go round the campment, and even therewith saw the said Carline coming out of the tent of the masters, who slept all together there, whereas their serving-men lay as they might, under cloaks and such-like, beneath the naked heavens, the weather being fine and dry as at that time. Stole the Carline then and went up to each one of the said men and made unked signs over him, and when all that was done stood up by herself amidst them all and laughed aloud. Then she called out: "O sweetling that I am preserving as a pearl of all price for the greatest warrior of the world, wakest thou or sleepest? Speak out and fear not, for these now will lie here like logs long after the moon is gone out and the sun is shining. These carles thou seest, and two of the masters lie therein in

their tent; but the third, the old one, I lured away far into
the thicket and laid him asleep there; so that his being away,
and the others hunting for him, might breed delay and quarrels amongst these runagates."

The Maiden lightly arose and spake in a clear voice: "My
mother, I am verily awake and ready for the road." So
she came to the Carline, and they went together to the horses
and dight their own, which were the best of the company's,
and without more delay gat to saddle and rode quietly down
along the pass.

So rode they till it was the afternoon, and they were
come out of the mountains into the first of the meadows.
Then they drew rein in a fair little ingle amidst goodly trees,
and gat off their horses and tethered them amongst the sweet
grass. Then spake the Carline: "I must now look along the
ways of sleep and see what is betiding." Therewith she drew
from her hardes a goat-skin bag, which she did over her
head, and then laid herself face downwards on the grass;
but the Maiden sat by her and watched.

Thus she lay for an hour, and tumbled and routed in her
slumber, and thereafter she awoke and sat up, and was much
besweated and worn; and she spake in a weak voice: "I
have seen what lieth behind and what lieth before; now
therefore I can do, and all will be well. For the chapmen
have awakened and have striven, the two young ones together, and then the two young with the old because of his
bitter mocks. But now they be got to the road again, and
though we be most like to prevent them at a place of refuge,
yet wise will it be to leave as little as may be to chancehap.
As to what lieth before, I have seen our way that it turneth
somewhat east tomorrow, and will bring us to a goodly Abbey that hath a noble guest-house, and there, by the help
of the Prior's safe-conduct and the gifts I shall give to the
saints and the stewards, we shall be put well upon our way.
But now will I do; and when thou seest me fall down and
lie like to one dead, be not afeard, but when I come to myself again then sprinkle my face with water and put a cup
of wine to my lips, and thereafter shall I be whole, and
we shall eat and drink and go on our way."

Then the Carline went about the way and gathered handfuls of the dust and small stones and laid them in the bag, and then lay down on the way and put the bag under her bosom and brooded it, as a hen broodeth her eggs, moaning and muttering the while, and thus she was a long hour. Then she arose and let her hair loose, and it was long and white and not scanty. In this guise she walked to and fro athwart the road, keeping her face turned toward the mountains, and kept taking handfuls of that dust and casting it up toward that quarter; and ever and anon she cried out: "Be mist and mirk, and bewilderment and fear, before those faces of our foemen! Be a wall behind us that they may not pierce through! Mirk behind us, light before us!" So she went on till she had emptied the said bag, and then she fell aback and lay on the road as one dead. And the Maiden did as she had bidden and meddled not with her. But at last, and it was another hour, she began to come to herself, and the Maiden sprinkled her with water and gave her wine to drink, and the old woman arose and was herself again and of good cheer; and she stowed away her bag, and they drew forth victual and ate and drank kindly and merrily together.

So they gat to the road again when it yet lacked three hours of sunset, but rode not after night had fallen lest they should miss their way. And no shelter they had that night but the grass and the trees and the well-bedecked heavens, and all that was sweet enough for them.

On the morrow they gat to the road early enough, and soon began to come amongst the cots and the homesteads, and saw the folk labouring afield, and none were otherwise than friendly to them; and a company of husbandmen, carles and queans, hailed them from the ingle of an acre where they were eating their dinner and bade light down and share, and they did so with a good will; and the upland folk looked with wonder on the Maiden and her beauty, and gave her much worship. But the Carline talked with them, and asked them much of their land and how it sped with them; and they said it was well with them, for that they dwelt in good peace, whereas they were under the dominion of the great Abbey, which dealt mildly with them, and would not suffer them to be harried; and they pointed out to the newcomers a fair white castle lying on a spur of the hills which went up to the waste mountains, and did them to wit that that was the bit and the bridle of any wild men who might get it into their heads to break out on to the wealth of the Holy Fathers. And there be many such, said they, about our land, and especially a good way east and south hence where the land marcheth on the Great Forest, which is haunted by the worst of men, who will not be refrained but by great might and great heed. "And now," said they, "we hear tell of that mighty and good lord, the Knight of Longshaw, that he hath of late prevailed against his foes, who be tyrants and oppressors; and if that be sooth, he shall do as much or more on the east side of the Forest as my Lord Abbot hath done in the west, and peace and good days shall abide with us." Much those twain heeded this talk, and they prayed for that good lord, him and his.

So they thanked that good folk and went their ways, and in an hour's time they found the path which would do their eastering for them toward the Abbey; and shortly to say it, they came to the guest-house thereof two hours before it began to dusk, and were well served by the brethren whose office it was.

LXIV

The Carline Endeth Her Tale

WHEN they arose on the morrow they began to think of departure, though they would have kept them in that guesthouse for many days; but both of the twain, and especially the Maiden, deemed that, if they might, they should be drawing nigh to that dwelling of the good Knight who had overthrown the League of the Barons; and they both deemed that thereabout, if anywhere, they should have tidings, even had they long to wait for them, of that new champion whom the wise Knight had gotten.

Now then the Carline did wisely, and she got to see the steward, and fell to talk with him, and did him to wit that, for all the simplicity of their raiment, they had both the will and the might to make a fair oblation to the Saint; and she took from the aforesaid necklace two sapphires and two emeralds, all great and very fair, and the steward's eyes danced in the head of him at the sight, and he said: "This is a fair gift indeed, and if ye will come with me into the church I will show you to the Sub-prior, and if ye have any honest desire, as is like, since ye have such love of Holy Church, he and I between us will help you therein. And if not, nought is your time wasted in seeing our church, which is of itself worth a long journey to behold."

So they went, well pleased, and when they were in the church they found that he had said nought but the sooth: so many pillars there were reaching up and toward the sky, so nobly wide it was, and as long as it should be. And there were many altars therein, all as well furnished as might be done; and long had it taken any lettered man to have told up the number of histories on the walls and in the windows, wherein they were all as if done with gem-stones; and everywhere the fair stories told as if they were verily alive, and as if they who did them had seen them going on the earth and in the heavens. So the two waited there ravished while the steward went to fetch the Sub-prior, and brought him presently, a kind and holy man, and humble of demeanour.

He spake to them and said: "My daughters, it is told me that ye need somewhat of our house in all honesty and holiness; now when ye have laid your gift on the altar, if ye will come with me and our steward here to the parlour, I will hearken to all ye have to say, and if the thing ye need of us can be done, done it shall be." They thanked him humbly and went and made their oblation, and prayed, and the Sub-prior blessed them, and brought them out of the church into the parlour, and there they sat down together.

Then the Carline opened her budget, and told how they two had suffered from war and rapine, and when they had been delivered from a foul caitiff by a good Knight who had cherished them with all honour in his house, and all went well a while, it endured not long, for needs must he go to the wars, and there was he slain: how they, to escape the malice of the mother of the said Knight, who was a proud and hard woman, and now that her son was dead neither loved nor feared aught, must needs flee away. "But withal," said the Carline, "even had that good and kind Knight lived and come back to us, needs must we have left his house and his kindness ere long. For this I must do you to wit," says she, "that we deem we have a weird and a fortune abiding us, and that through all trouble we shall be brought thereto in the end, and that the said Knight's house of Brookside was over-far from it. This therefore we ask of you, since ye have shown such kindness unto us as the man of Samaria to him who fell amongst thieves."

The Sub-prior smiled at her word and said: "Well, dame, neither the priest nor the Levite pass by the poor souls."

"Father," she said, "thou and thy house, are ye foes or friends to the Knight of Longshaw?"

The Sub-prior smiled: "Friends forsooth," said he, "so far as we may do him any good; but ye wot that we give him no carnal help with sword and spear, yea and little indeed might we give were we temporal lords, so far off as we be from Longshaw, and the river and the Wood Masterless lying all between us. And now indeed we begin to deem that the good Knight may yet come to his above, though ere he had given the Barons' League that great overthrow things seemed going much awry with him. Moreover we have heard of a new champion whom he hath gotten, and who counted for much in that battle with the Barons, and wellnigh as wise in war is he as the Knight himself, say men. But now, my daughters, what would ye with the Knight of Longshaw?"

With that the Maiden took up the word, blushing red like a rose, and she said: "With the Knight of Longshaw it is perhaps little that we have to do, although we wish him all good, but it is rather with that one of whom ye have heard tell that he is a new-come champion of the Knight's." The Sub-prior smiled withal and said: "But what have ye to do with this champion?"

The Maiden blushed no longer, but said: "I will tell you the story in as short a way as it may be told: I was a damsel living much all alone by the side of a terrible river, not lightly to be crossed, or indeed not at all. And on the other side of the said river was there a bold lad of about my years, and we fell into converse, speaking together very sweetly each from our own side of the water. And for a long time this seemed a no such evil fate for the two of us to endure; but time went on, and I grew into a woman and he grew into a man, and indeed as bold a champion as there is in our parts; and then indeed it seemed hard that, though we should meet in speech, yet never should mouth meet mouth or hand meet hand. But we lived on in hope, and trusted to what weird had wrought for us. And it seemed possibly not so unlike but that this bold and eager champion might go wide in the world, and somehow find out the country and the side of the river on which I was born and bred. And in the meantime was I determined above all things never to think of anyone else but this bold and beautiful champion, and even so it is with me now. And this good dame here, who is my very fostermother, and is somewhat wise, though I would hope not more so than Holy Church alloweth, has always bidden me to hope to see my champion again, and even so I do. And we both know that it is only amongst the Knight of Longshaw and his men that he is to be found."

Quoth the Sub-prior: "And when he is found, and ye let him know where ye are, will he come to you, think ye?"

"Even so we believe," said the Maiden. "Well," said the Sub-prior, "tell me what ye would have, and it shall be done for you." Said the Carline: "We would [come across the water and] have guide and guards through the Wood Masterless to some place where we may dwell alone. Can ye do this much for us? And we shall be well willing to pay with suchlike gems as ye have already seen of ours for such a small house."

"Well," said the Sub-prior, "that may well be, and tomorrow morn, if ye will take the whole thing on your own heads, I will send you [down to the ferry that lieth betwixt us and a House of Friars on the further side of the water. At a writing from us these good brothers may find you some such dwelling in the Wood Masterless as ye seek, and will furnish you with way-beasts and guides thereto]. But I leave it to you, Carline, whether ye do not risk greatly to take such a pearl with you into the place which is peopled by the worst of men." Said the Carline: "To tell you the truth, Father, I have pieces of wisdom by which I can blind the eyes of foolish men, so that they will see nothing of the delicate beauty of my daughter here." "Well," said the Sub-prior, and smiled.

So the very next morning it was as the Sub-prior said. [Two lay-brothers brought them down to the water-side, and at parting gave a writing into the hand of the Carline. And when they were safely over the mighty Flood, and landed on a pleasant strand where the water was shallow and the current none so swift, the ferryman spoke a word of them to one of the brotherhood who had stood watching the crossing of that boat. With a friendly greeting he turned and led the way to the Friary, a fair stone building, set with a wall both high and long. Here met the Carline and the Maiden with a kindly welcome, and were set in the guest-house to rest that night. And, said the good brothers, their matter might be seen to, and they would send them on through the Wood Masterless; and that there was such a house as the Carline would have, which is in good case, said they, though it may want here and there a nail or a plank.

And in the morning two of the brothers were bidden] array themselves and take sumpter-horses and good horses for the women, and to lead them to within such distance of the Castle of Longshaw as might seem good to the Carline, and that forsooth was but some dozen miles.

There then they rested; and from time to time the Carline would go her errands, and would see folk who would give her tidings of how things went in the world. And ever she found that the tale was the same. For the Lord of Longshaw might not stretch out a hand without thriving; and ever with him at council, or at privy talk, or in the front of the battle, was this marvellous champion, whom it availed nought for any man to gainsay. At last the time began to seem long for the Maiden; and the Carline from time to time, when she did not know that she was nigh, heard her bewailing that her man came not, and she heard her say one day: If he come not before long, then will be perished some deal of that delicate beauty which I would above all things deliver into his keeping, so that he may know that it was no mere shadow of a woman with whom he gave and took in talk on the other side of the Sundering Flood. And in very sooth she began to peak and pine, and the Carline took her to task therefor, and said that she herself would try to set this right. Till on a day the Carline knew for sure that the champion had now turned his head from all his valiances, and was thinking of nothing but of how he might come across her with whom he had had such merry days on the other side of the Great Water.

Short is it that is left to tell. The Carline knew of a certainty that he had been smitten in felony and grievously hurt, and that he had been carried to an hermitage and there healed; therefore she waylaid him on a time and brought him to the house wherein they dwelt. And there, whether it were by her planning or by mere chance-hap may scarce be told, but such a thing befel that the wrath of the champion blazed out in him, so that for some few minutes he might scarce tell what was before him. And then it was all over, and they two were sealed for one another for what yet abided them on the earth.

Now this is my tale, and belike it has been somewhat overlong, and therefore it scarce needs that ye bid this damsel tell a tale for her part, which were indeed better told by her casting to earth her grey cloak and showing her body fairly dight, For, indeed, this damsel belongeth to one who is your kinsman and dear friend: and seemly will she think it that she show her body so dight that it shall lack no fairness before you.

LXV

Osberne and Elfhild Make Themselves Known to Their People

THEREWITH the Carline sat down, and there was great cheer and rumour in the hall, and folk wondered what was to come next; but it is not to be said but that they had an inkling of what had befallen. Then Elfhild arose and cast off her grey

clóthes, and was clad thereunder in the finest of fine gear of
gold and of green, and surely, said everybody, that never was
such beauty seen in hall. And for a while people held their
breaths, as they that see a wonder which they fear may pass
away. And then a great shout rent the hall, and there it was
done. A tall man rose in his place, a grey cloak fell from
him, and he was clad all in glittering armour, and there was
none that did not know him for Osberne Wulfgrimsson, who
has been called the Red Lad. And he said in a bold and free
voice: "See, my masters and dear friends, if I have not kept
tryst with you; for it is of a sooth five years well told since I
departed from Wethermel with little hope in my heart. And
now forsooth is no hope in my heart, for all the hope has
budded and blossomed and fruited, and I am yours and ye are
mine while the days last. And this is the woman that I have
won; and O I would that it had been earlier, though God wot
I laboured at it. And now I think ye will be good to her as
ye will be good to me, and what tale shall there be except of
peace and quiet in these far-away upland vales?"

Song.*

So passed the hours into deep night at Wethermel, and
folk went to sleep scarce trowing in the wonders that they
had heard and seen. And there were few among them that
did not long for the dawn and the daylight, that they might
once again cast eyes upon Osberne and his beloved. And
hard it were to say which of those twain was the loveliest.
But surely about both of them there was then and always a
sweet wisdom that never went beyond what was due and
meet for the land they lived in or the people with whom they
dwelt. So that all round them the folk grew better and not
the worser.

---

*The song was not written. Ed.

LXVI

The Lip of the Sundering Flood

WHEN it was the morning and the sun shone through the house at Wethermel, those two arose and took each other by the hand, and no word they spake together, but went straight to the Sundering Flood, and there they walked slowly and daintily along the very lip thereof; and the day was the crown of all midsummer days, and it seemed to Elfhild that never on the other side had the flowers looked so fair and beautiful. So they went on till they came to the Bight of the Cloven Knoll, and there they looked across a while and yet said nothing. And Elfhild looked curiously toward that cave wherein Osberne first espied her, and she said: "How would it be if there were another one there?" He laughed and said: "There is not another one." But she said: "Dost thou remember that game I played with the shepherd's pipe, how that the sheep came all bundling towards me?" "Dearly I remember it," said Osberne. "Now," she said, "I will tell thee a thing. I have got the said pipe in my bosom now. It were good game to have it forth and try whether it has lost its power." He said: "Well, try it." She said: "Be there sheep about?" And there were sheep at no great distance.

And she drew forth the pipe and set her lips to it and played, and there came from it that very same sweet old tune that had joyed him so much long aforetime. But when they looked to see what would happen to the sheep, lo and behold they stirred not at all for all the sweetness of the tune, nor made as if they heard it. So they laughed, albeit each of them, and Elfhild in especial, was a little grieved that the power had departed from the pipe. And they looked down towards the water, and Elfhild half thought to see a little brown man sitting at the door of the cave. But there was nothing; only it seemed to them both that there came up from the water a sound that said, Give it me back again.

And Osberne said: "Didst thou hear that?" "Yea," she said, "I thought I heard something. What shall we do?" Said he: "Why should he have his pipe back again?" She said: "Let us see what will happen if we cast it down to him." "Good," said Osberne, and he took the pipe, and as deftly as he might he cast it towards the mouth of the cave, but it fell a long way short.

But lo, as it was on the very point of striking the water it seemed that it was wafted up to the cave's mouth, and it vanished away into the cave no slower than might have been looked for. And a faint voice came up from the water and said: I am pleased; good luck go with you.

So they sat down and pondered on these things a while, till at last Elfhild said: "Now will I tell thee a tale as in old days." And he said: "That is good." Then she began a tale which was sweet and pleasant, and little like to those terrible things that had happened to those two since they were sundered by the Flood. And it lasted long, and the afternoon was hot, and they were fain for coolness' sake to creep into the shadow of certain bushes that grew a little off the lip of the Sundering Flood. There they rested them, and when the shadows began to lengthen, they arose and went back hand in hand to Wethermel as they had come.

LXVII

A Friend in Need

IT was some three years after this that weaponed men came down into the Dale. It was told to Osberne, and he took his sword and went to meet them. He came across them as they fared slowly down the bent, looking weary and fordone. He looked at them, and he saw that there was nothing for it but that the chiefest of them, and there were but three, was the Knight of Longshaw. So he ran up to him, and cast his arms about him and kissed him, and asked him what ailed. And the Knight said, and laughed withal: "That has befallen me which befals most men: I have been overcome, and I believe that my foes are hard on my heels."

"Will they be a many?" said Osberne. "Not in this first stour," said the Knight. "Well," said Osberne, "I will go and look to it to get a few men together to show them out of the Dale." So he turned hand in hand with the Knight of Longshaw, and cried out to Stephen the Eater to gather forth; and in an hour or so they had enough men and to spare. By that time the pursuers came glittering over the bent, so Osberne and his gathered themselves together and stood till the others came. And when they were within hail, Osberne asked: "What would ye here in arms? We are peaceable men." Said the pursuers: "We have nought to do with you, but we would have the body of a felon and a traitor hight the Knight of Longshaw."

Osberne laughed and said: "Here he stands beside me; come and take him!" And the foe were some three score, all a-horseback. So they fell on without more words; but they made nothing of it, and the Wethermelers kept them aloof with spear and bill. Albeit Osberne did not draw his sword, nor did the Knight of Longshaw.

Then the foemen held off a little, and they said: "Hark ye, ye up-countrymen, if ye do not give up this man, then will we burn your house to the threshold."

"Yea," said Osberne, "ye have all day long to do it in, make no delay therefore. Or did ye ever hear who I am?" And they said: "Nay, we know not." Then he let his red cloak float over him and let his byrny show glittering, and he drew Boardcleaver and suddenly cried out, "The Red Lad! The Red Lad!" and all the others did in like wise. Then the foemen fled up the bent. And Osberne said: "Lightfoot men of Wethermel, here is a job for you: let not one of these men escape from out of the Dale." So they fell to, and hard they worked at it, and so they wrought that they slew them every one.

Then Osberne went back to the Knight of Longshaw and said: "See, master, it is still a name to conjure with. And now what wilt thou do? Wilt thou gather men in the Dale here? We can find thee a ten score or thereabout of as good men as need be."

"Nay," said the Knight, "I will not have them, for meseems I am getting towards the end of my tether, and I will not carry away your good men and true from your wives and your children." So therewith they went into the stead and were joyful together.

LXVIII

The Knight of Longshaw Gathereth Force

THE Knight of Longshaw abode at Wethermel in much content, and much it pleased him to look upon the beauty of Elfhild and the fairness of the life that men lived in the Dale. At last he said: "Now I must shake off my sloth somewhat, and it will be a case of farewell." "Will it?" said Osberne. "Yea," said the Knight, "for I will to Eastcheaping, and there I will set me to gather men, and I look to it that, ere three months are over, I shall have a good host on foot." "It is well," said Osberne.

So in two days' time the Knight went, with his two men that had fled into the Dale with him, to Eastcheaping, and Osberne rode with him. When they came to Eastcheaping the Knight said: "Now is the time for farewell." "Nay, nay," said Osberne, "there shall be no farewell this time at least; but I will help thee with the gathering of men, and when we have got an host I will be the leader thereof. This thou must not gainsay me." Said the Knight: "But gainsay thee I will, for unless thou gettest thee back to thine own people I will break up my whole purpose." "And why?" said Osberne. "Thou art blind not to see," said the Knight. "I come and find thee here as happy as any man in the world, wedded to a fair wife, the lord of a stout and a stalwarth people who love thee above all things. And I have that in me that tells me that if I carry thee away I carry thee away to death. For I have seen thee in a dream of the night and in a dream of the day living at Wethermel and dying on the field near the City of the Sundering Flood."

Said Osberne: "And shall I choose dishonour then?"

"Nay," he said, "where is the dishonour? Besides, take this for a gibe, that whereas time agone I could do but ill without thee, now I can do without thee well, for I have three or four fellows will come to my call as soon as they know that my banner is in the field again. Wherefore, I tell thee, thou must either be my unfriend, or get thee back home my friend and my lad." So when Osberne saw it would no better be, he wept and bade farewell to the Knight of Longshaw, and went his ways back home. Six months hence he heard true tidings of the Knight, that he had gathered an host and fallen on his foes, and had fared nowhere save to thrive. And it is not said that he met the Knight of Longshaw face to face again in this life.

It is further to be told that once in every quarter Osberne went into that same dale wherein he first met Steelhead, and there he came to him, and they had converse together; and though Osberne changed the aspect of him from year to year, as for Steelhead he changed not at all, but was ever the same as when Osberne first saw him, and good love there was between those twain.

Now is there no more to say concerning the Sundering Flood and those that dwelt thereby.

The World's Best Adult Fantasy Ballantine Books Spring — 1973

ORLANDO FURIOSO: The Ring of Angelica, Volume I, translated by Richard Hodgens

THE CHARWOMAN'S SHADOW
Lord Dunsany

GREAT SHORT NOVELS OF ADULT FANTASY, Volume II, edited by Lin Carter

A VOYAGE TO ARCTURUS
David Lindsay

THE SUNDERING FLOOD
William Morris

*IMAGINARY WORLDS
Lin Carter

*Soon to be available from Ballantine Books

To order by mail, send $1.25 per book plus 10¢ for handling to Dept. CS, Ballantine Books, 36 West 20th Street, New York, N.Y. 10003.

The World's Best Adult Fantasy
Ballantine Books
1972

To order by mail, send $1.25 per book plus
10¢ for handling to Dept. CS, Ballantine Books,
36 West 20th Street, New York, N.Y. 10003.